NIGHTINGALE LANE PUBLISHING

THE CHRISTMAS TREE MURDERS

Andrea Hicks

CHAPTERS

Prologue...1
Chapter 1...7
Chapter 2...22
Chapter 3...35
Chapter 4...43
Chapter 5...51
Chapter 6...65
Chapter 7...75
Chapter 8...88
Chapter 9...99
Chapter 10...114
Chapter 11...127
Chapter 12...134
Chapter 13...143
Chapter 14...148
Chapter 15...158
Chapter 16...164
Chapter 17...177
Chapter 18...180
Chapter 19...192
Chapter 20...198
Chapter 21...203
Chapter 22...214
Chapter 23...222
Chapter 24...229
Chapter 25...239
Chapter 26...250
Chapter 27...259
Chapter 28...272

Chapter 29...276
Chapter 30...279
Chapter 31...284
Chapter 32...298
Chapter 33...305
Chapter 34...309
Chapter 35...313
Chapter 36..317
Note from the Author...322

For my family
Who would I be without you?

Prologue

Camille had settled well in her new house in Birdcage Mews. It had been rather a shock to discover that her husband, Lord Henry Divine, known affectionately to his friends as Harry, had promoted his mistress to potential wife. She had been rather like a dark shadow to Camille, a cloud that hovered just above their union, out of reach and untouchable, and one that could not be dissipated, no matter how much vehemence she threw at it. Harry would not be moved, neither backwards nor forwards. He stuck manfully to his position, no matter how much she flounced, begged, cried, or even when she threw the Dresden figure at him. It had once been his beloved mother's, a piece coveted by him for that very reason. He had simply bent down retrieved the jagged pieces from the floor. After giving her a look that would curdle the milk in the silver jug on the tray brought in by the maid for their tea, and who had scuttled out again, so frightened was she of being caught up in the storm, left the room quietly and with such dignity it finally dawned on Camille; there was absolutely nothing she could do to evict the recalcitrant woman from the life they had made together.

She had been aware of her of course. Her husband would brook no entreaties from her, that as he and Camille were together, married for over ten years, he would have no need of a woman who had found fame as a star of the vaudeville stage, one that surely could only bring down his reputation as a Lord of the realm with a seat in the House of Lords, once filled by his father who had since passed away. Lord Neville Divine had also had a mistress, the wife of his best friend. You see, Camille thought. They are never satisfied, these men of title and property. One of anything is never enough. And what was the name of this paragon? Why, it was that warbling bird of paradise, The Fabulous Lady Delphinium.

And Camille was certain she was no lady.

Harry said he would pay for a house for Camille, not purchase one, which is entirely what she believed she deserved, but to take a lease on a house that she would never own. She felt it could have been because he wasn't utterly sure of his new ladylove, and did not want to go to the expense of buying and furnishing another house in case he changed his mind. It's not just women who change their minds after all. Camille had also found it quite astonishing when a man will do virtually anything to get under the skirts of a paramour. She realised that some would say she was being rather cynical, that he was simply trying to get into Delphinium's heart and out of Camille's, but as a cuckolded wife that scenario was not how she saw it at all. Well, she thought. Can you blame me? And his offer, although on the face of it appeared generous, (it will look to others as though he had Camille's welfare in his mind when everyone knew he couldn't give a hoot) … was in fact, not.

He had also demanded that their daughter, Ottilie, Lady Ottilie Divine, her rightful title, is to stay with him and his new paramour in the family home at Kenilworth House. He promised Camille that Ottilie would not be in the company of his "friend" often; that she will be tutored at home until the age of twelve, she is just ten, and will be sent to a ladies college in one of the Home Counties and then to a finishing school in Switzerland. Camille was outraged because she was aware that she was to be given no say in the matter of her daughter's education.

'Why does she need to be finished?' Camille had complained to her mother. 'She is perfectly acceptable as she is, a likeable, rather sweet, quiet child, and she will of course, "come out" when the time is right, no doubt to be married off by Harry to some chinless wonder who has more money than brains or personality. I feel for her, I truly do, and if it ever becomes within my power to change the course of her future, I can assure you I will do so most vigorously.'

'You did not go to finishing school,' her mother replied. 'I suppose we were rather Bohemian in our outlook.'

Camille's parents; her father, an eloquent, elegant, and wealthy aristocrat, her mother an African princess, had not made much use of the educational system open to the aristocracy for Camille. A traditional education had not been hers. Instead, they travelled the globe and not always in the lap of luxury, Camille's parents insisting she learn about how real life is and that it does not consist of being cossetted or wrapped in fur to keep out life's little chills.

'Travel broadens the mind,' her father would announce, and Camille's mind was as broad as it could possibly be.

'The point I am making, Mama, is that my broadness of mind and my physical charms are precisely the attributes that attracted Lord Henry Divine to me. You remember the occasion I'm sure, yet here we are, wrenched apart by that doxy, the so-called Fabulous Lady Delphinium, who has, to my knowledge, never travelled further than Hackney and whose name is definitely not Delphinium. I have carried out the due diligence of any pushed-aside wife. I have researched and investigated this woman who in her misguided dreams emulates Henriette-Rosine Bernard, or as we all know her, Sarah Bernhardt, and I know every inch of her, as I'm sure my husband does…albeit…in a different way.

'Lady Delphinium was christened Mabel Crocket. I have it on good and reliable authority she was born in a brothel to a prostitute, and who now styles herself as an actress. I have nothing against actresses per se, but if you're going to call yourself an actress, then, dearest, do act. Do not lay on your back in some stultifying room with the noises of other…partakers…seeping through the walls while some man takes your dignity and throws it into the gutter for a pittance.

'Oh, I'm not decrying any woman earning her own living. I think it's admiral even if it is something I would not want to do myself. Even Lady Delphinium, or Mabel, as I shall call her from now on, should be admired for lifting herself out of the…mire. What I can't bear is the deception. I will of course find a way of letting Harry know that the woman he is bedding is really a Mabel. It may change his view of her entirely.'

Camille's mother had shaken her head. She had always known that the aristocracy of England were keen to dally with other women when things became tedious at home. She had schooled Camille on the subject, but regretted that she had not pressed the point home in a stronger fashion.

'Be careful, my darling,' she had counselled Camille. 'You may find yourself with nothing. Women are not important in this world. It is men who make the rules and we seek to object to those rules at our peril.'

'But, Mama, this was not the life in which I was raised. You and Papa are wealthy people, and after all Harry was almost begging Father to allow him to marry me, promising the earth as men do. To be fair to Harry he looked after me until his concentration wavered and his interests began to wander to someone else. Papa is Lord Hapzenberg. Surely that must mean something to Harry. Papa is a man who was raised in all the countries of Europe. It is what he told me when I was a child, telling me stories of his youth. He is related to the Royal family in Switzerland, the country of his birth, and you, Mama, you were born in the Africas, an African princess no less. How dare he sully our good name.

'I know there was scandal when you and Papa were married, simply because of the burnished hue of your skin, the velvety lustre of your complexion that some in Papa's circle thought incongruous within the society in which he more often than not took pride of place, simply because of his status.'

Camille's mother smiled. 'When one has money, one can be…and do…what one likes, and of course I was accepted. Your father would not have countenanced anything less.'

'And you are a beauty still, a goddess I've heard some say, but I know you are also astute. I think you knew this would happen. I have tried to be a good wife, Mama. I used everything you and Papa taught me to become a wife that Harry would be proud of.'

'But that may have been your undoing, Camille. You are…opinionated, educated in life. Many men of the aristocracy do not look for such a woman to be by their side. Don't be under any misapprehension. He would still have strayed even if you had been the most subservient wife in history. It is the way of things,' she said. 'Men are not put together as women are. They are made to procreate, and when they see a likely candidate for coupling, they cannot stop themselves. Do not take it personally, my darling. We women have learned to accept it over the centuries. It is well-documented in our history books.'

Camille dabbed away her tears and shook her head.

'There is no other way to take it. She may call herself an actress but once a girl has sold her dignity, there is no going back. There *is* no way back.'

Chapter 1

Time changed everything, as it so often does.

After a rather strange and uncomfortable evening at The Hotel at 99 Nightingale Lane, Camille discovered, via a visit from the local constabulary, that her nemesis had been murdered. She was astonished, perplexed, as she came to terms with the mixed feelings coursing through her.

How many times had she imagined carrying out the dreaded deed, of doing away with the woman who had stolen her life, who had sought to warm the side of the bed where Camille usually laid her head, and take over the running of her beloved home, Kenilworth House. She had dreamt of it, wished it, she was ashamed to admit, but the blow that broke Delphinium and snuffed out her life was carried out by someone of whom Camille had no knowledge. The woman was young, not yet thirty, had a child, a boy believed to be the son of Johan Stern, a man who had taken his pleasure of her in one of the addresses so popular with men in Whitechapel, a close friend of Carrie Lawrence, owner of The Hotel at 99 Nightingale Lane. Lady Delphinium was too young to die, thought Camille. I wanted her gone, but not like this.

Camille spent a fractious few weeks in her new home, pacing across the drawing room floor, back and forth and back and forth again, because of course, as the cuckolded wife of Lord Henry Divine, she was the main suspect in Mabel's demise.

'The police,' she said to her friend, Lord Nathanial Fortesque-Wallsey, 'are looking no further than the ends of their noses because Lady Camille Divine must be guilty, because she was usurped by the victim in her husband's affections. Who else would have wanted to end the life of The Fabulous Lady Delphinium, the actress and songbird, *and one time harlot?*'

Her mind was in disarray and she knew instinctively something had to be done. She could not allow the actions of an unknown murderer, whom the police were seemingly not at great pains to find, simply because the noose was conveniently hanging over her head waiting to be dropped onto her neck, end her life and get away with the crime, absolutely free of blame and punishment.

She examined everything, the clues in front of her, the night of the murder, the people who were present at the hotel. She made a list of all those who could have been involved and came up with perhaps one of the most unlikely suspects. It was clear to her that there was one who had reason to want Lady Delphinium dead besides Camille, the woman whose husband had taken his pleasure for a coin.

She 'encouraged' others to investigate. The wife of a Lord could not be seen in those addresses that hawked unsavoury pleasures to the men who patronised them, the place in particular where Mabel had set out her wares. Oh, yes, she thought, the 'lady' has a past, one that my husband was well aware of, so very well aware, yet chose to ignore. In fact, it would seem to me, that the seamier side of life attracts certain men, those who tire of the fragranced and sensitive, and wish for something more, shall we say, rudimentary.

With surprising assistance from Elsie West, madam and brothel-keeper, and her illustrious sister, Carrie Bateman, now Lawrence, the real murderer, or, for correctness, murderess, was none other than Johan Stern's wife, Lizabet. She held a grudge against Mable for her part in supplying Johan with the dubious pleasure he was not receiving in the marital bed...more than once in fact, actions which resulted in the little boy now living with Johan Stern at his home in Victoria Square.

'Poor Lizabet now resides in an institution where I pray she is receiving the treatment she needs, Mama,' Camille unfolded to her mother, 'although unfortunately she will never know freedom again. She will be forever ensconced in that place. I wish her no ill-will. Perhaps she was unaware of the severity of her actions, that to take a life, regardless of how low, cannot be ignored.'

'And you will return to your husband, my darling?'

'I think not.'

'But, surely...'

'We are estranged and will remain so. I cannot forget so easily.'

Sometime after the dust had settled on Mabel Crockett's demise, Camille received a letter from someone she had no association with, who she knew by name only. It was from a woman who regularly frequented the same social circle as Harry Divine, Camille's estranged husband, Lady Phoebe Carruthers, who was of a similar age to Camille, married to Lord Edwin Carruthers and a mother to three children. She was surprised to receive it because she had been assured, or rather cautioned, by her husband, that the circles in which he moved were no longer available to her due to their estrangement, so the initial overture could never have been sought by Camille. However, the letter duly arrived, and this is what was written on the rose scented parchment, embossed with the Carruthers coat of arms...

My Dear Camille, (Camille thought this unusual as she had never actually met the writer)

I had wanted to write to you previously, but felt it was inappropriate, bearing in mind your husband and mine are the closest of friends, however, it was important for me to become known to you, and for you to know my feelings on the matter.

Of course, as a woman married to a man of similar standing, I am bereft for you. You should not have been treated so shabbily, and I can tell you with no hesitation that your situation has sent tremors of uncertainty through our female society. Which one of us will be next we wonder? Your husband has yet to be seen at any of the soirees I and my husband attend, although we feel sure it will only be a matter of time before he returns into the fold of his friends. We all hope that when this happens, you will be on his arm, my dear.

I have another reason for writing to you. I understand from Nathanial Fortesque-Wallsey that you are quite intrepid, that you made it your raison d'etre to discover the miscreant who murdered your nemesis, the Fabulous Lady Delphinium, that you 'encouraged' those who were present in that circle to point the police in the correct direction. Nathanial assures me you are of impeccable trust, that you are the perfect detector to discover what could have befallen another.

It is for this reason I beg of you to help me. My beloved maid, Nellie Bell, who has been a member of my staff for the last three years, and who has proved herself to be a loyal and trusted servant, has disappeared without a trace. I cannot tell you how bereft I am. She has been a devoted and dependable companion and it feels very much as though I have lost a member of my own family. My husband, Lord Carruthers, has directed me to find another maid, but Camille, I cannot rest until I find her, or, at the very least, discover what has happened to her. I need your help, my dear. I cannot employ any other detector as her disappearance would certainly become public knowledge, and without knowing her circumstances I feel this would be wrong. Also my husband forbids it.

I hope to hear from you very soon, Camille. You are welcome to visit me at my home, Denham House in Henrietta Street, or we can meet at a teahouse.

Yours with thanks and hope,

Phoebe

Camille walked to the window, flapping the letter in front of her like a fan, a frown crossing her face. This was a communication she had not expected, particularly from someone such as Lady Phoebe Carruthers, who had signed herself 'Phoebe' as though they were old friends. Phoebe was a celebrated woman, an artist, who had exhibited at all the grand art houses and galleries, which was the reason Camille was personally unfamiliar with her. She had not been available to attend any of the soirees Camille had attended with Harry because she was always at some exhibition or other. Lord Carruthers had never seemed to mind that his wife wasn't present, but after the situation Camille had recently experienced with Harry, she wondered if he actually cared. Certainly, from the tone of Lady Phoebe's letter he was not concerned for Nellie Bell, a woman who had worked for his wife for three years, and had seemingly given impeccable service.

His attitude towards the errant maid likely meant nothing as Camille was aware, knowing only too well that men who move in certain circles view their staff very differently from the women those staff serve. Camille revered her own staff, particularly recently when her most loyal and steadfast Knolly, Cecily and the quiet, but dependable, Phillips, had insisted on joining her at her new home in Birdcage Mews. She had often wondered what she would have done without them? Camille had not encouraged them to leave their previous employment and hadn't expected them to choose to join her as her staff. They had spent their many years at Kenilworth House serving Lord Henry Divine, positions that many in service would fight for, yet they were willing to leave an eminent household, one that was envied by many, and chose to serve their mistress who had been unceremoniously ejected from those illustrious environs, to live in a home that was definitely of no aristocratic consequence. Camille had learnt much from it. They had shown her, by their choice, that it was the person they served who mattered to them, and not the house in which they served.

Camille's husband had been none too pleased. He saw it as a personal affront, particularly from Knolly and Phillips who had known Harry since he was a boy. They had served his father when they were young and had just begun in service, and, on his death, served the new Lord, Lord Henry Divine, known as Harry.

Knolly and Phillips had made it quite plain that they did not agree with Harry's choice of amour, that they did not wish to serve her as they had Camille, their mistress for more than ten years. When Mabel Crockett's murder came to light she gave them both the choice; that since that lady would not be the chatelaine of Kenilworth House they could return if they wished, and resume their duties for her estranged husband, but to her astonishment, and joy, they both declined.

Camille glanced at the letter again. Lady Phoebe had suggested that she visit her at her home, Denham House, in Henrietta Street. She knew the house, a huge, palatial building, the outside of which was rendered in white, making it shine like an ethereal moon floating from its grounds, and surrounded by exotic trees and plants from all of Europe and the Americas. She and her husband were travellers, had visited all manner of countries, the essence of which were captured in Lady Phoebe's paintings. She had sold well and Harry had bought one of her paintings that captured the historical waterways of Venice in Italy.

Would Camille visit her at her home? She took in a breath of regret. Under usual circumstances she would have certainly visited her at Denham House, but the situation in which she found herself were far from usual. She made the decision to take up her invitation and join her at a teahouse where she could be sure that her visit would not be reported to her husband, and where she knew the servants would no doubt have their ears to the keyholes. Many a rumour had been reported from a maid who had taken her time over bringing a tea tray into a room, or removing it again and lingering by the door as the conversation continued. One can only imagine them hurrying down to the kitchen and reporting the information to the rest of the staff, which would go something like this. "Ere, you never guess what I just 'eard', she thought. And so, the maid would continue to regale her workplace family with juicy titbits of gossip. If the hostess was sensible, and not all were, she would stop the conversation in its tracks, particularly if she and her guests were discussing someone known to the servants, a member of the family perhaps, or a friend who often visited. No, she could not take the risk of discovery.

She decided to send Lady Phoebe a note, thanking her for her letter and assuring her that she would give it her best attention. She wasn't sure how much help she could be. Camille had had help after all. She felt strongly she couldn't take all the credit, although she was willing to say that it was due to her clear thinking that pushed the guttersnipe, Elsie West, in the right direction. She had only questioned her girls closely on Camille's suggestion. Had she known in advance who the culprit was? She always answered the question truthfully and said she did not, but had simply had suspicions, logical ones she thought, and one of those suspicions was Lizabet Stern. She had already struck Camille as a strange girl, disdainful and unaffectionate towards her husband. And now of course, she had been proved right.

Camille called for Phillips, and asked him to deliver the note directly to Lady Phoebe. When she handed him the letter, she couldn't help but notice he was looking rather tired.

'Are you well, Phillips?'

'A little tired, Madam,' he answered.

'When was the last time you had a holiday?'

He raised his eyebrows and looked at her quizzically. 'A holiday, Madam? Well...,' he scratched his chin. 'I do believe I have never had a holiday.'

'Never? You have never bathed in the waters at Brighton or Lyme Regis?'

Phillips frowned. 'No, Madam. His Lordship, Lord Divine, that is, never encouraged us to take holidays. He said our time was best spent in work. Idle hands...or something like that.'

Camille tutted and shook her head. 'So, if I were to give you some time off, do you have somewhere you can go? For a short holiday I mean.'

Phillips scratched his head again. 'Well, there's me sister. She lives in Bedfordshire, in a market town called Ampthill. Nice little place. Unspoilt if you know what I mean...Madam.' Phillips straightened up when he remembered who he was talking to.

'Then you must go there. Pack a bag, Phillips. Get a train or a coach or a carriage, and take the time you need. I'll see you again when you're feeling rested.'

'But, Madam. What will you do for a footman?'

'Manage, Phillips. Manage. It's what women do. Knolly and Cecily and I will rub along quite nicely I'm sure. You'll be missed of course, but you deserve some time to yourself. Do you have money?'

He nodded. 'I always put money by, Madam, for a rainy day.'

'Well, Phillips, it's just begun to rain. Take my note to Lady Phoebe Carruthers in Henrietta Street. Get a cab for which I'll pay, then continue to the station if that's where you're headed.'

'Are you sure, Madam.'

'I'm always sure, Phillips.'

A little later, Camille threw on her peach-coloured coat and matching cloche hat. She was fully aware that the ensemble set off her dusky complexion to its best advantage. She pulled on a pair of soft tan leather gloves and made to open the front door just as Cecily ran into the hall.

'Madam?' she cried, frowning.

'I'm going out, Cecily.'

'Why on earth didn't you call me. I always help you before you go out, don't I?'

Camille smiled at her. 'It's just my coat and hat, Cecily. I'm more than capable, and are you not doing some mending?'

'Yes, Madam, but, well...' Cecily sniffed. 'Things seem to be changing.'

Camille nodded. 'Yes, I agree, they are, but not for the worst of it. We women are capable of many things, Cecily, and I for one am able to put on my coat, hat and gloves without help.'

Cecily grinned and bounced a small curtsey. 'Of course you are, Lady Divine. I think you're capable of achieving just about anything. We've all said it.'

'Oh have you now,' Camille said to Cecily, returning her grin. 'So that's what you talk about in the kitchen is it? What I'm capable of.'

A pink flush tinged Cecily's face. 'Only in the nicest way, Madam.'

'That's good to hear.' Camille turned to leave, but then remembered. 'I've given Phillips some time off. Tell Knolly will you.'

Cecily bobbed another curtsey. 'Yes, Lady Divine. Of course I'll tell her. He needed it. He's very tired.'

Camille pulled a face which she was certain made her look glum and made an effort to adjust her expression. The last thing she wanted was for any of her staff to think she couldn't cope with a minor staff problem.

'I think Phillips may have to reduce his duties here. He's not getting any younger. Perhaps he could go to Ampthill permanently and live out the rest of his days with his sister.'

'Good luck, Madam,' Cecily said cheekily. 'He'll hang onto the bannisters for dear life if you try to make him leave.'

'He likes serving here?' Camille asked her, overwhelmed by Phillips loyalty.

'He likes serving you, Madam. He says you're a fair and caring employer, unlike...' Cecily pulled herself up, looking relieved she'd managed to stop talking before she'd said the words. 'Well, anyway. He wouldn't want to go.'

Camille opened the door, smiling to herself. She knew full well who Cecily was about to name. It was the man she was setting out to visit that very afternoon, her estranged husband, Lord Harry Divine.

'So, Camille. It seems you cannot keep away from Kenilworth House.'

Camille lowered herself onto the velvet chaise in the drawing room, her eyes trained on Harry's face, trying to discover how he felt about seeing her again. She felt a frisson of nervousness which annoyed her. Why should I be nervous about being in the home of my own husband, even if we are estranged, she thought. 'This was my home, Harry, and my daughter still lives here. Why wouldn't I visit?'

'Not to see me then, my dear?'

Her eyes wandered across Harry's body, lithe for his age, and still an attractive man, and couldn't help a sad expression crossing her face. 'And what good would that do?'

'I may have been a little hasty.'

She was astonished. Did her husband's affections change so easily. It was only a few months ago that he was mourning the demise of his lover, Lady Delphinium, also known, to her chagrin, Camille had no doubt, as Mabel Crockett, the prostitute.

'A little hasty! That's rich, Harry. You forced me from my home because you took a lover, presumably because you thought the boy she gave birth to was yours, and then you discover that he is not your son, and that it is unlikely that you will ever father one.'

Harry glared at her and she wondered if she had gone too far, but his comment made her seethe. 'Is there a need for you to be so explicit?'

She stood and stared across the room to where he was seated at a reading desk; the top could hardly be seen for books and papers.

'Yes, Harry, I believe there is a need for the truth, and that *is* the truth, as unpalatable as it may seem to you. I have been parted from my beloved daughter, by you, because you planned to fill my place in our marital bed with...another.'

'I was not in my right mind. I have been worried about not fathering an heir to the Divine line. My father stipulated to me how important it was that I father at least one boy, two or three if possible. We have not created one.'

'We have created a beautiful, intelligent and loving daughter. She is your heir, Harry. Times are changing. Do you not read the newspapers?'

'I suppose you mean those insufferable woman who stride about forgetting they're female and of the weaker sex.'

'The weaker sex? That idea has been bandied about for far too long and is totally reprehensible. How can we be the weaker sex when our bodies are put through so much. Do you think I've been weak, Harry, after everything I have been through these last months. I have been ejected from my home, separated from my daughter, and been accused of the murder of your lover, and yet here I am, standing on my own two feet without any visible means of support.'

Harry's mouth twitched as though he was doing his best to suppress a smile.

'I suppose you're one of them.'

Camille shook her head. 'And why would you suppose that?'

'Because of who you are. You're never short of an opinion.'

'Because I'm human, Harry, with a certain amount of intelligence. My sex does not determine my ability to understand things.'

'As long as you don't drag Ottilie into it. She doesn't need pert opinions. Her young mind must be trained to expect to marry, and to marry a man of my choosing. If she is to marry well she'll need to stay away from that sort of thing. A man doesn't want his wife telling him how to behave.'

She couldn't help but raise her eyebrows. She presumed he was alluding to her. 'That's a great pity, Harry. Any man could learn a lot from an intelligent woman. And what if Ottilie decides that marriage isn't for her. What will you do then?'

'Persuade her.'

Camille threw back her head and laughed, but not because she found Harry's words amusing. 'By the time Ottilie is of marrying age she will have a mind of her own. I wish you luck in persuading her.'

A heavy silence fell on them and Camille surmised that they would never bridge the gulf that had grown between them. Too much unpleasant water had flowed underneath and she had to acknowledge that her feelings for him had changed. Once upon a time she had loved him madly, thinking him gallant and magnanimous. Now all she could see was someone who had sunk into small-mindedness and resentment, a man who saw enemies at every turn.

'Where is Ottilie?'

'In her room, studying.'

Harry leant across the desk and took a cigarette from an ornate wooden box, then lit it with a match from a solid silver vesta case without offering one to Camille, the height of rudeness.

'It might be best if you don't disturb her, if you meant to see her during your visit.'

Camille made for the door and put her hand on the handle. 'She is nearly eleven years of age, Harry. She should not be all alone in her room studying every day. It isn't healthy. I've come to take her out. Please don't stand in my way. I'm her mother after all, and I have rights.' She held her breath waiting for him to explode and refuse, but instead, he shrugged.

'As you wish.'

Feeling on safer ground, she decided to push a little further.

'In fact, tomorrow is Saturday, so I thought she might stay with me. Knolly and Cecily have prepared a room for her for when she visits. I'll make sure she returns to you by Sunday evening. I'll bring her back myself.'

Harry nodded slowly and blew out a puff of smoke. 'See that you do. Please don't be late. I expect her back for dinner.' Camille nodded her agreement then left the room and went into the vast hall, grateful that their conversation was over and she could escape.

As she made her way up the stairs she realised she no longer loved Harry, that anything she had felt for him before his affair, was gone. He had loved another; in every way a man could love a woman. He had been a married man when he had fallen for Lady Delphinium and that meant adultery. Camille knew that when adultery had taken place she could get a divorce. Their parting had been so acrimonious and so public that Harry would not be able to deny it, and it would be then that she would insist that a girl needed her mother, and that Ottilie should live with her.

Chapter 2

'Oh, Mama,' cried Ottilie when she went into the small drawing room at Birdcage Mews. 'But this is such a beautiful house. Is it yours?'

'Unfortunately not, my darling. It belongs to David Lawrence who currently lives with his wife, Carrie Lawrence at The Hotel, at 99 Nightingale Lane.'

Ottilie put her dolly-bag down on the chair and removed her gloves, frowning as the realisation hit her. 'Isn't that the hotel where...the lady was murdered? You know the lady I mean, don't you?'

'Yes, Ottilie. I know of her.'

'She was Papa's new friend.' Camille nodded. 'Then I'm glad.'

Her eyes widened at Ottilie's vehement outburst. 'Ottilie! No, you must not speak like that about her. She was very young and didn't deserve to lose her life in such a way.'

'But she stole Papa from you. I know all about it. The servants think I'm not listening when they're talking about it but I hear everything.'

Camille knew she shouldn't ask but couldn't prevent herself. She had to know. 'And what have you heard?' She removed her coat just as Cecily came into the room with a squeal on her lips.

'Miss Ottilie.' She clasped her hands together. 'How I've missed you.'

Ottilie grinned. 'I've missed you too, Cecily. It's lovely to see you again.'

The door opened wider and Knolly appeared, breathless from running down the hall when she'd heard Ottilie's name. She held her hands out to Ottilie who grasped them, noticing how warm from the kitchen they were. The cook looked exactly the same and smelt the same too, of vanilla and sugar.

'Miss Ottilie, at last. Me and Cecily, we've been waiting for this day. We've both missed you so much.'

'Oh, Knolly,' cried Ottilie. 'I wish you'd come back to Kenilworth House. It's not the same without you and Cecily, and Mama of course. It's so...so colourless and quiet. There are no flowers like there used to be, no music and no laughter, and the new cook is a grumpy old thing. Please come back.' She turned to Camille. 'And you, Mama. I'm sure Papa is sorry for being so silly.'

Camille sighed and looked pointedly at Knolly and Cecily, who made their excuses and went back to the kitchen.

'I can't come back, sweetheart.'

Ottilie removed her coat and sat on the velvet chaise, her eyes glistening with tears. 'Why ever not? You belong there. And so do Knolly and Cecily. The new servants Papa has employed are horrible. They don't speak to me like Knolly and Cecily. I'm sure they sneer at me behind my back just because I'm the daughter of a Lord.'

Camille sat next to Ottilie and took her hands into her own. 'Are you unhappy, Ottilie?'

Ottilie tipped her head to one side. 'Not unhappy exactly. Everything is so different now. I love Papa, you know I do, but, well, it's like he's not the same Papa, not as he used to be. I just don't know why things couldn't stay the same.'

'You're learning about life, Ottilie. Nothing stays the same.' She put her arm around Ottilie's shoulders. It felt so good to be able to cuddle her daughter without Harry's disapproval.

'The servants say it's because Papa wanted a boy, an heir to his title.' She glanced up at Camille, her expression quizzical, hurt. 'Am I not Papa's heir? I am his daughter after all.'

'It doesn't work like that. Not at the moment anyway, but things are changing. As I said, nothing stays the same. Things change all the time, and women are becoming more stalwart in their feelings and opinions.'

Ottilie put her hand over her mouth as she giggled. 'You mean the suffragettes, don't you? Papa hates them. I heard him talking to Lord Carruthers about them.'

Camille took in a breath. Lord Carruthers. There was that name again. Camille smiled and tried to appear unconcerned. 'Oh, yes? And was Lord Carruthers at Kenilworth House?

'Yes. He and Lady Carruthers visited Papa a few days ago. Lady Carruthers is very nice, and so pretty. Her dress was dreamy.'

'And what were those naughty men saying?' Camille got up from the chaise and began to rearrange the flowers in the vase as though it was the most important thing she had to do, and that she really didn't care what was said.

Ottilie giggled again. 'I don't think I was meant to hear. After a while, Papa sent me to my room to study, but as I left the room I heard Lord Carruthers say that all suffragettes should be strung up.' Camille gasped. 'He said they were wicked women who shouldn't be allowed to continue bothering parliament with all their shenanigans. That is what he said.'

Camille had paled. 'And what did Papa say?'

'That he agreed they should be stopped, but perhaps it should be done through law rather than violence.'

Camille looked relieved. 'Well, that's something at least.' She ran a loving hand over Ottilie's dark curly hair. 'But, darling, you shouldn't be listening at doors. It's what servants do.'

'I wasn't really listening. They just happened to be saying those things as I left. I wish they hadn't really. I don't like the idea of anyone being strung up. Actually, I'm not really sure of what it means.'

Camille blessed herself, rolling her eyes as she thought how remiss her husband and his guests had been.

'And Lady Carruthers? How was she?'

'She looked lovely, Mama, but...well, she seemed quiet. I wasn't sure if she was ill. Papa asked after her health and Lord Carruthers sort of flapped the question away, saying that Lady Carruthers maid had gone missing and that Phoebe, that's her name isn't it, that Phoebe was pining for her. He said it was utterly ridiculous.'

Camille smiled to herself. 'My, my, you did hear a lot, my darling, in such a short space of time too.'

Ottilie nodded. 'Yes, I suppose I did rather.'

Camille hugged her daughter, remembering when she was just a girl and had been dismissed from a room just as the conversation between the adults had begun to get interesting. She felt quite proud that her daughter had the same sort of gumption, that she would listen regardless of the instructions of a few mere adults.

Camille frowned. The conversation that Ottilie had repeated had concerned her without a doubt. There seemed to be a turning of the tide, a surge of disapproval against the suffragettes who had come so far, many of whom had paid a terrible price. And Phoebe Carruthers was clearly suffering in the absence of her maid. It was quite likely that she had begun to see the girl as a friend, particularly if her husband was less than amiable or supportive.

Lord Carruthers sounded rather curmudgeonly. Camille was aware that he was a good deal older than Lady Phoebe as often happened within society families. Parents wanted to see their daughters marry well, to men of wealth and consequence, and that often meant that the husband could be decades older.

Camille's thoughts went to Cecily and Knolly, and also to Phillips who had served Harry's family for many years, including Harry's own father, the previous Lord Divine. What would she have done without them since she had left Kenilworth House? It seemed she wasn't the only one who had relied on the loyalty and affection of her staff.

The weekend passed very pleasantly. Camille and Ottilie spent much of the time shopping together, and in the evening on Saturday, after a day of shopping delights, Camille took Ottilie to her first play, The Lady and the Rose at Daly's Theatre in Cranbourn Street, just off Leicester Square.

'Mama, should we tell Papa we went to the theatre?' asked Ottilie as they both dressed for the theatre in their new clothes purchased from Janida's, the shop where anyone who was anyone purchased their finery, and to dine afterwards in a restaurant close by.

Camille laughed. 'Perhaps not, Ottilie. I don't like to keep secrets, but I think this one should be ours, a girl's secret. What do you say?'

'I say, tally-ho,' Ottilie shrieked. Cecily dissolved into fits of giggles that she tried to hide, taking her hand away from her mouth to help fasten Ottilie's midnight-blue shift dress.

'Ottilie,' cried Camille. 'Nice girls don't cry out tally-ho at every opportunity.'

'Papa says the hunters say it when they're on their horses chasing after the poor little foxes. It sounds so much fun but I don't think they should kill the fox. They do other things too, with the tail.'

'Yes, well,' said Camille. 'I think we've heard enough about hunters and foxes. Are you ready?' She turned to face her daughter. 'Oh, Ottilie, you look wonderful, doesn't she, Cecily.'

Cecily nodded; her hands clasped in front of her. 'She certainly does, Madam. How exciting, to be going to your first play.'

'Do you go to plays, Cecily?' Ottilie asked.

Cecily flushed and looked down at her hands. 'Er, no, I've never been asked. I think you need a beau for that,' she looked up at them both, 'or a Mama to take you.'

Ottilie's eyes flew to her mother and she suddenly looked excited. 'Cecily could come with us, couldn't she, Mama?'

'Oh, no,' cried Cecily, her hands flying to her face in embarrassment. 'That wouldn't be proper, Miss Ottilie.'

'Of course it's proper...I mean...alright. You're our friend, isn't she, Mama?'

'Well, yes...yes of course Cecily is our friend.' Camille studied Cecily. She knew Knolly had the evening off and had gone to her sister in

Whitechapel. 'Why don't you join us, Cecily?' She smiled at her maid. 'We can get you a ticket at the theatre. We're having supper afterwards. I'm sure you would enjoy it. Better than staying here on your own, surely.'

Cecily faltered. 'But, Madam, what on earth would I wear?'

Ottilie grabbed Cecily's hand and dragged her towards Camille's wardrobe, flinging the doors open. 'There you are, Cecily. Mother has heaps of dresses. Choose the one you like best.'

Cecily glanced at Camille and Camille pressed her lips together to stop herself from laughing, and raised her eyebrows. She walked across to the wardrobe and began to pull dresses from the rails, laying them on the bed.

'These should fit you, Cecily. Try them. And don't be too long. We have about half an hour before the cab calls for us. You have some cosmetics?'

Cecily nodded. 'Just a little.'

'Perfect.' Camille pulled a headband from a box on top of the wardrobe, complete with diamante sparkles on the band, and two short feathers in lilac. 'There. It will go perfectly with your blonde hair. Don't be long, Cecily.'

Cecily watched their retreating backs as they left the bedroom, then hurriedly went to her own room to wash before returning to Camille's bedroom and choosing a stunning lilac creation that Camille had laid across the bed. It was a little loose on her slim body, but it changed her appearance completely.

She spotted some new hairpins on Camille's dressing table, and quickly pinned her wayward blonde hair into a chignon, silently promising to replace them out of her wages, adding the diamante headband. Then she looked down at her feet.

'Shoes,' she cried. She ran out of the room and began pulling boxes from her own tiny closet in the room she shared with Knolly. When she found the box she was hunting for she took it to her bed and removed the top, Inside were a pair of black velvet Mary Jane shoes with a diamante button. 'I never thought I'd wear you,' she said, 'but tonight is the perfect night.'

She pulled on some stockings and then the black velvet shoes. Taking a deep breath, she added some lipstick, saved for a rainy day, with a shaking hand, and pinched her cheeks, to make them blush as though she were wearing rouge. 'There,' she cried. 'All ready.'

'Cecily,' called Ottilie up the stairs from the hall. 'The cab's here. Are you ready?'

'I'm ready, Miss Ottilie,' she called back, then went out on to the landing to join Ottilie and Camille. Both gasped when they saw her.

'Well, well, Cecily,' said Camille. 'You are a dark horse.'

Cecily smiled and Ottilie took her hand. 'Sit next to me, Cecily. We're three girls together.'

Camille laughed, shaking her head. She had broken yet another rule, but wasn't in the least bit sorry.

When the play had drawn to a close, Camille, Ottilie and Cecily made their way into the foyer. They had loved the play, Ottilie had been transfixed, and Camille made a note to find some other suitable events to introduce her daughter to the world. As they were about to leave, Camille spotted Phoebe Carruthers, who had attended the play with her mother. She saw Camille at the same time and immediately left her party to speak to her.

'Camille,' she breathed. 'How good it is to see you. Thank you for your note.'

'Has there been any news?' Camille asked.

'None. I'm so very worried. It is not like her. Nellie has been so loyal, such a wonderful companion. My husband does not approve of course. He feels that when women become close it signals some trouble or other, but I'm ashamed to say I have ignored his opinion. I will not rest until I discover what has happened to her.'

'Why ashamed?' asked Camille frowning. 'Surely, it is only human nature to be concerned about a girl who has gone missing, regardless of her station in life.'

Phoebe took Camille aside, away from Ottilie and Cecily who stared after them, then at each other.

'Can we meet? Perhaps Monday. In Selfridges restaurant. It is mostly frequented by ladies so there is no danger of my husband visiting.'

'Are you not concerned that some of those ladies may tell their husbands you have met with me, and who will tell my own husband. He has forbidden me to associate with anyone in our social circle?'

Phoebe shook her head. 'You are seemingly unaware of the support you have, Camille. I'm quite sure Harry, who has sunk in my estimation I must confess, has kept this from you, but many of the women in our circle applaud the way you have conducted yourself since that awful debacle, and condemned Harry's part in it. Really, he has behaved like quite the cad. To evict you from your home and refuse admittance so you may see your daughter is such a devastating cruelty. I'm so pleased to see that Ottilie is with you and your companion this evening. She should be with her mother. A father cannot look after a young woman in the same way, nor prepare her for what is to come later in her own life.' Phoebe looked past Camille at Cecily. 'Who is your companion? I am not familiar with her. Is she from the counties?'

Camille turned towards Ottilie and Cecily who were now chatting like old friends. She smiled then turned back to Phoebe. 'Cecily is my personal maid, Phoebe.'

Phoebe's hand flew to her mouth as she gasped. 'You have brought your maid to the theatre?' Camille nodded as Phoebe smiled. 'Good for you. I knew you were a kindred spirit. She looks lovely. One of yours I expect,' she said eyeing the dress Cecily wore.

'Yes, and she looks wonderful.' Camille threaded her arm through Phoebe's. 'My life has changed, Phoebe. I live a very different life from the one I led at Kenilworth House, and to be honest, it has made me realise how stifled I was, by tradition, by conformity, by Harry if I'm to be completely frank.'

Phoebe looked astonished. 'But are you not concerned about your living, Camille? Does Harry not give you an allowance?'

'He does, and it is quite adequate for our needs, although no more than that. I say "our" because eventually I hope that Ottilie will live with me.'

'Then I shall pay you for your services. You will become a woman of means under her own hand.'

Camille's eyes widened and she grinned. 'That is dangerous talk, Phoebe, particularly in front of your husband I hear.'

Phoebe shook her head. 'You have heard of his views of the suffragette movement then? He is firmly against it, and is astonished that Parliament is taking it seriously. I for one would welcome some say in my own life. I am one of the lucky ones, my painting and art exhibitions allow me some freedom. They have saved my life in some ways, because without it I think my life would be very dull.'

'I must join my girls, Phoebe. I'll meet you on Monday as planned in Selfridges restaurant. Shall we say half past twelve?'

'Perfect,' replied Phoebe, looking brighter than she had when Camille had first observed her. 'I'll look forward to it. I'm so relieved we are doing something to find poor Nellie.'

'Mama, why were you and Lady Phoebe talking for so long? I didn't know you were friends.'

'We have only met recently, Ottilie. Her maid, Nellie Bell is missing and she is very worried about her.'

Cecily startled, her eyes widening with surprise. 'Nellie? Is missing? Ooh, sorry, Madam. I shouldn't be involved in your conversation.'

'No, no, Cecily. You know Nellie? Nellie Bell?'

'I do know her, Madam. We maids who serve in notable houses all know each other, a bit like a club I s'pose.'

Camille smiled wryly. 'And share gossip I shouldn't wonder.'

Cecily reddened. 'Well, sometimes. But not about you, Madam. Not what you would call gossip, anyway.'

'Perhaps we'll discuss that another day, Cecily. But this Nellie. How well do you know her?'

'As well as I know any of the other maids, Madam. She's a lovely girl, very forthright if you know what I mean.'

Camille glanced at her, frowning. Nellie Bell didn't sound like any maid she had ever encountered. 'Forthright, Cecily? In what way is she forthright?'

'She speaks her mind, 'specially about women and their place in the world. Some of the maids don't like it, saying they're proud of what they do, like I am, Madam. But Nellie thinks women should have more chances in life. She says no way will she be landed with a load of squalling kids.' Cecily looked embarrassed as she got into her subject. '*Her* words, Madam,' she said glancing at Ottilie. 'Not mine. I don't think the same way. I'd like a family one day, but I do agree with her when she says women and girls should have more chances in life, more "opportunities" is the word she uses. She goes to rallies as well, you know, the ones where they march and hold banners. She showed me her suffragette clothes, very plain, quite austere really, not something I'd want to wear myself that's for sure. They made her look, sort of hard. I can't think of a better word, as if she wasn't prepared to give up what she believed in without a fight.'

Camille sat back in the cab and took a deep breath. She realised that with very little effort she had begun to form a picture of Nellie Bell, her personality and her beliefs. It seemed the girl was not frightened of speaking her mind, of having pertinent opinions about a very contentious subject, the cause for which women everywhere had lifted a banner of solidarity. She was surprised to hear how frank and outspoken she was, because this did not chime at all with the girl Lady Phoebe had described.

When Phoebe had spoken of Nellie, Camille had pictured a rather timid individual, a loyal, subservient type who would never leave her beloved mistress willingly, yet Nellie Bell clearly had ideas and opinions that would not be best favoured by some others. Camille knew only too well how much hot water one could get into, simply because of an opinion voiced at the wrong time amongst the wrong group of people. Women who did so were frowned upon. Harry had made it quite clear. Is this what had happened to Nellie Bell? Had she made her opinions plain to the wrong person? Or had she simply tired of being a ladies maid and made another life for herself, perhaps with another family or with a young man she kept a secret, without telling Lady Phoebe Carruthers she was leaving? Camille knew these were the questions she would need to find the answers to, because without them they would never discover what had happened to Nellie Bell.

Chapter 3

Camille stepped up to the etched glass double-doors that led her into the Selfridges ground-floor department, where scarves, stockings, Christmas trinkets, jewellery, and the chocolate she loved so much were on display. The store was beautifully decorated for Christmas, Camille could see no expense had been spared, and she acknowledged it was truly a wonderland of festive treats which would tempt even the hardest heart.

There were silver and white trees on every counter, glittering as if covered by a fall of fresh snow, and above her head the chandeliers sparkled, sending out prisms of light into every corner of the vast shopping floor. This was a paradise to which she would return, but next time she would bring Ottilie and they could throw themselves into the Christmas spirit and shop until they were truly content. Camille was quite sure Harry would never consider such fun for Ottilie.

She spotted a sign pointing diners to the restaurant which was on the first floor. Glancing at her watch she could see it was a little after twelve thirty. She inhaled a deep breath, wondering what the next hour would bring her, and made her way up the stairs to the restaurant floor. The landing was covered in a bright Turkish carpet complementing the panelled walls in dark oak, rather too masculine for her taste, but when she went through the restaurant doors after giving her name to a young girl who stood behind a lectern overseeing the reservations, she was pleasantly surprised by the change of décor. The restaurant had a light and airy feel about it. The tables were small, most seating either two or four, and were interspersed with huge ferns in large oriental urns. The walls were painted in a pale apple green and the room had been very tastefully decorated for Christmas. There were no gaudy lights or tinsels to be found; everything had been beautifully complemented in white and silver. The overall effect was quite stunning.

'Camille!'

Phoebe Carruthers was seated at a table for two by a long window that had been dressed with sheer white lawn curtains and silver tasselled tie-backs. She looked every inch the artist, dressed in a bright red low-waisted shift dress, with a brilliantly coloured scarf swathed around her neck and shoulders. Large drop earrings hung from her ears, and her wrists were encircled by vibrant bracelets that matched the colours in her scarf. Each time she moved they made a chinking sound.

'Phoebe, how are you?'

Camille went across to the table and kissed Phoebe on both cheeks, and was immediately attended upon by a handsome young waiter who pulled her chair out for her and waited until she was seated before pouring them both water from a carafe. He left them to peruse the menu.

'Thank you for meeting me, Camille. It must have been a difficult decision for you, to put yourself into the fray once again, an ordeal surely after what happened. I think you're terribly brave.'

Camille shrugged and shook her head. 'I'm not sure it's bravery, Phoebe. One gets used to a certain life, but I have discovered that there could be other lives out there for us. I wouldn't go as far as to say that Harry did me a service by dismissing me from his side, but I think I'm all the stronger for it.'

'But you must miss Kenilworth House?'

Camille nodded looking sad, the corners of her mouth turning down at the thought of her beloved former home. 'I do miss it, the gardens, the staff. The way the sun glinted through the windows in the library in the morning. It was truly beautiful, and I know Ottilie loves it too, but we miss each other terribly. If pushed to answer, I think she would forego Kenilworth House to live with me.'

'Would Harry allow it?'

'That remains to be seen. When you saw us at the theatre it was the first time she had been allowed to stay with me since...well, since last year and everything that happened.'

'Were you terribly frightened?'

'More than you could ever imagine. It was difficult to keep body and soul together sometimes. But I managed it and it made me strong, although I would never want to repeat the experience. To be accused of murdering another human being is...awful.'

'Which is why I contacted you, Camille. You are the only person I could think of speaking to about Nellie. Some of the other women in our circle, well, they support suffrage, but not the giving up of their maids, and they feel that their staff should count themselves fortunate to have a job. I don't feel like that. I'm grateful that Edwin and I can afford to have staff...we certainly couldn't manage without them. I don't look down on them because they are in service. It's a job like any other.'

'I agree entirely,' nodded Camille, 'but in all honesty I have only recently come to know it. When Cecily, Knolly my cook, and Phillips my footman decided to leave Kenilworth House and follow me to Birdcage Mews, I was utterly astonished. They have become very important to me. Without them...well,' she blew out a breath, 'I don't know what I would have done. I have been very fortunate.'

Phoebe covered Camille's hand with her own. 'Let's order, and then we'll discuss Nellie and what we can do to find her.'

They both ordered a light soup, a Vichyssoise to begin, and followed it with a Waldorf salad, a dish imported from the Waldorf-Astoria Hotel in the United States.

'I hear it's very good,' said Phoebe. 'Harry Selfridge has just put it on the menu. It was invented by a friend of his, Oscar of the Waldorf-Astoria in New York.'

'Sounds delicious,' replied Camille, 'and not too dangerous for the waistline.' A bottle of light white wine was delivered to their table by the sommelier. Phoebe poured them both a glass and Camille watched in surprise as she almost devoured the glass of wine in one go, then topped up her glass to the brim.

'About Nellie,' Camille pressed. 'Did she have a gentleman friend?

'Not that I know of,' replied Phoebe. 'One would expect her to take her full complement of off days if she had, yet sometimes she stayed in her room reading, or walking around the park opposite our house in Henrietta Street.'

'Did she ever accompany you and Lord Carruthers on your trips abroad? I understand you often went travelling for your art.'

'It's true, we did, although for the last couple of years we've holidayed in Scotland. Edwin's family have a lodge up there and truly, the scenery in the Highlands is equally as dramatic as some of that I've seen abroad, if not more so. I did a lot of painting up there. Nellie came with us to Scotland, but before she joined us I had another maid, Iris, who came abroad with us regularly. She left Denham House because her mother was very ill and needed someone to look after her.'

'So Nellie has been with you for just, what, two years?' She and Phoebe halted their conversation while their soup was served.

'Three. She only came abroad with us once, and it was a short stay in New York. Edwin had some business to attend to there. Usually when we go abroad we stay for much longer.'

'Did Nellie meet anyone in America or Scotland?'

'Do you mean a man?'

Camille plunged her spoon into her soup and sipped it. 'Anyone.'

Phoebe shook her head. 'I don't think so. I don't see how she would have had time in New York, and the lodge where we stay in Scotland is remote, far from any town and surrounded by forest. There's a village where we get supplies, but really, I don't know how she could have formed any relationship with another person. Obviously we do meet people when we travel, but Nellie doesn't get time off as such. She spends much of her time at the hotel we stay in, or the lodge.'

By the time the Waldorf salad was served, Camille thought it was time she asked Phoebe about Nellie's opinions of suffrage and women's fight for equality.

'You knew about it?'

'Yes, I knew. It was why she and I grew so close. I'm sure by now you know my feelings on the subject, Camille. Like you, I have been married to a man that quite likely I wouldn't have chosen for myself, although, from what I've heard, you and Harry seemed to be very much in love when you were first married.'

'We were.'

'Still?'

'I feel differently now, and certainly I think the whole world knows *he* does.'

'If I'd had the law on my side, I would have gone to a university to study art. It's what I always wanted, but when I told my parents they simply laughed. My father said I must be out of my mind to want to go to such a place where who knows what went on. I remember telling him that I wanted to study art, fine art if I could get a place, not embroil myself in imagined shenanigans, but he said it was out of the question, that women didn't do such things, and that I should leave the studying to men as everyone knew men had bigger brains than women. He said the university place would be wasted on me and that no seat of learning would be in its right mind if it took me as a pupil.' Her eyes sparkled with tears at the memory. 'It was then that he informed me that Lord Edwin Carruthers had asked for my hand in marriage. He said he had accepted on my behalf, that it was the perfect match, and that I would be looked after for the rest of my life. By looked after, he meant told what to do, how to feel, how to be.'

That Phoebe Carruthers was passionate about her belief in the rights of women to conduct their own lives was clear. There was no doubt in

Camille's mind that she felt her life had been wasted on a man she had not chosen for herself.

'Do you love Edwin, Phoebe?'

'No. I have never loved him, but I have done my duty, both to him and to my family who have done very well out of the connections they have made due to my marriage to him. We have three children whom I adore. They are my saviours, my reason to continue. I carry on for their sakes, but once they are old enough I hope to make a different life. Rather like you have.'

'Did Nellie know of your feelings?'

Phoebe gave an enigmatic smile and played with the tiny silver spoon in the saucer holding her coffee cup.

'I'm sure she was aware that I didn't love Edwin. He isn't the easiest man to live with, he flies off the handle a lot if things don't go the way he thinks they should, although she would never have said anything to me. She didn't need to. I could see it in her face, that she wondered why I was married to such a man. It made me feel...well, less than I wanted to feel. She was very attentive to me, as though she understood that the life I lived was not the one I wanted. The children adore her, she was very good with them, kind, almost like an aunt. I found it very touching. I like her and I miss her. I'm also terribly worried because this disappearance is so out of character.'

'Do you remember the young woman who accompanied Ottilie and me to the theatre?'

Phoebe grinned. 'You said she was your maid.'

'Yes, and she knows Nellie, quite well it would seem. She is also aware that Nellie has very strong views about suffrage. Were you aware of it?'

'I know she is a supporter.'

'Did you know she went to rallies?'

'I didn't know that.' Phoebe frowned then took a sip of coffee. 'You think there's a connection?'

'There might be. A lot of men don't like the thought of laws being passed to give women more rights. I think it's worth looking in to.'

Phoebe placed her hand gently over Camille's again. 'If you can find her, Camille...of course I'll pay you for your time. And please...please don't put yourself in any danger.'

Camille lifted her coffee cup to her lips and raised her eyebrows. 'To find a missing girl...there might be no other way.'

Chapter 4

Two days later, Cecily took Camille her morning cup of tea to the bedroom as usual. Camille had a restless night, neither asleep or fully awake, with so many things jostling for the upper hand in her mind. She had begun to dream about someone snatching Ottilie away from her outstretched arms, trying to save her precious daughter from a person unknown, a fog, a silhouette. It was very disconcerting and galvanised her even further to discover the whereabouts of Nellie Bell.

Cecily handed Camille her favourite cup and saucer and then hesitated by the side of the bed.

'Is everything alright, Cecily. You look rather awkward.'

Cecily rubbed her chin ferociously with nerves, making it bright red in the process, then held out a newspaper she'd been holding behind her back.

'They've found a body, Madam.' Her eyes welled and Camille frowned, certain she could only think the very worst. 'They don't know who it is yet, but it is a woman, well, a young woman anyway, it seems.'

Camille held out her hand for the newspaper. A headline was blazoned across the top of the front page, lurid as is the usual with some of the rags, yet this seemed to be warranted.

'WOMAN'S BODY FOUND ON STEPS OF SELFRIDGES.'

'It says she was found under that huge Christmas tree they've put outside, y'know, the one with those beautiful sparkly birds.'

'Under a Christmas tree? How odd.'

Camille began to read the article which documented in depressing form the discovery of a woman's body under the Selfridges Christmas tree just as Cecily had said. 'I wonder why she was left there,' Camille said to herself as much as to Cecily. 'Perhaps it's a kind of symbolism.'

'What does that mean?' asked Cecily. 'It don't say that in the article.'

Camille slipped out of the bed and Cecily ran to get her robe. 'We need to find out who that body belongs to, Cecily.'

'You don't think it's Nellie do you, Madam?' Her hands flew to her mouth. 'Oh, please say it's not her. She don't deserve that.'

'No one deserves it, but it happens too often and usually it happens to a woman. I'm not sure how we can find out, unless we go there, to Selfridges. There will be a crowd there no doubt, and we can listen to the gossip.'

Cecily looked at Camille quizzically. 'We, Madam? Do you mean me?'

Camille nodded and made for the bathroom. 'Yes, Cecily, I mean you. Get your hat and coat. It has been unseasonably warm this year, but we don't want to draw attention to ourselves. Make sure it's dark, no feathers or anything sparkly. Something plain.'

Cecily ran to her room mumbling under her breath. 'I can do plain. Plain is all I've got, and I've never owned anything with a feather in it.'

Camille and Cecily joined the increasing crowd around the steps of the huge, elegant frontage of Selfridges where they were jostled by the curious wanting to get a first look at the poor soul who would no doubt make the front of the newssheets the next morning.

'I can't imagine Harry Selfridge is enjoying this at all,' Camille murmured to Cecily. 'This will be the busiest time of year for his store and it could definitely make shoppers want to go elsewhere.'

'I wouldn't go elsewhere,' said Cecily, peering at the etched glass doors in awe, 'that's if I could afford to go in the first place, which obviously I can't.' Camille glanced at her with raised eyebrows. 'Sorry, Madam. I weren't complaining or anything. I'm very happy.' Cecily pulled a face and bit her lip then shrugged. 'Anyway, it looks beautiful, don't it? Look at all the lights, and those chandeliers. They're a bit like the ones at Kenilworth House.' She glanced at Camille and pulled a face again. She saw Camille smile to herself. 'Keep putting my foot in it, don't I, Madam?

'You're going to have to sort that out if you're going to become my righthand woman.'

Cecily's eyes widened. 'Your righthand woman, Madam? In what way?'

'I need someone with whom I can toss ideas about. Someone who has a mind of precision, a sparkling intuition. Do you think that someone could be you, Cecily?'

Cecily thought for a bit. 'I could always try, Madam. I don't know what pre... pre...'

'Precision, Cecily. It means meticulousness, someone with a precise mind is exact and accurate, not vague and woolly headed.'

Cecily nodded. 'I reckon I could be like that. I'm good at remembering things.'

'Yes, Cecily. It's what I thought, and we will discuss some remuneration for you so that one day you may be able to purchase in a shop like Selfridges, but at the moment we need to find out who owns the body under the Christmas tree. If it is Nellie Bell our work is done.'

'But how will we find out, Madam?'

'You know her, don't you? Nellie Bell?'

'I s'pose I do. At least, I know what she looks like.'

'And that's all we need.'

'But how...how will we get to the front? Look at all these people. I'm almost ashamed to be one of them, Madam.'

'Me too, but we're detectorists, so therefore we need to be here.'

Camille put two fingers in her mouth, and while Cecily looked on in astonishment, gave a loud, piercing whistle.

'I think there's another body,' she cried out in the loudest voice she could muster. 'Off Regent Street, by Saville Row.'

The crowd seemed to move as one, like a heaving wave, the occupants running off down the street. They had seen all they wanted to see of the body lying under the Christmas tree and were hoping to see yet another. Camille shook her head in disgust.

'The macabre always wins out,' she said with distaste. 'Despicable. Right, Cecily, time for you to earn your new salary. Go and look.'

'At the body, Madam?'

'Yes, yes, at the body. Find out if it's Nellie Bell. Quickly, we must waste no time.'

Cecily ran forward and Camille watched as she bent to take a look at the body. A police officer grabbed Cecily's arm and pulled her away.

'Oi. What d'you think you're doin'?'

Camille stepped forward, a smile on her face which she bestowed on the police officer, a portly young man with a red complexion and tufts of red hair escaping from his police officers' helmet. 'Oh, officer, we are sorry, but my poor girl here thinks the unfortunate young lady lying under the Christmas tree is her sister.' Cecily's eyes widened. 'Don't you Cecily?

'Er, yes, yes, my sister's been missing a while.' She glanced at Camille then at the police officer. 'I'm hoping it's not her.'

The police officer's face settled into one of sympathy and he pushed his hands into his pockets. 'Oh, well, miss. Is it her? Do you need to get closer. There's no clue on her who she is so if you could throw some light on it the authorities would be grateful.'

'Go closer, Cecily,' said Camille, pushing Cecily closer to the body lying prone under the lower branches of the huge Christmas tree. 'Have a good look and be sure of who it is...or isn't.'

Cecily stepped forward, clearly reluctantly, and bent her knees so she could get a proper look. She straightened up, her face pale, the skin around her eyes almost translucent. She swallowed hard, unable to speak. The police officer peered into her face, frowning.

'You alright, miss? Is it her?

Cecily shook her head. 'No,' she said, her voice little more than a squeak. She shook her head again, her eyes glassy with shock. 'No, it's not her.'

The police officer pursed his lips. 'Oh, so you don't know who she is?'

'No, officer, I don't.'

He nodded. 'At least it's not your sister.'

'No, no it's not my sister.'

Camille put her arm through one of Cecily's and dragged her away from Selfridges. Cecily was so frozen with shock she could barely move.

'Are you alright, Cecily? Was it terribly awful?'

'Yes, Madam.'

'Come. We'll find somewhere to sit. I think you need a stiff drink.'

'Well, I know at least one person who won't need a stiff drink any time soon. I've never seen anything like it.'

They walked for a while and found a small hotel in Duke Street. The glow from the windows was very inviting, and as they stepped through the entrance the warmth hit them like a fur-lined coverlet.

'Lovely,' said Camille. 'Just what we need, and look, a crackling fire. Let's sit, Cecily. Are you hungry?'

'No, Madam.'

'Just brandies then.'

She called over a waiter and asked for two warm brandies which he brought to them almost immediately.

'Sip, Cecily. Sip carefully, and savour each sip. Let it slide down and it will warm you through.' She waited, aware that Cecily was in shock, not wanting to push her too soon. After a few moments of warming by the fire, she heard Cecily breathe out, then relax against the back of her chair. Camille leant forward and patted her knee. 'Better?' she asked Cecily.

Cecily smiled; her cheeks now flushed with the warmth in the room. 'Yes, Madam. I'm sorry if I seemed rude. I've never seen a dead person before.'

'I've never seen one, so I think you were very brave. And I want to thank you for coming with me and going along with my ruse...my pretence if you will. We had to get a look at the poor girl. Was it Nellie?'

'No, Madam. It was not.'

'Did you know her?'

'I don't think there was any chance for me to know someone like her, Madam. She was a lady of means. Her clothes were beautiful, she wore jewellery that sparkled in the lights of the Christmas tree...but her face.'

'Her face?'

'I think she had been beaten, Madam. Both her eyes were blackened, her cheeks bruised, and her hair had been pulled out of its chignon. There was blood running from her scalp as though someone had tried to pull the hair from her head,' Camille nodded, her face contorted into a horrified frown, 'and there was something on her cheek.'

'On her cheek? What do you mean, Cecily?'

'A word...a word had been carved into her cheek.'

Camille's eyes widened and she stared harder at Cecily. 'Carved? You mean with a knife?' Cecily nodded. 'What word?'

'The thing is, Madam, it's not a word I know. It was Emi, then the number one.'

'Emi one? That's not really a word, and why the number. I wonder what it means? Which cheek? Which cheek was it carved into?'

Cecily frowned, deep in thought. 'Her right cheek, Madam. Yes, definitely, her right cheek.'

'Her right cheek, and all we must do now, is to find out who the poor soul is who lies, as we speak, under the lower branches of Selfridges Christmas tree.'

'And how do we do that, Madam?'

'My thoughts are that if the lady is a lady of means as you say, she will be missed. Her absence will be noted and no doubt the police will know, which will filter into our newssheets. I don't think the police will be able to keep the identity of the poor woman under their helmets for too long. There is always someone who lets that kind of information out into the world. I think we must wait until she is unmasked. When she is it will be another clue as to why she was killed and why a word was carved on her cheek.'

'But what about Nellie Bell, Madam? Are we giving up on her and investigating the murder of this lady?'

'Oh not at all,' said Camille, draining her glass and readying herself to leave the hotel. 'But I don't believe in coincidences. When a number of things happen together they are often linked. That is what my instinct is telling me, and I always listen to my instinct.'

Chapter 5

'You were right, Madam,' said Cecily as she went into Camille's bedroom with her breakfast tray.

'Was I? That'll make a change. What was I right about?'

'It's in all the newspapers, the lady who was left under Selfridges' Christmas tree.'

'Oh, yes.' Camille sat up and pulled the breakfast tray towards her, more interested now. 'Who was it?'

Cecily pulled the newspaper from under her arm and unfolded it so she could see the front page. 'Lady Phoebe Carruthers, Madam.'

Camille's hand was stayed as she raised her cup to her lips, her face blanching in horror. 'What?' She lowered the cup to the tray and got out of bed, grabbing the newspaper out of Cecily's hand. 'No...no, it can't be her. I had lunch with her only three days ago. We discussed Nellie's disappearance.' She scanned the front page, her eyes brimming with tears.

'My Lady,' said Cecily, putting a hand on her arm. 'Please, sit down, Madam. You've had a shock.'

Camille sat on the chaise longue and looked up at Cecily. 'Did you not recognise her, Cecily, when you saw the body at Selfridges?'

'No, Madam. Not at all. It didn't look like her. I remember Lady Phoebe from the theatre. She seemed so nice, and so pretty. Delicate, like.'

Camille pulled Cecily down to sit next to her on the chaise. 'When you say it didn't look like her, what do you mean?'

'Her face, Madam. It was so bruised and battered. I don't think her own Ma would have recognised her.'

'What about her hair. Even I could see from where I was standing by the steps that it had been pulled out of its chignon.'

'Yes, Madam, pulled out the chignon, and pulled out of 'er 'ead.'

'Her head?'

'Yes, Madam, pulled right out of her scalp. Covered in blood it was, where someone had yanked it fair clean off.' Cecily looked wistful. 'She 'ad beautiful 'air an' all.'

Camille shook her head. 'This is an utter nightmare. Lord Carruthers must be beside himself. And her children. The poor, poor children. I should visit them. Pay my respects.'

Cecily rose from the chaise looking uncertain. 'Is that wise, Madam?'

'You don't think I should go?'

'It's just that...after what happened between you and Lord Divine... they're friends, aren't they? Lord Divine and Lord Carruthers?'

Camille nodded. 'Yes, they are, which is why we're going.'

'We?'

'Yes, Cecily. We. Are you or are you not my righthand woman?'

'I s'pose I am, Lady Divine. If you say so.'

Camille turned to her and smiled. 'I do.'

The cab pulled up outside Denham House in Henrietta Street, the house where Lady Carruthers had lived. Camille could not deny she felt nervous at seeing Lord Carruthers. He was an old and close friend of Harry's, they were of a similar ilk, an old London family with a family seat and extensive wealth. Camille was only too familiar with how these men thought and behaved, and what their expectations were. They were seen as pillars of society, men whom one would look up to, usually regulars in the House of Lords, and members of the Old Boy's Club, where anything that went on stayed in the four walls and never left. It was how Harry was able to keep his affair with Lady Delphinium a secret for so long.

'Are you alright, Madam?' asked Cecily as they went up the front drive to the huge white house that seemed to float above the garden. 'This must be a bit difficult for you.'

Camille glanced at her from the corner of her eye. 'Well, I must admit this isn't the most comfortable I've ever felt, but needs must.' She nodded as though agreeing with herself, confirming that her decision had been the correct one. 'Now, Cecily. Down to business. When we...if we get into Denham House, I need you to be on your metal.'

'My metal, Madam?'

'Yes. Keep your eyes peeled. That means have a really good look at everything. There may be clues.'

Cecily frowned. 'I'm sorry, Madam. I don't know what you're talking about.'

Camille stopped just before they got to the vast front door.

'Let me explain. The thing is, Cecily, it was Lady Phoebe who was so worried about Nellie Bell's disappearance. She wouldn't have contacted me if she hadn't thought something had happened to her, and she was absolutely sure she didn't leave Phoebe's employ at her own volition.' Cecily squinted and Camille sighed. 'She didn't leave because she wanted to, she left because...someone...forced her.'

'Or killed her.'

'Cecily!'

'Well, Madam, ain't that what you mean. Lady Phoebe was bashed to death for some reason, and that sort of word was carved on her cheek. It was a strange word, and not a word. Emi, and one, like in a number book. Must mean something to someone, and that someone went to a lot of trouble to get rid of her. So the way I sees it, if they went to that much trouble, they must have 'ad a reason, and they want everyone to know that the word is important to them. And surely, Madam, we need to find out what that reason is and why the word, if it is a word, is important. And...you said you don't believe in coincidences. Well, nor do I now, not now I know it was Lady Phoebe Carruthers what was left under the Christmas tree and it was 'er what was worried about Nellie's disappearance.'

'So, like me, you think there's a connection?' Cecily nodded. 'I'm glad to hear it, Cecily. We really must be singing the same song, and in tune, if we're going to discover what's going on.'

'And I think we should totally agree that there is an obvious link between the two events.'

Camille stared at her. 'Yes, well, we're in agreement then.'

'Yes, Madam. We are.'

A maid answered the door, her eyes red-rimmed, her face wet with tears.

'Yes?' Her voice wobbled as she spoke.

'I've come to pay my respects to Lord Carruthers on the loss of his wife. My name is Lady Camille Divine.'

The maid showed them into the vast hall and asked them to wait. Cecily looked about the room as they sat on two high-backed, rather austere hall chairs.

'Bit modern, Madam,' she whispered. 'Not sure I like it. And that funny picture on the wall. What is it?'

'It's one of Lady Carruthers' paintings. She was an artist.' Camille squinted her eyes. 'I think it's a bird, a foreign one alien to these shores if I'm not mistaken.'

'Alien to reality if you ask me,' whispered Cecily.

Camille's lips twitched into a smile which she hid from Cecily as she thought how amusing she could be. 'Well, that's art for you. It doesn't necessarily need to be representative.' She heard Cecily take a deep breath.

'Oh, right. Well...that ain't.'

The maid returned, wiping her red nose on a large handkerchief as she began to sob again.

'Lord Carruthers said he'll see you, Madam,' she gulped, 'but he's not alone, Ma'am. He's with Chief Inspector Owen.'

Camille raised her eyebrows. 'Oh. Really. Well, yes of course.' She turned to Cecily. 'This could prove to be very interesting,' she whispered as she removed her cloche hat and duster coat. She turned to the maid again. 'Could, my maid sit with you in the kitchen do you think?'

The maid nodded. 'Yes, Ma'am, of course.' She glanced at Cecily. 'All the staff have congregated in the kitchen. We don't know what else to do. Lady Carruthers always gave the housekeeper our chores daily. She was so efficient was Lady Carruthers, took care of the staff she did. And now she's gone.'

Camille gave Cecily a long look. 'Perhaps you could go with this young lady into the kitchen once she has announced me, Cecily.' Cecily nodded. 'And get them talking,' she said sotto voce.

Camille followed the maid into the sitting room where she found Lord Carruthers, Chief Inspector Owen and a woman she didn't know. She nodded to them as she went in, and the maid curtseyed to them then left the room.

'Lady Divine.' Lord Carruthers and Inspector Owen rose as Camille entered the room. The lady, of course, remained seated, but Camille could not ignore the look of superciliousness that she sent in Camille's direction. Camille walked forward. She rose her arm to shake Lord Carruthers' hand and wished she hadn't when he took her hand in his in a very clammy and weak handshake. 'Thank you for visiting us at this dreadful time. May I introduce my sister, Lady Maud. I don't think you've met.'

Camille turned her attention to the woman, who, when introduced to Camille, lifted her chin and peered at Camille through narrowed eyes. She was dressed severely in black in the old-fashioned way, her skirts reaching the floor, her dress made in heavy black satin. She wore a black hat on top of a greying chignon that had been pin-curled, a short net veil reaching the bridge of her nose. Her skin was papery and had clearly never seen a cosmetic. Camille was instantly repelled. 'No, we have not. Lady Maud. I'm delighted to make your acquaintance, although one wishes it were not at such a sorrowful time. Lady Phoebe was a kind and generous woman. I'm sure the whole family will be bereft at her loss.'

Lady Maud gave an almost imperceptible nod but said nothing. Camille turned back to Lord Carruthers, a look of sorrowful regret on her face which of course she was feeling, but she could not help but think Lord Carruthers had been released from his marriage to Phoebe, and that his sister was not perturbed by the fact. From what Phoebe had told Camille there wasn't a lot of love lost between her and her husband, and Camille knew that their marriage had been arranged and was not a love match. This often was the case in their society, and now, as she stood relatively close to Lord Carruthers, she could see he was much older than she had first thought, his sister even older.

'I'm so sorry, Lord Carruthers. Phoebe was a beautiful, talented and gentle woman and will be sorely missed.'

He nodded. 'That she will.'

Camille turned to Chief Inspector Owen. 'Chief Inspector Owen. We meet again.'

Owen nodded and took Camille's proffered hand in a strong, purposeful handshake. 'Yes, Lady Divine, and under sad circumstances yet again.'

'The nature of your job I would have thought, Chief Inspector Owen. There can't be many circumstances in your line of work that are happy ones.'

Owen observed her with a steady gaze. 'As you say, Lady Divine. The nature of the job.'

Lord Carruthers indicated for them to be seated, then rang the bell for tea. Camille looked at first Lord Carruthers and then averted her gaze to Chief Inspector Owen, thinking, correctly, that she had interrupted something.

'Please continue, gentleman. As a friend of dear Phoebe I can only be interested in your conjecture. As a woman of a certain society, I am hoping that this...evil person...will be intercepted and brought to justice as soon as maybe.'

Chief Inspector Owen turned to her, crossing his legs left over right, and folded his hands in his lap.

'You were a friend of Lady Carruthers, Lady Divine.'

Camille sent the maid away who had brought in the tea tray and began to pour tea into four cups. 'I am, er...was, Chief Inspector Owen, we were relatively new friends you might say.' She passed Lord Carruthers a cup and saucer. 'Milk or lemon, my Lord?'

'Milk. Can't tolerate lemon,' he said abruptly.

'Chief Inspector?'

'Milk for me too please, Lady Divine.'

'And Lady Maud?'

'Lemon. There's no necessity for human beings to drink milk after they've been weaned.'

Camille raised her eyebrows thinking how droll and unprepossessing Lady Maud was. She passed her a cup of tea and was expecting a word of thanks, but none was forthcoming.

Camille was hedging and she hoped that Chief Inspector Owen didn't realise. She wasn't sure whether she should tell him about her meeting with Lady Phoebe, and the disappearance of Nellie Bell. She was quite certain that Lord Carruthers wouldn't have mentioned it and she needed time to think.

'And what was your relationship, Lady Divine? asked the chief inspector. 'As new friends you were not close.' He sipped his tea without taking his eyes from her.

'I...I...had not known her for very long.'

'How long?'

'Not more than two weeks, but of course we mixed in the same social circle so had at least some knowledge of each other, at least we did until Lord Divine and I...'

'That isn't very long, Lady Divine, not long enough to form a friendship I'd say. Did you meet somewhere?'

Camille nodded. What have I got to lose, she thought. I'm involved in all of this whether I like it or not.

'Lady Phoebe wrote to me. She was very distressed at the disappearance of her personal maid, Nellie Bell. She had heard about the situation that occurred at The Hotel, when Lady Delphinium was murdered, and how it was finally resolved. She felt that because I had gone some way to help to find the person involved that I could help her in this instance.'

A look of amusement flashed across Chief Inspector Owen's face, then a slight frown. 'As a detectorist, Lady Divine?'

Camille took a breath. 'You're patronising me, Chief Inspector. Not very gallant of you.'

'Please forgive me, Lady Divine. It was not my intention to be patronising, but I am surprised. I would have thought you would have had other pursuits to keep you occupied, bearing in mind your station in life.'

Camille felt herself getting angry. 'You mean knitting circles, charitable events, and whatnot. I'm assuming that is what you mean.' She heard Lady Maud give a 'tsk tsk' and chose to ignore it.

'Something like that.'

'Well, Chief Inspector, we live in a new world where woman are quite capable of doing more than casting wool onto a knitting needle. Or perhaps you hadn't noticed.' She turned away and sipped her tea.

Lord Carruthers cleared his throat. 'Your husband has recently come out of mourning, Lady Camille. I take it you have not seen him recently.'

'I have seen him. He and I have reached a rapprochement, particularly with regard to Ottilie. She is all I care about, Lord Carruthers.' She turned to him. 'What will you do now?' she asked him. 'The children?'

'Nothing will change. They're all at boarding school and that will continue. The boys at twelve and thirteen will continue their education until Eton and they will then be boarded there. Lady Mathilda, who is the youngest at ten, will go to a Swiss finishing school and then married off. It's what happens isn't it? It happened to you, Camille.'

'Not so, Lord Carruthers. I loved Harry, wanted to marry him. I thought he loved *me*.'

Edwin Carruthers took a cigar from a decorative box on the table, nipped off the tip and lit it with a match.

'That...is an unusual event. Love is an unusual emotion between those of us in high society. Phoebe and I were an excellent match. We produced three wonderful children, and she was free to pursue her artists' bent, which took us to some wonderful places in the world. We had a life to be envied. I'm sure many did envy us.'

'What did Lady Phoebe think had happened to her maid, Lady Divine?' asked Chief Inspector Owen.

Camille shook her head. 'She didn't know, but she was beside herself, terrified that some dreadful event had happened to her. Apparently it was utterly out of character. She had attended Lady Phoebe loyally for more than three years with barely a day off. They were friends I think, as much as lady and maid.'

'Lot of fuss about nothing,' humphed Lord Carruthers. 'I told Phoebe she should just forget about her and hire someone else. Maids are two a penny. And now look what's happened.'

Chief Inspector Owen placed his cup and saucer on the tray. 'Why do you say that, sir? Do you think the events are connected?'

'My wife would not listen to me, Chief Inspector.' Edwin rubbed his eyes with his fingers. 'I told her no good would come of it but she just would not listen. I can only assume that she went looking for the damned girl. Was in a place she shouldn't have been and went and got herself killed.'

'And what place would that have been, Lord Carruthers,' asked Chief Inspector Owen.

'Lord knows,' he answered looking cross. 'I certainly didn't. I suppose it was wherever women like her went.'

'And what kind of woman was she?'

'One of those damnable suffrage types. My wife, my Phoebe admired her, thought it was brave of her to hold such opinions bearing in mind her station in life. Have you not noticed? It's the women with breeding that are forcing these damnable stupid laws through Parliament. Apparently she'd been one of those women who'd known others who been force-fed in prison, had actually been in prison herself for some misdemeanour or other. In prison! Can you believe it? If I'd had anything to do with taking on staff I would have marched her out of the house tout suite. Don't want women like that under my roof.'

'Quite right, Edwin,' uttered Lady Maud. 'It's a travesty indeed. These women are nothing but trouble-makers. They don't know how fortunate they are.'

'And your wife? Was she a sympathiser?'

'Oh, indeed, indeed, but I forgave her. She didn't discuss it with me as she knew what I thought about it. But...I'm not a stupid man. I'm quite sure she dabbled. Damned silly waste of time.' He glanced at Camille. 'I take it you're not one of them, Camille. I would imagine you have more than enough on your plate, what with being ejected from your family home.'

Camille looked uncomfortable, thinking how rude Edwin Carruthers was. 'If it's all the same to you, Lord Carruthers, I will continue to look for Nellie Bell. It was the last conversation Phoebe and I had and I want to fulfil my promise to her.'

Lord Carruthers rose from his chair and Chief Inspector Owen followed suit. They were being dismissed.

'Your time is your own, Lady Camille, to waste as you please. I now have to make a life without Phoebe, and a funeral to organise.' He lifted his chin towards the door. 'If you'll forgive me.'

Camille rose from her chair and put a hand on his arm. 'I'll be thinking of you and the children. Please let me know when Phoebe's funeral is to take place.' Edwin Carruthers nodded, and for the first time since Camille and Chief Inspector Owen had been in his company, he looked bereft.

Camille left the house and went down the steps with Chief Inspector Owen who had left his car by the side of the house. Cecily was waiting for Camille on the drive.

'Everything alright, Cecily?' Camille asked her.

'Oh, yes, Madam,' she replied. 'Very...interesting, you might say.'

'May I offer to take you both home?' Chief Inspector Owen asked them. 'I can take you to Birdcage Mews. It will be no trouble.'

Camille smiled. 'That's very kind of you, Chief Inspector. Thank you. We accept.'

Chief Inspector Owen pulled the car up at the gates of the mews and switched off the engine. Camille turned to him and smiled.

'Thank you, Chief Inspector. It was kind of you and saved Cecily and I from waiting for ever for a cab.'

He bowed his head. 'Just one thing, Lady Divine.'

She raised her eyebrows. 'Yes, Chief Inspector?'

'May I recommend that you allow the police to do the policing. We're trained for it, and detective work can be...dangerous. Perhaps if Lady Carruthers had come to us with her concerns she might still be alive.'

'Is that what you really think, Chief Inspector, or are you saying that for my benefit? For your information, her husband forbade it. He asked her not to involve the police so your vexation should really be with him.'

'I would say the same to everyone, Lady Divine. You are not experienced in the world of detecting, have not had knowledge of those sorts in our society who think life is cheap. Lady Phoebe is dead, killed by a murderer or murderers unknown, and her maid is missing. Until we find the person responsible, your undertaking of this work Lady Phoebe asked you to agree to will be extremely dangerous.'

'So like me you think both events are connected, Chief Inspector?' Camille looked at Cecily in the back seat from the rear-view mirror. 'Of course, she had a word carved into her face did she not? I'm sure you're aware of that. Emi and the number one, wasn't it? I wonder what it means.'

'Lady Divine, I advise you...'

'Thank you for the ride, Chief Inspector,' said Camille as she got out of the car, nodding at Cecily as she went, to do the same, 'and if I discover anything interesting, I'll let you know.' She peered into the car. 'Don't worry, Chief Inspector. I'm tougher than you think.'

Chapter 6

'So, Cecily. What did you find out?'

'They'd had a massive row.'

'Who?'

'Lord and Lady Carruthers. The day she was murdered. They had a slanging match.'

Camille removed her duster coat and hung it on the hall stand. Cecily followed her into the sitting room, her eyes sparkling. She felt she'd done a good job finding things out, even though she wasn't sure about her new status of righthand woman. She'd told Knolly about it and Knolly had said it sounded a bit dangerous.

'Would you refuse then, Knolly?' Cecily had asked her.

Knolly had pulled a face. 'Bit hard to refuse Lady Camille anything. She's so good to us, ain't she?'

'She is,' Cecily nodded. 'And I'm not happy about her going off on her own, neither. Safety in numbers.'

Knolly had nodded. 'There's truth in that,' she answered. 'Just use your noddle, Cecily. It's what God gave it you for.'

'Do we know why they argued, Cecily. It could be very important.'

Cecily removed her cloche and coat, and folded the coat over her arm. 'Something to do with Lady Carruthers wanting to paint,' she looked up to the ceiling in an attempt to remember the wording, 'a selection of portraits documenting those who fought for suffrage. That's what the butler said, anyway. It seems Lord Carruthers wasn't happy about it. He was shouting at the top of his voice saying it was ridiculous and that to side with silly women who should know better would ruin her career as an artist. They said Lady Carruthers was in tears, and that she was begging him to stop shouting. Then they heard her run upstairs and minutes later the main door slammed and they think that that was when Lady Carruthers left the house.'

'Did *you* ask the staff about the day Lady Phoebe was murdered?'

'Didn't need to, Madam. It was all they was talking about. They're all beside themselves that they've lost their mistress. Seemed they loved her. Said she was kindness itself and was always concerned about their welfare. Now they're all worried about their positions for fear of losing them, especially this time of the year. Some of 'em 'ave got kids, children, Madam, and they said they're already stretched what with the shortages from the war still biting. Doesn't sound good does it?'

'You're right, Cecily. It certainly doesn't sound good.' Camille sat on the chaise deep in thought.

'Would you like some tea, Madam, and some of those little cakes what Knolly made?'

'That would be lovely, Cecily. Thank you.' Then. 'Just one thing before you go. Did anyone mention Nellie Bell?'

Cecily nodded. 'One of the girls did, a maid, about the same age as Nellie I'd say. She said it was strange what was 'appening in the house, that they'd had more than their fair share of bad luck and she 'oped it wasn't catching.'

'I see. Did any of them say where they thought she might have gone?'

Cecily shook her head. 'They were as surprised as anyone that she'd done a bunk. That was how they put it.'

'So they think she left because she wanted to.'

Cecily frowned. 'Umm, well they didn't say she didn't, but...they didn't say she did neither.'

Camille smiled her thanks and Cecily scuttled off to get the tea. Camille shook her head and stood by the French window looking out onto the garden. She thought about Lady Phoebe, her beautiful face with the sparkling eyes as they had sat in Selfridges restaurant, and then how Cecily had described it when Phoebe's body had been laying under the Christmas tree, beaten, battered, and with strange lettering carved on her face. She shook her head again and sighed. She had liked Phoebe very much, had hoped they would be friends. A sadness hit her. Her life had changed irrevocably since the middle of the year when she had had to leave Kenilworth House. Many of the people she had called friends before she and Harry had parted were no longer friends, had not contacted her. She knew why. There were rules in their society. Harry was Lord Henry Divine and she was sure his close friends would have instructed their wives that they were no longer to have anything to do with her. What those men didn't know, was that many of those wives were supporters of the suffrage movement, had attended rallies and arranged places for refugees to stay, those who had run from a torn-apart Europe during the 1914 – 1918 war. She had wanted to open Kenilworth House to those poor creatures who had had to leave their homelands, but had not ventured to discuss it with Harry. There had been no point. She knew exactly what his answer would have been, because he, like Edwin Carruthers, thought that women should know their place and were only good for a number of things, all of which made men's lives contented and made them appear to be in total control.

'It's too bad,' she said to herself. 'It really is too, too bad.'

Cecily brought in a tray with three cups and saucers and a large teapot, complete with a cake stand on which there were various cakes and bite-size sandwiches. Camille frowned.

'Cecily, I know it's Christmas but really...I will never eat all this.'

'You have visitors, Madam.'

Camille's heart sank. 'Oh, who? I didn't hear them arrive and certainly there are no visits planned.'

'It's Lord Fortesque-Wallsey and Mrs West. I can always say you're otherwise engaged. They're waiting in the hall.'

Camille sighed and nodded. 'Alright, show them in, Cecily. Frankly no amount of cakes will be sufficient to stem Mrs West's appetite. It seems her appetites are her main priority.'

Cecily stifled a grin and left the sitting room to invite Lord Nathanial Fortesque-Wallsey and Mrs West to join Camille. She showed them in then bobbed a curtsey and left, thinking that there would no doubt be a call for more food. Mrs West was certainly a good eater and would make her way through the cakes in no time.

Camille held out her hand to Nathanial and he took it and kissed it, allowing the ends of his moustache to tickle the back of her hand.

Camille knew why he did so, and she eyed him with twitching lips, knowing his preferences were not for the likes of her.

'Nathanial. So good to see you. I don't have many visitors these days. My so-called friends seem to have fallen off the edge of the earth. And Mrs West. You're here once again. You and Nathanial must be very close.'

'Yeah, we are,' said Elsie, picking up the huge teapot, then raising her eyebrows to Camille. 'Shall I be mother?'

Camille nodded and turned to Nathanial. 'Not at the House, Nathanial? Do you not have more to do with your precious time than floating around London with your ingenue and visiting women who have been ejected from their marital home?'

Elsie passed Camille a cup of tea and widened her eyes. 'What the 'ell did all that mean?' Without waiting for an answer she took a tea plate and a pair of tongs and helped herself to the biggest cake on the plate, slices of puff pastry filled with fresh cream and raspberry jam. 'Don't know what these are called but they're my favourites. Your cook is a genius, Camille.'

'Mille Feuille.'

'Wot?'

'It's what the pastry is called. Mille Feuille. It's French.'

'Oh, right. My Rose would know about that. Learning French she is. With a tutor what I'm paying for.'

Camille nodded and watched Elsie as she proceed to demolish the pastry. 'Perhaps he or she could teach you how to speak the King's English,' she said under her breath. She rolled her eyes and turned her attentions to Nathanial who was watching Elsie with amusement.

'So, Nathanial. You didn't answer my question. To what do I owe this visit, not unwelcome of course.'

His face changed and a look of utter sadness crossed it. 'Phoebe,' he said. 'Such a terrible loss.' Camille nodded. 'It's just that I wondered if you had been able to help her. I know she was stricken at the loss of her maid, was distracted with worry over the girl.'

'She wrote to me, a letter that I have kept and will show to the police. I met her in Selfridges restaurant and she explained that Nellie Bell was a loyal and caring maid, quiet and attentive, yet I also discovered she had had an interest in the suffrage movement. According to Cecily, she was not so quiet when extolling the virtues of the suffragettes and their causes, that she was an active member, and had not only attended rallies, but had been sent to prison as so many of those women were. I had been very shocked to hear it, but I got that information from Lord Carruthers himself.'

Nathanial crossed one leg over the other, seemingly deep in thought.

'He...Edwin Carruthers did not hold with the cause of suffrage. Were you aware of that?' Camille nodded. 'In fact, when it came to the vote, he made no bones about being totally against it, particularly when the Representation of the People Act was mooted in 1917. He was incandescent with anger. I remember it very clearly. My father was still alive then and had taken me to the house as a visitor, telling me that I should familiarise myself with the goings on at the house because one day I would be sitting as a Lord of the House.' He looked sad again for a moment. 'Clearly he had not planned for it to happen quite so soon. He died just before Christmas 1918, Spanish Influenza, like so many others. The Representation of the People Act was passed that year, meaning that women of thirty and over could vote in elections, particularly if they held property. It did not go down well, and not only with Edwin Carruthers.'

He leant towards the coffee table and took a tea plate and sandwich tongs, helping himself to one small smoked fish sandwich. Camille poured him a cup of tea that Elsie had failed to do in her eagerness to get the biggest cake.

'So, are you saying that Edwin Carruthers wasn't the only one who wasn't keen on the suffragettes?'

Nathanial snorted. 'Not keen? That's one way of putting it, Camille. I would say they were very much like Edwin, perhaps not quite incandescent, but flaming mad that their time was taken up with what they deemed a triviality.' He took a small bite of his sandwich, chewing as he thought, and then a sip of tea. 'The thing is, Camille, these men, those in the House of Lords, come from old families where tradition and ceremony is everything. Look at what Harry was willing to do to ensure an heir, or who he thought was his heir. No one thinks it more ridiculous than I, I can assure you, but not all men think as I do.'

'Ain't that the truth,' said Elsie, stuffing the last of her third cake in her mouth.

Camille sighed. 'Can you not contribute something useful, Elsie? Why do you feel it's necessary to accompany Nathanial on his visits to me? Do you consider yourself a friend?'

'We could be if you'd stop being so toffee-nosed. Nathanial is a Lord and he and I are friends.'

'Yes, but what kind of friends? I'm trying to find some poor girl who has gone missing, perhaps not of her own choice. And *our* friend,' she nodded to Nathanial, 'Lady Phoebe Carruthers is now dead, killed by an unknown hand who carved a word into her cheek. Does that not horrify you, or are you so inured to the depths of depravity that an innocent woman's death means nothing to you?'

Elsie wiped her mouth with the back of her hand and stared at Camille.

'Talking in riddles again, Camille. I didn't understand half what you said, but I think you're saying I'm a tart what don't care.' Camille stared hard at her and widened her eyes. 'Well, you're wrong. I do care, which is why I'm here. I don't just come for the cakes y'know, although they're very nice, and your tea has improved too, more like what I'm used to instead of that Lapsy Chong stuff you gave me last time.'

Camille shifted her position on her chair and sighed, lifting her cup to her lips, wondering what on earth Elsie could do to help her find Nellie Bell.

'So, Elsie. What can you do to help me find Lady Carruthers's maid?'

Elsie rose from her chair and began to walk about the room, teacup in hand. She peered at the pictures on the wall, the photographs, the little knick-knacks Ottilie had given Camille as presents for Mother's Day and birthdays, little things she had lovingly made herself.

"Ave you checked her room? The one she stayed in at her place of work?'

'You mean Denham House, on Henrietta Street.'

Elsie nodded. 'If that's where she worked. You might find something out about what kind of person she is, or what made her tick. You 'ave to get to know her, don't you? I mean, exactly what do you know about her?'

'Not much,' Camille admitted. 'Only what Phoebe told me, that she was quiet and loyal.'

'But you said Cecily said she was more outspoken when it came to the suffragette movement.' She inclined her head to one side and thought. 'I know someone who's in the suffragettes. She might be able to help, you might even know her. She's as posh and toffee-nosed as you.'

'Then how do you know her, pray?'

'She works for me sister, Carrie Dobbs that was, then Carrie Bateman, now Carrie Lawrence. She's had more names than I've had 'ot dinners.'

Camille glanced at Nathanial. 'I doubt that.'

'She's the chef at The Hotel. She's got one of them Cordon whatsits. Went to school in Switzerland. She goes on them rallies what the women go on. Got Carrie to give a home to some Belgian refugees during the war. She did it gladly. She's a good sort, my sister. Salt of the earth. Like what I am.'

'What's this woman's name?' asked Nathanial. 'I might know her.'

'Dorothy Tremaine. Lives on Victoria Square. She 'ad my Rose to stay at her house when I was...well...unavailable. It's where she first started her learning. 'Ad a tutor and everything.'

'And she works for your sister?'

'She does. Do you know her, Nathanial?'

'I do. Rather attractive if I remember rightly. Got quite a brood if she's the person I'm thinking of.'

'Can I meet with her?' asked Camille. 'She might know of Nellie, if they were in the same group together. I think it's what happens. There are different groups of suffragettes all over London.'

'I'm going to see me sister tomorrow morning. You can come with me if you like.'

'Can I not visit her at Victoria Square?'

Elsie laughed. 'Well, she might welcome *you* there but I can't see her putting the red carpet out for me.' She sat down and put her cup on the table. 'I won't show you up, I promise, Camille. It's me sister's gaffe and she has rules,' she said, softening her voice. 'Even I'd get thrown out if I didn't keep them. And you know The Hotel, don't yer? It's not like you 'aven't been there before.'

Camille sighed and closed her eyes. 'I'm afraid I do. The memories of that place give me nightmares.'

'No, Camille, it's not The Hotel that gives you nightmares. It's what happened there. It's the nicest of places, honestly. Me sister's got the place running like clockwork now. Just come with me in the morning.' She grinned. 'I'll meet you outside if you don't want to be seen in the street with me.'

Camille nodded. 'Yes, yes I'll meet you outside.' Elsie looked at her with raised eyebrows as though waiting for something. 'Yes, well, thank you, Elsie. For your...help.'

Elsie grinned at Camille's reticence to thank her, and helped herself to another cake. She opened her mouth wide to bite into it.

'You're welcome.'

Chapter 7

It was fiercely cold. The third week of December had blown in like a hurricane. There was hardly a leaf left on the trees lining Nightingale Lane and the pavements sparkled with frost. Elsie stamped her feet on the pavement outside The Hotel, wishing that Camille would hurry up. A moment later a cab drove into the street and pulled up in front of her. Thank God, thought Elsie. This weather would freeze the balls off a brass monkey.

'You're 'ere then?' she called out as Camille got out of the back of the cab.

'How observant you are,' replied Camille. 'I just hope this visit is worth the cost of the cab I've just taken.'

Elsie's mouth dropped open. 'Why the 'ell didn't you walk? It ain't that far.' She followed Camille up the steps to the front door of number ninety-nine, The Hotel.

'Not in this weather.'

'I got the tram. It's good enough for me.'

'I've never journeyed in a tram.'

'Lucky you.'

Elsie pushed past Camille and greeted Gerald, the doorman.

'Alright, Gerald. Can you let us in. It's freezing out 'ere.'

'Certainly is, Madam. Let's get you inside.' He bowed to them both and opened the door.

The warmth hit them as they went into the hall. Edmund Kitchener, the receptionist, glanced up as they made their way towards him. Camille observed him visibly take in a breath.

'Mrs West,' he said. 'How lovely to see you.'

'She in?' Elsie asked him.

'If you're referring to Mrs Lawrence, yes, she's in the kitchen with Mrs Coyle and Mrs Tremaine. Would you like me to announce you?'

'Announce me? Nah, it's fine. Don't trouble yourself. I'll go down the back steps.' She turned to Camille. 'Lady Divine here needs to see Mrs Tremaine.'

Edmund bowed to Camille. 'Lady Divine. It's a pleasure.'

'Thank you, Edmund. How are you?'

'I'm well, Madam, thank you. Mrs Tremaine is working in the kitchen. If you'd like to take those steps there,' he indicated behind him, 'they will take you down to the kitchen lobby.'

'Many thanks, Edmund. It's good to see you again.'

'And you, Madam.'

Camille followed Elsie as she stepped behind the reception desk and ran down the kitchen steps.

'He don't speak like that to me,' said Elsie, huffily.

'Really,' answered Camille. 'I wonder why?'

As Elsie got to the kitchen lobby she called out to her sister. 'Carrie. You in here!'

Camille smiled as Carrie came to the door, a look of surprise crossing her face. 'Lady Camille. How lovely?' She frowned. 'Wouldn't you prefer to come to the sitting room? It's much more comfortable there.'

'Actually, Carrie, it's Mrs Tremaine I've come to see. Perhaps you and I could take tea at a later date, but I see you've got your hands full at the moment.' She smiled at the bonny little girl Carrie held against her hip.

'Yes, this is Harriet. She was born last February. I can't believe she's nearly a year old.'

Camille reached forward and took one of the little girls chubby hands. 'Oh, she's beautiful, Carrie, and her hair, so dark, just like you and Mr Lawrence.'

Carrie laughed. 'Yes, there was no chance of us having a blonde between us.' She tickled the little girl. 'Say hello, Harriet.' The little girl giggled and turned shyly away as Carrie beckoned Camille and Elsie into the kitchen.

'Dorothy, Lady Camille would like to speak with you. Is it a good time?'

Dorothy turned from the stove where she was putting a pie in the oven. She pushed her blonde hair away from her face and tucked it under her cap. She blew out a breath and pulled out some chairs from the pine table.

'Please, Lady Camille, take a seat. I'm sorry but I can't leave the pie. If the pastry burns Ida will have my guts for garters.' She giggled. 'That's one of Ida's sayings, not mine.'

Camille smiled as she sat at the huge pine table in the centre of the kitchen.

'I'm sorry to interrupt you in your work, Mrs Tremaine, but I needed to see you rather urgently.'

Dorothy looked surprised and then intrigued. 'Oh?'

'I hope I'm not stepping on your toes, Mrs Tremaine, but I wanted to ask you about your suffragette activities.'

'Right, well, we haven't had a rally for a while. When The Representation of the People Act was passed we realised that it was a terrific milestone, but it didn't go quite far enough.' She frowned. 'But what is your interest, Lady Camille? Are you looking to join us?'

Camille smiled. 'I'm looking, yes, but *for* someone, Nellie Bell. I believe she was an ardent suffragette, had been on many rallies and had been imprisoned and knew some women who had been force-fed. I know this happened to many suffragettes, but I wondered if you knew the name.'

Dorothy scratched her head, pushing her fingers under her mop cap, a habit she'd picked up from Ida.

'Um, well, nothing springs immediately to mind.' She pressed her lips together, deep in thought. 'Perhaps you would allow me to make some enquiries, Lady Camille. I'm sure some of our ladies would know the name, particularly if the woman had been in prison. Is she missing?'

Camille nodded. 'She was Lady Phoebe Carruthers's maid.'

Dorothy gasped. 'Oh, my goodness. Isn't that the poor woman who was murdered and left outside Selfridges. Heaven only knows what Harry must have made of it.'

'You mean Harry Selfridge?'

Dorothy nodded absentmindedly. 'Yes. He's a friend.' Her hand flew to her mouth. 'How dreadful. Poor Phoebe. She was a wonderful artist.'

'You knew her?'

'Only socially, at events, that kind of thing. We were not close friends, but she had an interest in the suffrage movement. We have one of her paintings on our drawing room wall. A cityscape of London. It's quite stunning. But I'm astonished that anyone would want to murder her. She seemed to be a quiet, quite delicate little thing,' she frowned, 'although I must admit I thought her husband was a boor, Edwin Carruthers isn't it?' Camille nodded. 'Too loud for my taste. Phoebe was such a talented painter. Why on earth would anyone want to do away with such a wonderfully talented woman?'

'She's not the only one, neither,' said a voice behind them.

Ida came into the kitchen with a newspaper, folded so that the front headline was on show. 'Look at this.' The headline was lurid. WOMAN'S MUTILATED BODY DISCOVERED AT THE PALACE OF WESTMINSTER.

Camille gasped. 'No! Please, God, not another. Where at the palace?'

Ida unfolded the newspaper and read as far as the middle of the article. She looked up frowning. 'The body was left under that huge Christmas tree they always put there for the kiddies.' Ida bit her lip. 'Ain't that like the other one, what was her name...?'

'Phoebe," said Camille, downcast. 'Lady Phoebe Carruthers. I knew her.'

'Oh, my dear,' said Ida, putting the paper on the side so Camille couldn't see it. 'Let me make you a cuppa.'

'What do they mean, mutilated?' asked Elsie, saying the unfamiliar word slowly. Carrie glanced at her, frowning her annoyance with her sister who never seemed to know when to keep quiet.

'It means she was cut about,' said Camille, 'and I'm wondering if it was in the same way as Lady Phoebe.'

'Why, my dear?' asked Ida gently. 'What on earth did they do to her?'

Camille took in a deep breath as she stared off into the distance.

'They, the killer, carved a word into her face, seemingly after she'd been beaten and bruised. My maid, Cecily, who was with me that evening when we went to find out if the body was of Nellie Bell, said that Phoebe was unrecognisable. She'd met her you see, at the theatre. She came with Ottilie and me, a treat, and to prevent her from sitting on her own in a new home. She knew Phoebe, would have known immediately if the body had been hers, but of course she was so changed, so...broken by whatever the person did to her. We didn't know whose body it was until the next day when the newspaper reported it.' She stopped to wipe her eyes with a lawn handkerchief. 'Why...why would anyone do such a dreadful thing to an innocent young woman?'

'How old was she dear?' asked Ida, placing a china cup and saucer in front of Camille along with a lemon tart, Ida's panacea to every ill. Camille smiled her thanks and sipped her tea.

'About twenty-eight, twenty-nine, maybe a little more perhaps, that's all. My age more or less, a little younger. Not so old.'

'Certainly not,' agreed Ida.

'You said she had something carved into her face, Lady Camille,' said Carrie, shifting Harriet to her other hip as Ida passed the child a ratafia biscuit.

Camille nodded as she placed her cup back on the saucer. 'A word, of sorts. We weren't sure what it meant. Emi, and then the number one.'

'Just Emi?' Camille nodded again. 'Wonder what that means,' frowned Carrie. 'Is it the initials of something, or p'raps a name, shortened maybe?'

'No one seems to know, not even the police.'

Dorothy looked surprised. 'You've spoken to them?'

'Chief Inspector Owen was at Denham House when I called to pay my respects yesterday. He has told me not to involve myself in the investigation, but I'm sure they will not be looking for Nellie Bell. She's hardly important when someone like Phoebe Carruthers is murdered.'

'But that's terrible,' said Ida. 'She's as important as anyone else.'

'Do they say who it was who'd been found at the Palace of Westminster?' asked Camille. 'I hate to say it but I might be familiar with her.'

Ida picked up the newspaper again, squinting at the article. 'A Miss Rowena Porter.'

A gasp came from Dorothy who stood up from the table and grabbed the newspaper from Ida's hands. 'Oh, my God, not Ro, not lovely Ro.'

'Oh, Dorothy,' cried Carrie. 'Don't say you know her.'

'I do,' sobbed Dorothy. 'Yes, I do. My cousin was sweet on her at one time. She's such a lovely girl. One of us too. One of us. A stalwart. Believes in everything we stand for.'

'Did,' said Elsie, They all turned to look at her and she returned their stares. 'Wot?'

'Do you have to, Elsie?' said Carrie, crossly. 'You can see how upset Dorothy is.'

'I know she's upset but all this talk ain't helpin' anyone is it?' She shook her head with frustration. 'I said to Camille yesterday, you need to get a look at the maid's room, and find a link between them what's been murdered. How can you expect to find the killer and what happened to the maid if you don't find out about them. You have to get to know them, where they went in the daytime when their family weren't about, the company they kept, that kind of thing.'

Camille reluctantly nodded. 'I hate to say it, but Elsie is correct. We need to get into Nellie's room at Denham House.'

'Where's that?' asked Ida.

'Henrietta Street.'

'Blimey, now you're talking. Them 'ouses are worth a pretty penny.'

'So how will you get someone in there, Lady Camille?' asked Dorothy as she wiped her eyes on her apron. 'Edwin Carruthers might think it's a bit strange if you ask to go poking around her room.'

'I was thinking of asking Cecily, my maid, to go. She could say she was a friend of Nellie's which is almost the truth. They did know each other even if they weren't close. She could say that Nellie had something that belonged to her and she needs it. It was all I could come up with.'

'I could go with her,' said Ida.

Carrie looked horrified. 'No, Ida. Why would you offer to do that?'

'Because you and I both know that the police won't be spending time on finding Nellie Bell. They'll be too interested in finding out what happened to the ladies what have been murdered. They'll have all of high society on their backs if they don't, and I doubt that poor Nellie Bell's got anyone looking out for 'er. She's one of us, in service. I'd feel terrible if I just turned me back on 'er.' She turned to Elsie. 'And you Elsie.'

'Me? What 'ave I got to do with it? I ain't in service. I'm a businesswoman.'

Ida's face changed. Her usual expression of kindliness fell from her face. She went across to Elsie and stood in front of her and spoke to her in a low and steady voice.

'You are now, Elsie, but you've got a short memory, my girl. Don't forget I came to Bucks Row didn't I? Remember? I saw how it was with you, how you were living, and, what you were doin'. So don't come all that high and mighty, hokey pokey with me. You're no different to me, or to my Frances what cleans the rooms here, or that poor girl who's gone missing.'

Elsie sighed and rolled her eyes. 'Alright, alright, don't go on. Bloody 'ell if it weren't for me Her Ladyship here wouldn't even be sitting at your kitchen table. It was me what suggested she come and speak with Mrs Tremaine.'

'About the suffragettes?' asked Dorothy.

'That's right.' She picked at her teeth, then held her nails out for her inspection. 'And if you want my opinion, I reckon it's got somethin' to do with them.'

Dorothy threw up her hands. 'Why, Elsie? Why would you say such a thing? You don't know anything about them.'

Elsie shrugged. 'Intuition.' She looked at them and smiled cockily. 'I 'ave got some y'know.'

Dorothy laughed, but without humour. 'Are you saying that you think these poor women were killed by suffragettes, or...or that girl was disappeared by suffragettes? Why would they do such a thing? They're trying to help women, not kill them.'

Elsie pushed herself away from where she was leaning against the cupboard.

'Of course I'm not saying that, you daft bat.' Dorothy gasped and Elsie laughed. 'Well, the thing is, that's what you're treating me like. I'm saying the connection is that somehow they're connected by either knowing, or being, a suffragette.' Dorothy opened her mouth to say something, but Elsie stopped her. 'And...you need to find out if your friend, Rowena was it, had a word, or letters, or whatever it was carved on her face.' She pulled out a chair from the table and sat, and indicated for Carrie and Ida to do the same. When they were all settled and looking at one another, she said, 'So. What's the plan?'

Camille took a breath and took control.

'A visit first. Cecily will go with a tall tale.' She looked at Ida. 'And will you accompany her, Mrs. Coyle? I must confess I would feel happier if you went together. You could even say you were one of Nellie's relatives. I'm fairly sure Edwin Carruthers knows nothing about her or whether she had relatives. It's quite likely if you were to go to the garden door the maids would give you admittance without

Lord Carruthers knowing. After all, I'm sure he has a lot to attend to at the moment.'

'Yes, I'll go with Cecily,' said Ida. 'When would you like me to go, Lady Divine?'

'I think tomorrow morning, early. Catch the staff while they're busy with their morning chores so they won't have time to think about it. Meet Cecily outside. You can't miss the house. It's rendered totally in white and very exotic looking. There are palm trees and tropical types of plants in the grounds. I'll tell Cecily to meet you there.'

Ida nodded, then glanced at Carrie. 'That's if Carrie is alright with it, and Dorothy can manage without me for a couple of hours.'

Carrie nodded. 'Yes, Ida. Of course. You seem determined.'

'We've got to stick together, us women. Watch each other's backs. I'd like to think someone would do the same for me if anything untoward happened.'

'Elsie,' said Camille. Elsie glanced at her. 'Are you willing to help us?'

'Depends what you want me to do.'

'Could you talk to your girls. Maybe one of them has heard something. You have a relationship with the police don't you?'

Elsie snorted. 'A relationship? I wouldn't call it that. They come for a bit of how's-your-father and they get what they come for.'

'Isn't there a high-up one that you know, Elsie?' asked Carrie. 'Someone who gave you some information when Lady Delphinium was murdered.'

'Might be.'

Camille rolled her eyes. 'Can you have a word with him?' Elsie gave her a sharp look. 'Please.'

Elsie nodded. 'Yes, Lady Camille. Of course I can. I'll see to him meself.'

Camille saw Carrie close her eyes momentarily and pressed her lips together to stop herself laughing. 'Lovely.'

'And what will you do, Lady Camille?' Elsie asked her, smiling sweetly.

'I'm going to the Palace of Westminster to find out if anyone can tell me anything. There are always soldiers or policemen on the doors, checking people as they go in and out, so I'll have a word with someone there. There will no doubt be a funeral soon for Phoebe. I will go as a mourner, for of course, that is what I am, and make a note of who is there. I've been reading that sometimes the perpetrator will go to the funeral of the person he or she murdered. It's a macabre way of finding pleasure in knowing what happened to the deceased person when no one else does.'

'That's 'orrible,' said Ida.

'Yes, it is,' answered Camille, 'but it might give me a clue.'

'I'll come with you,' said Carrie. 'To the Palace of Westminster. You don't want to go alone, surely, Camille. The two of us will be safer and two heads are better than one, aren't they?'

Camille smiled. 'Thank you, Carrie. I would welcome your company. Two women together will see so much more.'

They quietly sipped their tea, then Camille rose from the table and put on her lace gloves.

'Well, ladies, I want to thank you. When I began this journey I was completely alone. Then Cecily agreed to join me, after some persuasion, and now all of you. I can't thank you enough and it heartens me to see how much you care for the poor girl, Nellie, and of course for Phoebe Carruthers and Rowena Porter.'

'So, do you think if we discover information about the original murder, we'll find out about the others?' asked Dorothy.

'I think that is very possible, Mrs Tremaine. Very possible indeed.'

'Dorothy please. If we're going to work together then we should be first names only don't you think.'

Camille nodded. 'Yes, indeed, Dorothy. And will you speak to the women in your society? What is it called again?'

'The National Union of Women's Suffrage, but there are many different factions, for instance we have one particularly for West London suffragettes.'

'That may be a good place to begin looking,' said Camille. 'Both bodies have been found in London, and I hate to say it, but I think Elsie is correct in thinking that the thread between them could be something to do with the suffrage cause.'

She glanced at Elsie who smirked at her, but then smiled. Camille returned her smile, thinking that perhaps they could find some common ground. After all, they were all women who cared, even Elsie.

Chapter 8

Carrie and Camille got the tram to Millbank and alighted on the corner to walk down Abingdon Street.

'A tram,' Camille said. A first for me I think, and I rather enjoyed it. Everywhere looks so beautifully festive,' said Camille. 'I can hardly believe we're looking into why women are being murdered and left under Christmas trees. It's so macabre.'

Carrie nodded. 'I agree. I feel very nervous, Camille. Since what happened at The Hotel,' she glanced at Camille apologetically, 'I can't help feeling a sense of anxiety every time something like this happens.'

'It is a strange thing, isn't it? Both women were women of some note, both were obviously by themselves when they met up with their killer.'

'And I s'pose we should wonder why they would be out unaccompanied of an evening. I wouldn't go out at night without someone else.'

'Maybe they weren't on their own.' Camille stopped suddenly and stared at Carrie. 'Maybe they were at the theatre, or at an event and they were coerced into a situation that put them in danger.'

Carrie pulled a face. 'I think that's a bit of a stretch if you don't mind my saying. How would we find out?'

'By asking their loved ones, those nearest to them.'

Camille continued to walk towards the Palace of Westminster and Carrie hurried to catch her up.

'Also, perhaps your illustrious sister could ask her contact in the police what the women were wearing when they were murdered. It would certainly give us a clue as to where they were before they were killed. And also if they were expected to be there, or were they somewhere which their families were unaware of, although Edwin Carruthers didn't make any mention of it. I understand there was an argument between Edwin and Phoebe on the night she was killed and she left the house by herself. Upset I believe.'

'But would he have mentioned it though? I s'pose he was in mourning, grief-stricken at what had happened to his wife.'

Camille frowned. 'Mm, I'm not sure grief-stricken would describe it.' She thought for a moment. 'More matter-of-fact, I'd say, as if he was almost expecting it to happen.' She shook her head. 'No that's too strong. It's difficult to explain. It's as though he just wanted to get on with it. He wasn't remotely concerned about his children because they were at boarding school. He said they would just continue as they were, that the boys would go to Eton and his daughter would be 'finished and married off'.

'Finished?'

'Finishing school in Switzerland.'

'Why?'

Camille shrugged. 'It's what we do...in society. We're finished in a school for girls that turns us into young ladies so we can make good marriages.'

'Is that what happened to you?' Carrie glanced at Camille.

'No, it didn't. My parents were more interested in allowing me to travel. They thought it would expand my mind and make me more independent. They took me out of school and we travelled together.'

'Carrie nodded. 'Do you think they were right?'

Camille looked at her and smiled. 'Yes, I do.'

They reached the gates of the Palace of Westminster and both could not help but look up towards the spires. The gothic façade of the building loomed up in front of them, and the windows sparkled with lights as the afternoon drew in. Carrie looked across at Westminster Bridge which crossed the River Thames flowing past the iconic building. She took a deep breath.

'It's so beautiful. The Clock Tower. It's...stunning.'

'Yes,' breathed Camille. 'Your first time here?'

Carrie nodded. 'Yes. I'll bring David next time, although he may have seen it already.'

'You can go inside, but I don't think it will be necessary today. Perhaps next time. When you're with your husband. I just want to speak to the soldier on the door and hope he was here when they found Rowena Porter.'

'He might not want to speak to you. He might not be allowed to.'

'That's true, but I have some money in my purse.' Camille glanced at Carrie. 'We'll just have to make it worth his while.'

They made their way to the front entrance where a soldier stood guarding the lobby. Camille made to walk towards him until she heard Carrie gasp.

'What is it, Carrie?'

'The tree. Look. It's the tree.'

Camille turned in the direction of where Carrie pointed, and there it was on the opposite side of the path on a lawn edged with streetlights, the Christmas tree where Rowena Porter's body had been left. It was very grand, so tall they could only see the top of it because of the huge star, beautifully lit and decorated.

'Stunning,' said Camille.

'And sadly the last thing that poor girl saw before she was killed.'

'No, Carrie,' said Camille sotto voce, mindful of people passing by. 'The killer was the last thing she saw.'

'Sir,' said Carrie. 'May my friend and I speak with you?' Carrie had approached the soldier standing guard at the entrance. She stared up at the tall, broad soldiered man, her expression guileless, her eyes wide. She was glad he was young. Perhaps he'll be open to monetary persuasion she thought.

The soldier frowned, trying not to look too closely at her. 'Miss?' He lowered his eyes without moving his head. 'Can I help you?'

'Our friend, the girl who was left under the Christmas tree.'

'Your friend, Miss. She was your friend?'

Camille stepped forward. 'Our friend.'

'Were you here?' asked Carrie. 'When she was found?'

His face clouded over and he nodded. 'I was...' he glanced at Camille... 'Madam.'

'What was said, Officer? About poor Rowena. We were very close to her.'

'I'm not sure I should...'

Camille took some notes from her purse. 'Of course we don't expect you to tell us for nothing. You should be reimbursed appropriately.'

The officer looked right and left as though checking to make sure no one was watching, and then his eyes returned to Carrie and Camille, and to the money she held in her hand. 'I could get into trouble.'

Camille chuckled. 'There's no one here,' she said in a whisper. 'Quickly.' She thrust the notes into his pocket. 'Now, please. Tell us.'

He frowned and looked irritated than began to speak very fast. 'She was mutilated. Her face was bashed in, all the bones broken they said. Her hair was covered in blood.'

'What was she wearing?' asked Carrie softly.

'Satin. A satin gown...for the evening. They said she must have been somewhere, and had met her killer wherever she had been.'

'Do the police not know where she had spent the evening?'

He shrugged. 'She was found first thing this morning after her family had told the police she had not returned home. They searched, the police and the family. I s'pose they won't know much yet.'

'Who found her?'

A tear suddenly ran down his cheek as his face crumpled. 'I did. I'm one of the officers who is always on this door. I can see the tree from here, thought how lucky I was to be so near all the beauty of the festivities, but then, this morning, I saw what looked like a ball of rags under the tree and went to investigate. It was early, before five, so there weren't many people about. What I found...' He rubbed his hand across his face. 'I've never seen anything like it before. I'm a soldier but I've not seen battle. I was too young to be in the war. She wouldn't have been recognisable to her family. She was so broken.'

'Did she have a mark on her cheek? A word, letters?' asked Camille.

He nodded. 'There was something, yes. Letters. And a number. It was very rough, scratched, carved into her cheek. It looked like Emi, and the number two, but I couldn't be sure. It could have been something else. No one knew what it meant.'

'Do they think the Christmas tree was significant?'

He frowned. 'What d'you mean?'

'The other body that was found. It was placed under a tree outside Selfridges.'

'I don't know, Madam. I'm sorry.'

'Could you find out?' asked Carrie, and Camille smiled at her, wishing she had asked the question.

'Er, I don't know. Why would they tell me anything? I'm a new soldier. No one takes much notice of me. I could lose this job and I love it, apart from finding the lady.'

Carrie nodded and Camille stepped back. 'Of course,' she said. 'You have been helpful. Your mother will be proud of you.'

A smile swept across his face. 'I hope so, but you should go now. You've been here too long and questions will be asked.'

'And if we return? Will you be here?'

'You'll have to take pot-luck, Madam.'

Camille and Carrie walked towards Westminster Bridge, then took a detour down Whitehall.

'Will you join me for tea, Carrie? I know of a sweet little teashop on the corner of Richmond Terrace. We could discuss our findings. Two heads are always better than one.'

Carrie thought of Harriet and her heartstrings quivered. Her little girl was with Frances, Ida's daughter. They loved one another, and Frances was always ready to play with Harriet. Carrie knew she was in good hands.

'That would be lovely, Camille. It will do me good to get out of The Hotel for a while.'

They chose a table near the window, so they could marvel at the bright lights in the centre of London. They chose a pot of tea for two and a selection of small cakes which they both eyed with pleasure.

'These look gorgeous,' said Camille.

'It's nice here, Camille. You've been before?'

'Harry used to bring me here,' said Camille, biting into a tiny cream puff.

Carrie looked embarrassed. 'Oh, Camille, I'm so sorry. I wouldn't have said anything.'

Camille chuckled. 'Please, Carrie, don't worry. I think I'm all but over it now.'

'But it must have hurt. It would have hurt anyone. I remember when I thought David was married and he hadn't told me. I was, well, almost ready to explode with sorrow.'

Camille wiped her mouth on a napkin. 'I loved him, you know, very much. You're correct about the sorrow, but my mother taught me that one hides ones feelings, that we keep our facial expression much the same as it has always been and continue into life without letting things rock the boat. I did it for Ottilie to be honest. The last thing I wanted was for her to see me in a floppy mess. Her father was already doing that.'

'He was in mourning for Lady Delphinium for a long time it seemed.

'Indeed, but I discovered he mourned the loss of his potential son much more.'

'Rather sad.'

'Sad for all of us. It broke our family in two.'

There was companionable silence while they sipped their tea until Camille broached the subject of the missing maid.

'I wonder where she is?'

'The maid?' Camille nodded. 'There could be a reasonable explanation as to why she went missing. I know you say she was close to Lady Phoebe, but I have to ask myself, would someone necessarily tell their employer if they were going to, well, runaway, because it feels she might have.'

Camille rested her chin on her hand and stared out of the window. 'So, Carrie. Why would someone run away without telling anyone where they were going? What would make you want to run away?'

Carrie shook her head. 'I just can't imagine running away from everything I know and love. I was made to once.'

'Runaway?'

'Well, not exactly. When I got pregnant with John, my mother arranged a marriage for me with a soldier who was being posted to India. I had absolutely no choice. I didn't run away from everything and everyone I loved, I was sent away, and it was very hard.'

'You survived, Carrie. In fact, from what I've heard, you triumphed.'

Carrie smiled, her mind going back to the days she spent at the mofussil in Secunderabad. 'I s'pose you could say I did triumph, but I didn't do it on my own. I had help from some wonderful people.'

'And you think it may have happened to Nellie Bell?'

'Oh, I don't know. People knew what had happened to me, Camille. They knew I'd married, not that I'd been forced, but that I had travelled to India with my husband. With Nellie, hmm, I'm not so sure. Your own maid knows her doesn't she?'

'Yes, but not well. They were not friends, more acquaintances because of their work as maids. It seems it's a bit of a club. They probably talk about us, say all the things they would love to say to our faces.' Camille laughed.

'What about Cecily? Do you think she's loyal?'

Camille downed the remainder of her tea and nodded. 'Completely. She followed me from Kenilworth House where she had an excellent position working in a notable property in the centre of London for a lord of the realm, to come to my new home, a deal smaller...'

'And not so notable,' laughed Carrie.

Camille laughed with her. 'And she is happy it seems. Knolly, the cook, followed me too, as did Phillips, a footman who had worked for the Divine family for many years.'

Carrie gazed off into the distance.

'Alright, lets note what we know. Nellie is a woman in her late twenties, early thirties. She's passionate about the cause of suffrage, and she's loyal. She was very close to her mistress, they became friends, so much so that Phoebe was desolate at her disappearance. Phoebe was convinced that something had happened to her, but then, Phoebe is murdered. Another body is found in similar circumstances, and Rowena Porter is of the same social standing as Phoebe, at least, she comes from a good family, one with connections.'

'That's right.'

'And at the moment it's really all we know.'

'Except for the word...on the cheek. It must be significant, a code or a name shortened.'

'Shortened from...?'

'Emmaline, Ember, Emilia, Emeraude. These are names that would be familiar in our society.'

'So someone might have shortened it, and people who shorten names are usually those who are close to us, people with who we wouldn't take it the wrong way if they shortened our Christian name.'

Camille sat up. 'You're right. We would only allow someone to shorten our name if they knew us well.'

'So it would seem that these women were killed by someone who knew whoever 'Emi' is, quite well.'

They left the tearoom on the corner of Bridge Street and walked down Whitehall to where they hailed a cab.

'Tomorrow we discover more,' said Camille as they settled into the seats. 'Cecily and Ida will go to Denham House in Henrietta Street and hopefully will be given admittance to Nellie Bell's room.'

'The police would have already searched her room, surely,' said Carrie. 'Isn't it the first thing they would do?'

'Possibly. But don't forget, they're men mostly. The police force has been swelled with men now that our soldiers are home from the war, and those who were already in the force before they left for France and managed to survive, have simply returned to their jobs. Cecily and Ida are women, and they know the things that mean most to us. I have every faith in them.'

Carrie nodded. 'Me too. If there's anything there to be found, I know Ida will find it. She's like a dog with a rag. She won't give up until she's forced to.'

Chapter 9

Ida arrived outside the house in Henrietta Street. She was clearly there before Cecily of whom there was no sign. She looked up the drive at the imposing building thinking that she had never seen anything like it. The house seemed to float in the gardens surrounding it, which were full of plants Ida had never seen before. There were trees with strange barks, and leaves that sprouted out of the top and hung down like petals, shrubs spiney and gorse-like, and in the frost that had descended over London that morning, looked quite festive, although Ida wasn't sure she liked them. She preferred the traditional flowers she was used to, the ones she grew in the garden at Nightingale Lane, particularly the peachy-pink roses which had been her mother's favourites, and her herb garden that she tended with such care.

She stared up at the house again, thinking how glad she was that she didn't work in a house like the one in front of her. Nightingale Lane was the house where she had spent much of her working life and wouldn't have changed it for the world. She thought the house in front of her was a monstrosity.

She sighed as she waited. She didn't know Cecily, but Camille had described her, and Ida looked up and down Henrietta Street where she felt so very incongruous in the opulence, wishing the girl would hurry up so they could get on with it.

Ida hadn't looked forward to their task today. She didn't like lying to people, particularly those in service as she had been, and still was in a way, but there was nothing for it if they were to discover any more clues to Nellie's disappearance. Ida frowned to herself, thinking that people didn't just disappear like that as though they were once there and then not, gone in a puff of smoke. She was sure the girl had either gone because she wanted to or because someone had made her, not that she was experienced in such a thing, but it seemed the only explanation.

She spotted a girl running up the street, puffing and blowing as though she had run a long way. She stopped directly in front of Ida, apologising profusely.

'Oh, Mrs Coyle. I'm so sorry to keep you waiting. The tram I was on came off its runners and we all 'ad to get off which meant I 'ad to get here on foot.' She leant a hand against the wall, holding her side as though she'd got a stitch.

'Oh, my girl,' said Ida. 'Rest yourself, for goodness sake. Your face is all red. Bend over, that's it, bend over and the stitch will go. You'll make yourself ill if you don't get your breath back.'

Cecily did as Ida instructed and within a few minutes had steadied her breath. The stitch that had been so painful disappeared as quickly as it came and she smiled at Ida.

'Thank goodness for that. Made me feel quite sick it really did.'

'Are you alright now?' Ida asked her and Cecily nodded. 'S'pose we'd better get on with this. Not looking forward to it I must confess. Don't like lying to people.'

'Nor me, but what else can we do? Lady Camille thinks it's the only way we'll find anything.'

They walked up the long curving driveway towards the front of the house and Ida tutted.

'Strange place this. Not sure I like it.'

'I don't,' said Cecily. 'Looks like something from the continent. Lord and Lady Carruthers have been all over them foreign places because of her painting. It's probably why this house looks the way it does. I reckon there's houses like this on the continents what they've been to.'

Ida wrinkled her nose. 'It'd look a lot better with a few roses around it.'

Ida and Cecily skirted the house, looking for a garden door. There were lots of ornate railings with strange looking finials and ornate pots littering the edges of a narrow path that seemed to lead to the back of the house.

'We need to get to the kitchen,' said Ida. 'They'll be run off their feet and won't question us too closely, I 'ope. I reckon this path will lead us there.'

They followed the path until they came to a short flight of steps leading down to a door in the side of the house.

'That'll be it,' said Ida. She glanced at Cecily. 'You ready?'

Cecily nodded. 'Shall you do the talking or shall I?'

'I don't mind,' said Ida.

'You do it then,' said Cecily. 'You look like you could be her aunt.'

'Not her grandmother then?' Cecily smiled.

Ida knocked on the door and it was opened by a maid who stared at them with huge round eyes as she wondered who the two strange women were.

'Hello, dear,' said Ida. 'I'm Nellie Bell's aunt and this here,' she indicated Cecily,' is Nellie's best friend. She lent Nellie something before she...well, wasn't seen for a while, and needs it back. We need to go to her room to find it if it's not too much trouble.'

The girl opened her mouth and shouted at the top of her voice. 'Mrs Bevis. There's someone 'ere to see yer.'

The girl left and was replaced by a short woman with a red face. Mrs Bevis, Ida decided.

'Good morning to you, Mrs Bevis.' She repeated her story.

Mrs Bevis shrugged and opened the door wider for them to enter. 'Don't take too long about it, Missus. The master will be up and about in an hour or so and he won't want to see two strangers poking about the 'ouse. Who did yer say yer was?'

'Nellie's aunt.'

'Didn't know she 'ad an aunt, but she never said much at all to be honest. Never mentioned any family that's for sure. You must be worried, Missus, not knowing where she is.'

'I am worried,' said Ida, feeling awful that she had told this friendly woman a bare-faced lie. 'We all are.'

They were given instructions about the back stairs and how to get to Nellie's room in the attic, which brought back some old memories to

Ida. The house might look odd, she thought, but it was run on the same lines as the one she had always worked in.

'Here it is,' said Cecily. They faced a door painted a dark-cream like all the others. She put her hand on the doorknob and pushed it open.

The room was very much like the attic rooms had been at the house in Nightingale Lane before it had been bought by Carrie and turned into a convalescence hospital. There were two iron beds covered in pale green coverlets, one flat pillow on each. Between the beds was a small cabinet on which there was a stub of candle and a small clock. There was a bookcase on the floor and a shelf on which were some cheap ornaments, little trinkets from days at the seaside, a little china boat with white sails, a lighthouse, and a photograph.

'This looks familiar,' said Cecily.

'It certainly does,' said Ida. 'I s'pose we'd better start looking.'

'What're we looking for?'

Ida shrugged. 'I dunno, ducky. I can only think that the police 'ave already looked in here, but girls hide things they don't want anyone else to see, don't they? Letters, photographs and whatnot. I reckon they're the things we need to be looking for.'

Cecily nodded and went across to the shelf, picking up each ornament and turning them around in her hands, inspecting it for anywhere where something might be hidden. 'It would be so much easier if we knew exactly what we were looking for. I'm trying to think of things I wouldn't want anyone else to see.'

'Like a letter from a lover,' said Ida.

Cecily glanced at her. 'Well, yes, not that I've ever had one.'

"Bout time yer did then, girl.'

Ida ran her hands down the side of the bed, then pulled it out a little way from the wall, peering into the gap that was left.

'Nothing there.' She pushed the bed back against the wall, then opened the door to the cabinet, and got down on to her knees, puffing, and wincing at the pain her rheumatic bones were giving her. She looked into the cupboard but all she found were the girl's uniform and some boots. She closed the door, heaved herself up and sat on the bed. 'So she wasn't wearing her uniform when she disappeared,' she said.

'Wasn't she?' asked Cecily.

'It's in the cupboard, which means she must have been wearin' her off-time clothes, meaning she was likely going somewhere in particular when she disappeared. No one wears their uniform when they're going out do they?'

Cecily shook her head. 'No, I s'pose not.' She sat on the bed next to Ida. 'D'you think she was meeting someone?'

'I do, girl. That I do. Come on, keep looking. There's got to be something here.'

They scoured the room until Cecily got to the bookcase on which there were about twenty books, all romances.

'Bit of a romantic,' said Cecily. She frowned. 'I'm surprised.'

'Are you? Why?'

'She didn't strike me as the romantic type. More of a blue-stocking type, intelligent, knows things.' She opened each book and held them upside down, shaking the pages. When she got to the book directly in the middle of the row of books she picked it up and glanced at the cover. 'Therese Raquin,' she read, although pronounced very badly. She turned to Ida. 'Is that French?'

'I believe it is.'

Cecily turned the book upside down and shook it. A folded sheet fell out of the middle.

'Oh, Ida, look.' She bent to pick it up and unfolded it. 'It's a letter.' She glanced up. 'Should we read it? It feels wrong, reading something private.'

Ida tutted. 'That's what we're here for, girl. Give it me.' Cecily passed the letter over to Ida and waited while Ida read it. She nodded. 'Just as I thought. It's a love letter. She had a lover.'

Cecily's hand flew to her mouth. 'Oh, my goodness. Fancy that. D'you think that was who she was going to see the day she disappeared?'

'Might have been. But why wouldn't she tell anyone?'

Cecily shook her head. 'I can't imagine. You'd think she'd be excited, proud she 'ad a beau. Maids talk about things like that all the time don't they?'

Ida pulled a face. 'Not if it was someone she shouldn't be seeing.'

Cecily's eye's widened and she paled. 'What, you mean, like...a married man?'

'It's possible. Happens all the time.' Cecily tried all the other books but there was nothing inside any of them. Her eyes rested on the cabinet.

'D'you think there could be something be'ind the cabinet, Mrs Coyle. If I 'ad something I wanted to hide I might put it there.'

They grabbed the cabinet between them and pulled it from the wall. It was extremely heavy, old-fashioned and not made for moving. There was a small rug on the floor in front of the cabinet between the two beds and Ida pushed it across the wooden floor with her foot.

'That's better. It'll give us more room. Pull, girl. Pull your side.' They both pulled with all their might until the cabinet moved forward.

Cecily knelt on the bed and peered behind it. 'There's something there,' she gasped. 'A little box.'

'Can you reach it?'

Cecily squeezed her right arm and shoulder down behind the cabinet, her cheek scraping along the back corner of the furniture which made her wince. She pushed harder until the tips of her fingers reached the box. 'A little more,' she puffed. She pushed harder until she could get her fingers underneath the box, then enclosed it in her palm. 'You'll have to pull me, Mrs Coyle. I think I'm stuck.' Ida grabbed hold of her left arm and pulled her out of the gap, bringing Cecily back onto the bed. Cecily rubbed her hand across her face where the corner of the cabinet had pressed into her cheek.

'Ooh, that 'urt.'

'You alright, Cecily?'

'Yeah, I'm alright. Let's get out of 'ere. I've 'ad enough. We can open the box once we've left. I don't want to stay 'ere any longer. It's giving me the creeps.'

They went back down to the kitchen where Mrs Bevis was fixing up the master's breakfast tray with a silver cruet set and the best linen. She looked up as they went through the kitchen porch door.

'Find what you were looking for?' she asked them, not really concentrating, too busy wanting to please Lord Carruthers in his time of mourning.

'No,' said Ida, but never mind. It weren't nothing valuable. A loan of a hat, that was all.'

'Oh, right. Maybe she was wearing it.'

Ida nodded her agreement. 'You could be right there, Missus. She probably were.'

'Well,' said Cecily as they hurried down Henrietta Street to the tram stop on the corner of Garrick Street. 'What's in the box?'

The got to the tram stop which was thankfully empty, and sat on a little bench placed there for travellers. Ida took the box from her coat pocket. It was covered in red velvet and had two tiny gold hinges on one side. Ida lifted the top and gasped.

'Oh, my goodness. Oh, my goodness me. Look at them.'

Cecily peered over her arm and her mouth dropped open. 'Mrs Coyle. They're beautiful.'

Inside the box was a pair of earrings, crafted with a large diamond as an ear bob, then finished with a droplet of three diamonds beginning with a tiny one at the top, and ending with the largest one. 'They are, ducky, and worth a fortune I'll be bound.'

'Why would a maid have something like that in her possession, and why were they hidden behind a cabinet?'

Ida glanced at her, her eyebrows raised. "Cause she didn't want no one to know she had them. Isn't that why people hide things?'

'She hid the letter too. Maybe the letter and the earrings came from the same person.'

'Likely I would have thought. A present p'raps, from someone she shouldn't be seeing.'

'Either that, or the person she's seeing don't want anyone else to know.'

Ida breathed deeply. 'Whatever the reason there's something fishy here, and I ain't liking the way it's smelling. Lady Camille will be glad of this information. God knows why the police didn't find it. Bloody useless they are, and thank the Lord for it. It means we know more than they do.'

Cecily thought for a while. 'Who signed the letter, Mrs Coyle? Who was it from?'

Ida took the letter from her pocket and unfolded it, squinting at the signature. 'Just 'Yours', and then an initial, 'B''.

'Yours, B? Wonder who that is?'

'Who knows. We'll give all of this to your mistress to see what she makes of it.'

Ida and Cecily arrived at Nightingale Lane just as Dorothy was putting the kettle on to boil for elevenses.

'Oh, there you are,' she cried, her eyes sparkling with anticipation. 'Did you find anything?'

Ida put the letter and the jewellery box on the pine table. 'We did, Dot. And it's all very interesting. The police didn't find this. Flippin' useless they are, but they don't know women or their little hiding places.

'Or why they need to hide things,' said Cecily. 'And Nellie certainly had something to hide and knew where to hide them.'

Dorothy poured three large cups of tea and placed three jam scones on a pretty china plate. 'There you are,' she said looking excited. 'Now sit and tell me all about it. Lady Camille will be thrilled.'

Ida and Cecily proceeded to tell Dorothy about their adventure at Denham House and where they'd found the letter and the earrings.

'And you say the letter was found in a book? Which one?'

Cecily thought for a moment. 'Therese Raquin, I think it was. French isn't it?'

Dorothy grinned. 'It certainly is. Gosh, fancy her having that on her bookshelf.'

Ida glanced at her. 'Is it saucy?'

Dorothy laughed at Ida. 'Saucy?' She pulled a face. 'That's one word for it. I should say it is, but it's also very dark. Not the happiest book that's ever been written I understand.'

'Have you read it then?'

'I might have,' grinned Dorothy, winking at Cecily who put her hand across her mouth and giggled.

'Anyway,' said Ida, frowning at Dorothy. 'I've asked Edmund to get a message to Lady Divine to meet us here. Where's Carrie? Is she here?'

'She's with the suppliers in the sitting room. I shouldn't think she'll be long.'

Within the hour they were all in the kitchen sitting around the pine table, apart from Elsie, who was detained, she'd said. Ida rolled her eyes and shook her head.

'We can only wonder why, but I 'ope it's in a good cause,' to which they all laughed.

Lady Camille removed her lace gloves and opened the jewellery box. She gasped as the sparkling jewels were reflected in her eyes.

'Oh, my goodness. Earrings, and superb ones at that.'

'Are they, Madam?' asked Cecily. 'Do you think they're real diamonds?'

'Oh, yes, definitely real diamonds, and what sparkle. I'd wear these without a doubt. And you found them in Nellie's room?'

'Behind a cabinet,' said Ida. 'So she'd hidden them.'

'She might have stolen them,' said Dorothy.

'That's a possibility,' said Ida, 'or they may have been a present from this person.'

Carrie leant forward and took the letter from Ida, reading it quickly.

'He swears undying love,' she said quietly. 'That would be hard to resist. And signed, Yours, B.'

'B,' said Camille. 'I wonder who B is?'

'It's a start though isn't it, Madam. We have some initials, which is more than we had before.'

'You're right, Cecily. It certainly is. And Carrie and my visit to The Palace of Westminster wasn't uneventful. We were fortunate to meet with the guard who found poor Rowena Porter.'

'You spoke to him?' asked Dorothy.

Camille nodded. 'We did...and Rowena had the letters 'Emi' on her cheek, and the number two. He was desolate, beside himself at the injuries she had sustained. He said no one would have recognised her, but what she was wearing, a pink satin covered with beads, showed that she had clearly either been somewhere, or, was on the way to meet someone.'

'Was she married?' asked Ida.

Dorothy shook her head looking downcast. 'No, and I think my cousin lived in hope of them forming some sort of relationship, but she was resolute at the time, saying she wasn't sure of what she wanted for her life.'

'Was she in the suffragettes?' asked Carrie.

'Oh, yes. It's how my cousin met her. I had a cocktail party at Victoria Square, and invited her, and the other suffragettes in my group of course. My cousin, Reggie, fell for Rowena almost immediately. She is...was...very striking, dark, almost black hair and stunning violet eyes. She was really a beauty, and I can only imagine that Reggie is beside himself with her loss. It's in all the newspapers so he would surely know by now.'

They were startled by Elsie's arrival in the kitchen, her loud voice haling them all.

'You're all 'ere then?' she said as she dragged a chair out from the table. 'Like a witches coven.' They all stared at her as she howled at her own joke.

'Did you find anything out, Elsie?' asked Carrie, looking exasperated.

'Might 'ave. Need a cuppa first, and one of them jam scones what you've all 'ad.'

Ida got up and made another pot of tea, pouring it into all the cups and pushing the milk jug and sugar bowl towards Elsie, and fetching the cake tin.

'There you go, Elsie,' she said. 'Now you've been fortified p'raps you can tell us what you know.'

'Rowena had dabbled,' she said, pushing a big piece of scone into her mouth.

Dorothy frowned. 'Dabbled? What does that mean?'

'She'd had relations with someone, y'know, bedroom ones.'

'I don't believe it,' cried Dorothy. 'Not Rowena.'

Elsie shrugged. 'Why not Rowena? You don't know everything she did in her life.'

'No, but, but she might have been forced.'

'Apparently there was no evidence of a fight, down there, so to speak, although obviously she was beaten to death.'

Dorothy put her head in her hands. 'Oh, my God, this is just getting worse and worse.'

'And what about Phoebe?' asked Camille. 'Had she had...relations.'

Elsie shook her head. 'Nope, not according to my friend.'

'He's your friend now is he?' said Carrie. 'I thought he was a customer.'

'Like I've told you before, Carrie,' said Elsie, taking a large gulp of tea. 'I have to keep in with certain people, and this detective I know is one of them.'

Camille and Carrie looked at one another. 'His name's not Owen is it?' asked Carrie.

'No names. No pack drill,' answered Elsie. 'We can't give out names or our customers would go elsewhere if they thought we were talking about them. It's the whores' promise. What goes on in the bedroom stays there. I'd be out of business otherwise.'

'Well, whoever he is, he's given Elsie something we can put towards all the information we have,' said Camille. 'Now we have to put it all together and come up with something.'

Chapter 10

Camille hailed a cab for herself and Cecily, and made her way back to Birdcage Mews. At last she felt she was making some headway. Finding Nellie Bell had become very important to her. She had made a promise to Phoebe Carruthers that she would find the young woman she was so worried about, the one with whom she'd had a close connection. Camille understood how Phoebe could have considered her personal maid to be a friend, particularly as her marriage to Edwin Carruthers was likely not as happy as they would have wanted those in their society to think. In fact, this was quite usual within the circles in which they mixed.

Marriages were so often arranged. Once a girl had come home from being finished in Switzerland, knew how to walk, to embroider, to run a household, with the help of numerous staff of course, and knew to speak only when spoken to and to forget any opinions she may have held previously, she was ready to come out, to be put on the market for a husband. Phoebe's parents had done very well for her, securing a man who was well-known in the right circles, had wealth that went back hundreds of years, and a title to go with it, which of course was passed to his chosen wife. Camille could only assume that Phoebe was a woman cut from the same mould as she was. To Camille's husband's chagrin, Camille had always been outspoken, had in fact, been encouraged to be so by her parents, which in itself was unusual. She was well-travelled which had given her an experience of people that most girls of her age did not have. She was quite sure that Phoebe was of a similar personality, having travelled across the world with her artistic talent which meant having exhibitions in many capitals of the world.

Camille wondered if Edwin Carruthers had ever felt jealous of his wife's artistic talent. It wouldn't have surprised her. Men like him, and Harry Divine, always wanted to be top of the tree, the one who was the more famous half of the couple, and would brook no change in the dynamic which had been the backbone of their society for many years. Most girls accepted it because they had seen their mothers treated in the same way, could not envisage another way of living, certainly not earning their own income, and relying solely on their husbands for their livelihoods, their opinions, and for the very society in which they mixed. It seemed to Camille that the most important talent for some was to host the perfect dinner party, usually for friends and guests of their husbands, and that many vied for the position of top hostess.

Her thoughts went to the letter Ida and Cecily had found at Denham House, in Nellie's room. That it had been hidden could in no way be in doubt, and in the novel by Emile Zola no less. Therese Raquin of all things. Camille shook her head and stared out of the window. Why on earth would a girl like Nellie Bell have a copy of Therese Raquin? Did she purposefully choose that particular book to hide her letter? And if she did, why? Why choose that particular book?

When they arrived at the house in Birdcage Mews she went straight into her sitting room, calling Cecily to join her.

'Yes, Madam?'

'My books?'

'Your books, Madam?'

'I brought them with me, at least...I thought I did. Please don't say they were left behind. I don't think Lord Divine will let me take them if they were. He sees everything as his, even the embroideries and soft furnishings that I chose without his knowledge. Those books were just about the only things I owned at Kenilworth House apart from my clothes. It's important, Cecily.'

'I think they're in one of the guest rooms, Madam. I'm sure they were never unpacked. You seem to have had so much on your mind since you've lived here, there's been no time for you to read. I'm sure they came with us. Phillips brought the trunk in.' She frowned. 'I remember it being very heavy. He struggled with it if my memory serves me right.'

'Would you mind searching the trunk for me, in fact get all the books out and put them on some shelves if there are any in there. I confess I can't remember what all the guests rooms are like, only the one where Ottilie slept when she stayed. Oh, and for heaven's sake don't put any of them in her room. They're not the sort of thing she should read.'

'Are you looking for anything in particular, Lady Divine?'

Camille nodded. 'Therese Raquin. It's the same book in which Nellie Bell hid her love letter. The thing is, Cecily, it is what I would call a particular book.'

'A particular book? Why would it be particular, Madam?'

'Find it for me, and I'll tell you. In fact, you can read it for yourself. I'm sure you'll know exactly why it's particular.'

Cecily joined Camille in the drawing room, a book in her hands. She turned it over, grimacing, then rubbed dust down her apron.

'It's a bit mucky, Madam.'

Camille nodded absent-mindedly. 'Yes, some might say that.' She glanced up. 'Oh, I see what you mean.'

'I think I'll take it into the kitchen, my lady, and give it the once over or you'll get dirt all over your lovely dress. The dust has settled something terrible up in that bedroom. Might need a clear out.'

'Well, perhaps when we've sorted this business out we'll do just that, but right now I need to do some research. Yes, Cecily, take it into the kitchen and clean it up would you?'

Ten minutes later Cecily returned with the book in her hands, looking much happier.

'What might you find in there, Madam, which would help you find Nellie?' She passed the book to Camille. 'I read the back cover. I hope you don't mind. Sounds like a right to-do.'

'It's rather a dark story, Cecily. Therese is made to live with her aunt after her mother dies. She has a cousin, Camille,' Camille lifted her eyebrows and grinned when Cecily's mouth formed the perfect 'O', 'and when Therese is of age her aunt forces her to marry her cousin. He is a spoilt boy and rather sickly, and Therese does not love him. While working in their shop, Therese meets Camille's childhood friend, Laurent, and begins an affair with him. They meet regularly, but want to be together, and know the only way they can be together is to kill Camille.'

Cecily gasped, covering her mouth with her hand. 'Oh my goodness. They don't murder him do they?'

'They do. They drown him. Everyone thinks it was simply a boating accident, but of course Therese and Laurent know it was not. They do everything they can not to be discovered, as lovers or murderers, but then someone proposes they marry to mend their broken hearts which they do, but they are stricken with guilt over what they have done, and commit suicide.'

'That's a dreadful story, Madam,' said Cecily shaking her head in dismay. 'Why would anyone write a story like that? Not very jolly is it?'

'It's far from jolly, Cecily, but something is telling me that it may have some bearing on Nellie's disappearance.' She held up her hand as Cecily was about to ask her what it was. 'Don't ask me what it is about the story, Cecily, but...I do think it was significant that Nellie should hide her letter from her lover, we're assuming he was her lover, in such a book.'

'The police didn't find it, did they?'

'The police are dolts.'

'Even Chief Inspector Owen?'

Camille glanced up at Cecily. 'No...I think he is more than capable of solving the puzzle, but the officers around him are less than efficient, and without the clues we have found I don't see that he has all the information he needs to run an investigation. I cannot imagine what he will say when he discovers that it was a cook and a maid who discovered the most salient of clues, and not the officers he sent to Denham House to find them.'

'I can't think he's going to be very pleased,' Lady Divine. 'Are you going to tell him? About the clues, I mean.'

'All in good time, Cecily. For now I think we will keep them to ourselves.'

The following day, Camille made her way to Nightingale Lane in a cab. She felt compelled to discuss matters with Dorothy Tremaine who was an enthusiastic member of the suffragettes, and in particular the London branch. Elsie's comment that at least one of the links between the women was the suffragette movement had struck a chord with her, and she felt it was certainly worth pursuing.

'She's taking a day off, Madam,' said Edmund Kitchener, the receptionist at The Hotel. 'I would imagine she would be at home at Victoria Square, although of course I cannot guarantee it. Would you like to telephone her to make sure?'

'Would that be permissible, Mr Kitchener? Would Mrs Lawrence approve of it?'

He smiled. 'I cannot imagine that Mrs Lawrence will have any objections.' He handed her the earpiece. 'I will dial the number for you.' When Dorothy's number had been dialled he handed her the candle telephone complete with mouthpiece and made himself scarce. Camille smiled to herself. Ever the gentleman, she thought.

A maid answered.

'Tremaine residence.'

'Oh, yes, hello. This is Lady Camille Divine. I'd like to speak with Mrs Tremaine if she's available.'

'I'll go and see, Lady Divine.'

A few moments later Dorothy answered. 'Camille? Is everything alright?'

'Yes everything is fine. I'm at The Hotel looking for you. I understand this is your day off.'

'I needed to spend some time with the children, and Ida and the others said they could manage without me for a day. What can I do for you? It's a pleasure to hear from you of course.'

'I wanted to speak with you about the London suffragettes but I'd rather not discuss it on the telephone. Would you have an hour to spare?'

'Yes of course, Camille. We're at 44 Victoria Square. Will you get a cab?'

'I can get one at the end of Nightingale Lane.'

Half an hour later, Camille was seated in Dorothy's upstairs sitting room. Four little faces were facing her with large inquisitive eyes and she couldn't help but smile.

'Gosh, Dorothy. What a brood you have. How on earth do you manage to run such a family, a home, and work at The Hotel?'

'Strangely enough, I don't see working at The Hotel as work exactly. I feel it is more of an extension of my life and makes me a far happier woman than if I were at home all the time. I adore the children of course, but I believe very strongly that every woman needs something for herself. Being the chef at The Hotel is my thing, and I have learnt so much from those I work with. It's all quite fascinating.'

'They're of a different class of course.'

Dorothy shrugged, then leant towards the coffee table to retrieve a cigarette from a marble box, offering it to Camille, who refused with a shake of her head.

'They are, yes, but it's something I don't give much thought to, if any. When I met Carrie aboard ship on the way to India, something drew me to her, even though it was quite plain she was not one of the upper echelon. She was singled out, in fact, she singled herself out because she wouldn't have anything to do with any of us. She was treated appallingly by the other girls in our group, and I wasn't very proud to be one of them, so I kept my distance from them. She was...incredibly strong. Did you know she gave birth on the ship on the way to Bombay?'

Camille raised her eyebrows and looked aghast. 'No, I must admit I didn't. What a ghastly thing to happen. How on earth did she cope?'

Dorothy laughed. 'Took it all in her stride, that's how. It barely made her tremble. Well, that was the outward appearance anyway. I'm sure she suffered, particularly with the man she was married to at the time, Arnold Bateman.' Dorothy shivered. 'Dreadful man.'

'Dead isn't he?'

'Yes, and not particularly mourned I'm afraid.' She stubbed out her cigarette and looked at Camille with narrowed eyes. 'Anyway, you didn't come here to discuss my life. You wanted to discuss the suffragettes?'

'Was Nellie Bell one of your group? I know there are different groups in and around London. Are you still part of it?'

'The suffrage movement will continue until every woman is entitled to vote for her own future. At present only women over thirty with property can vote which is ridiculous. Of course, it is men who have made these laws, and there are still men in the Commons and in the Lords who would have women stuck in the last century with no say over their own lives. There is still such a long way to go.'

She sighed. 'The point is, Camille, we don't discuss other members of the society and their actions, or anything about their lives, so this rather goes against the grain for me, although I know it's important at the moment, if we're to find out what happened to our friends. It is opportune that you decided to visit me today as I had planned to contact you with some information I discovered yesterday. You and I have something in common at least, although it's a sad connection, that one of our friends was murdered, beaten to death. And of course the disappearance of Nellie Bell.' Camille nodded sympathetically, hoping Dorothy was about to tell her something of importance. 'Nellie Bell wasn't a member of my own group, the Westminster group, but I have learned that she was a member of the Whitechapel group, a very active member.' She drew in a deep breath. 'There was also some gossip about her.'

'Gossip? What sort of gossip?'

Dorothy ran her fingers through her hair, clearly in distress that she was discussing Nellie Bell's business when she felt it was of no concern of hers. She went to the door and called up the stairs.

'Nurse Finch. Could you take the children for half an hour please? The tutor will be here in about an hour and I have something I need to do.'

Moments later a nurse entered the room. She gently chivvied the children to go up to the nursery.

'But I want to stay with you, Mama Dorothy,' said Seraphina the eldest of the girls.

Dorothy smiled warmly at her. 'I know darling, but I really must speak with Lady Divine, and then I'll come up to the nursery and we'll have lunch together. How does that sound?' Seraphina nodded and smiled and followed the nurse and the other children up the stairs to the nursery. Dorothy shut the door firmly behind them and smiled at Camille. 'They're such good children. No trouble whatsoever, but of course Seraphina is getting older and wants to be with me all the time.'

'She's not your child, is she?' asked Camille gently.

'No, my sister Leonora's eldest. Little Dotty was her baby. She would have been so proud of them.'

'And Nellie? What was it you discovered about her?'

Dorothy returned to her seat and lit another cigarette. 'We think she was having an affair with a married man.'

'And do you think the letter we found was from him?'

Dorothy nodded. 'I would say it must have been from him.'

'Does anyone know who he was?'

'Apparently she told one of the younger girls who had only recently joined the movement that he was older, and was someone of a different class. She swore this girl to secrecy by the way, but when she discovered Nellie was missing she immediately told one of the organisers who made it known throughout the society. It was hoped that one of the women could shed some light on Nellie's disappearance. The popular view is that she ran off with him.'

Camille frowned. 'But she didn't take anything with her. She wasn't wearing her uniform it's true. It was found neatly folded in the cabinet next to her bed, but surely she would have taken those earrings, particularly if he had given them to her. Why would she have left them hidden behind a cabinet? It doesn't make sense.'

'Perhaps she was simply going to meet him. You say she wasn't wearing her uniform. Was her coat in the closet?' Camille shook her head. 'So she had planned to go out.'

'It would seem so.'

Dorothy bit her lip. 'There's something else.' Camille stared at her expectantly. 'She had been married at some point.'

'Had been?'

'Well, still is unless she is a widow. She could have been widowed during the war of course.'

'I don't suppose you have a name.'

'Bell was her married name. And she told her friend that she lived in Pratt Street when she was married, so I think there's every chance you could find out which house she lived in and whether her husband is still alive.'

Camille felt a surge of excitement go through her. At last a step towards a discovery and hopefully some progress made. She leant forward and grasped Dorothy's hand.

'Thank you so much, my dear. I know you didn't wish to divulge this information, but let me assure you, you have done the right thing. If we can discover what happened to Nellie it may lead us to discover what happened to dear Phoebe and Rowena.'

Dorothy leant towards the coffee table and picked up a newspaper, shaking it out to display the front page.

'And Lady Letitia Harvey-Milton. She was found last evening, hidden under the lower branches of the Christmas tree by Nelson's column, beaten to death.'

Camille covered her face with her hands. 'And her face?'

Dorothy shook her head. 'If she has been mutilated in that way it has not been reported, at least not yet.'

'Why is this happening, Dorothy?' Camille breathed. 'I suddenly feel rather frightened.'

'Yes, I must admit a frisson of anxiety went through me when I read this morning's headlines. Now there are three mysterious murders and all women within a society with which you and I are familiar.'

'We seem to be looking at two connections, the circles in which we move, and the suffrage movement.'

Dorothy frowned and pulled her lips into a straight line while she thought hard. 'But can we honestly say that it connects without a hitch to the disappearance of Nellie Bell? It appears to be unlikely.'

'I don't think we'll know until I've spoken with her husband.'

Dorothy's mouth dropped open and she looked astonished, her eyes registering fear.

'Surely you won't speak with him, Camille. Will it not be dangerous? Do you know of Pratt Street? I wouldn't want to go there. From what I've heard from Carrie and her sister, it's on the edge of a den of iniquity. I believe they call these places rookeries. They are where all the thieves and vagabonds make their homes and their plans to rob the likes of us. Surely to go there would be putting yourself in the path of danger.'

'I know it's not terribly salubrious, but I also know it's the only way we'll get the information we need. She was apparently married to this man. If she wasn't widowed by the war then he is presumably still alive, and we need to know why they are no longer together. It's unusual isn't it, for a man and a women to simply part, particularly since we have just been through a war.' Dorothy raised her eyebrows and Camille smiled. 'My situation was very different as you know. We live in a different world from the one Nellie and her husband occupy.'

'Yes,' Dorothy nodded, 'that's true, but just be careful, Camille. Please don't go alone.'

'Oh, I shan't. It's Phoebe Carruthers' funeral on Christmas Eve, a fine day to organise a funeral I must say, but at least her children will be home from boarding school. I'll take Cecily with me and afterwards, go on to Pratt Street and try to find Nellie Bell's husband. It's the only way we'll discover what happened.'

'And what will you do if he doesn't speak with you?'

'That's when I will go to Chief Inspector Owen with our findings.'

'And it's what you will say to Mr. Bell, that you will speak to the police if he doesn't tell you what happened between them. A push in the right direction so to speak.' Dorothy smiled at Camille.

'Absolutely.'

Chapter 11

Camille rose early on Christmas Eve, taking her breakfast in the small dining room instead of on a tray in her bedroom. She wanted to be ready for the day ahead which she knew would be a testing one; Phoebe's funeral was to be held at ten thirty at St Bride's Church in Fleet Street. It was a famous church that Phoebe liked to frequent because of its long history and association with artists and writers. Camille's thoughts went to her children, her two boys and the little girl who would grow up without their mother. To lose her in circumstances beyond their control such as illness or accident was one thing and quite awful enough, but for Phoebe to be murdered by another, broken and mutilated, was quite something else. She wondered how they would come to terms with it.

A knock at the dining room door interrupted her thoughts and she glanced up to see Cecily, and behind her, peeping over her shoulder, Nathanial Fortesque-Wallsey.

'Hello, old girl. Bearing up?'

Camille gave a watery smile and shook her head. 'Funerals. One can accept it more perhaps when the person is elderly, but Phoebe? She was so young.' She glanced at Cecily. 'It's alright, Cecily. Lord Fortesque-Wallsey is an early visitor but I think we can spare him some morning coffee.' She turned her attentions to Nathanial. 'And breakfast? Have you had any?' Nathanial shook his head. 'And eggs and bacon for poor Lord Fortesque-Wallsey who hasn't had a morsel to eat.' Cecily giggled, then put her hand across her mouth.

'Oh, Cecily and Knolly won't mind,' said Nathanial. 'They're a good sort, aren't you, Cecily. You and Knolly.' He glanced at Camille. 'Our Cecily's got a soft spot for her favourite Lord, haven't you, Cecily?'

Cecily's face began to turn red and she could hardly speak, becoming tongue-tied because of the attention Nathanial paid her. 'I...I, well, um, I'll go and get your breakfast, sir.' She bobbed a shaky curtsey and ran out of the dining room.

'Oh, Nathanial, honestly. Do you have to do that to her? She gets so flustered, poor girl.'

Nathanial grinned. 'I know. It's why I do it.'

A few moments later, Knolly entered the dining room holding a steaming plate with a teacloth.

'Here you are, my Lord. I thought I'd better bring it in seeing as you've turned our Cecily to jelly. I don't know what you said to her, but she's all over the place.'

'Me?' exclaimed Nathanial, wide-eyed. 'I'm as innocent as a newly born babe.' He winked at Camille as he tucked into the bacon, eggs and fried tomatoes on the plate.

'Are yer now?' grumbled Knolly. She glanced at Camille and rolled her eyes. 'No babe I've ever known and that's a fact.'

Nathanial shrugged and continued working on his breakfast. 'You should come and work for me, Knolly. I'd double your wages if you did.'

Camille slapped him on the shoulder with her napkin. 'Nathanial! Please don't come here as a guest and try to steal my staff. It's such bad form.'

'Don't worry, Madam,' said Knolly. 'You've nothing to fear. I wouldn't go to the Fortesque-Wallsey's for a pension.'

Camille smiled smugly at Nathanial and he shook his head. 'Can't imagine why,' he said, his eyes crinkling at the corners as he smiled.

Camille laughed. 'Perhaps it's because *you* live there.'

Knolly shook her head and left the room, a smile playing on her lips. They were all fond of Lord Nathanial. He was easy to like, not a bit stuck up, and liked to have a joke with them, although she was aware Cecily was a bit too star-struck. He was a handsome man after all, but Knolly knew that he had a different life to the one most people would have expected of him, although she wasn't meant to know about it. People are strange, she thought, some of them downright queer, but nevertheless, as long as they were good sorts, it don't matter, do it?

'So, Camille,' Nathanial said, wiping his mouth on a napkin. 'What do you think today will bring? That breakfast was top-notch, by the way. Knolly gets better and better. I'd love her to come and work for me.'

'Have you ever heard of loyalty, Nathanial? It's why my staff came with me to Birdcage Mews and why they stay with me.'

He leant back in the chair and crossed one leg over another, a pose if ever Camille had seen one. 'The funeral.' Camille nodded. 'Do you wish me to come with you. You can't mean to go alone.'

'Cecily is accompanying me, and afterwards I must go to Pratt Street.'

He uncrossed his legs and sat up, frowning. 'Pratt Street? Oh, no, my dear, not there. Why on earth would you want to visit such an awful place?'

'Because it's where Nellie Bell's estranged husband lives. At least he does if he wasn't killed in the war or taken off by the Spanish influenza. No one seems to know what has happened to him, or why they are apart.'

'And if you find him, what then?'

'I want to ask him why they parted.'

Nathanial pulled a face. 'And are you going to give him a reason to tell you. He might be pushed to tell you to mind your own business.'

'Indeed,' said Camille. 'But if he does, no harm done, and I will at least know that he is still alive and that she wasn't widowed. If he's still alive they parted for a reason, and I would really like to know what that reason is.'

Just as Camille stopped speaking there was a knock at the door, and they could hear voices in the hall. Cecily entered the dining room again and bobbed a quick curtsey.

'It's Mrs West, Madam.'

Camille glanced at Nathanial. 'Did you tell her you'd be here?'

'I think she might have some news for you.'

Tutting, Camille beckoned for Cecily to show Elsie in. 'I hope she's not drunk,' she said. 'That woman is too fond of the gin,' to which Nathanial snorted a laugh.

'Mrs West, my Lady,' said Cecily as she showed Elsie into the room.

'Elsie, my darling,' cried Nathanial rising from his chair as Camille's eyes rose to the heavens. 'How lovely to see you.'

Elsie frowned and waved him away. 'What you on about, Nathanial?' she said waving him away. 'You saw me this mornin', in your bedroom if I recall correctly.' Camille put her head in her hands. 'Anyway, I 'aven't come to see you. I need to speak to Camille.' Camille looked up and widened her eyes, hoping that Elsie had brought some useful information with her. 'It's about the latest murder, the one what was in the papers recently. Letitia Harvey-Milton. My man on the inside,' she tapped the side of her nose, 'he reckons she weren't as badly beaten as the others, says he thinks the killer's running out of steam.'

'Did she have a mark on her face?' asked Camille.

'That's what I've come about. She 'ad 'Emi' four, marked on 'er cheek. Not in a word like, but in a number, like in a book of numbers.'

"Emi' four,' said Camille glancing off into the distance. 'So...we've had 'Emi' one, Phoebe, 'Emi' two, Rowena Porter, and now 'Emi' four, Letitia Harvey-Milton.' She rose from her chair and stood by the window. 'There's one missing,' she said. "Emi' three. There's been no 'Emi' three.'

Elsie sat at the dining table without being asked and poured herself a coffee. 'What d'you think that means?' She sipped at the cup and blanched at the hot beverage as it burnt her lip.

'That 'Emi' three hasn't been found yet.'

Both Nathanial and Elsie stared at her. 'There's another?' asked Nathanial.

'Well, yes, of course. The murderer is numbering all his victims, although God knows why. But 'Emi' three hasn't been found, at least not to our knowledge.' She looked hard at Elsie. 'Did your contact mention another murder, Elsie, one that hadn't been made public?'

'You're wrong there, about it not being found. I think it has been found. He mentioned it was an 'orse.' She looked around the table. 'Any of what Nathanial 'ad going? I left the house early to give you that little snippet. Dunno what you'd do without me.'

Nathanial threw back his head and laughed out loud. 'A horse? Oh, come now, Elsie. A horse indeed!'

'It's what he said. He said an 'orse was found lying under the Christmas tree by Horse Guards Parade at the back of Downing Street. It had been shot right through the 'ead and then it's cheek had been carved into.'

'Carved into?' cried Camille.

'Like the women what were found. 'Emi', then the number three. He said it's put 'em all out, the police I mean, 'cause they've been looking for a killer of women, but now it seems he don't like 'orses neither.'

'But why a horse?' asked Nathanial, shuddering at the thought of it all. 'Are you sure, old thing?'

'Course I'm sure,' answered Elsie giving him one of her looks. 'I'm not deaf, and I speak English, same as 'im, and he said it was an 'orse.'

Camille and Nathanial stared at each other, both astonished at the unwelcome news, both wondering what the connection could possibly be. Camille left Nathanial and Elsie arguing over the details and went into the kitchen to seek out Knolly.

'Knolly, could you rustle up a plate of breakfast for Mrs West please. She's about to die from hunger apparently. Only the good Lord knows why they don't eat in their own homes.'

Knolly chuckled. 'It's no trouble, Madam. Cecily's gone up to get ready to accompany you to the funeral. I've lent her a black hat, and she's got a black coat and shoes.'

'Actually, Knolly, Lord Fortesque-Wallsey will be escorting me to the funeral. Tell Cecily I'll come by in a cab afterwards as I have an appointment elsewhere, and I'd like her to come with me.'

'Alright, Madam. I'll let her know.'

Chapter 12

The sun insisted on throwing out its rays of warmth and brightness on an event which should have been overlaid with the damp mistiness of a winters' day, enveloping everyone in the chill that usually accompanied Christmas Eve, a more fitting atmosphere for a terribly sad day. On any other day, the building could only be described as rather dour. Instead the sun's brilliance dappled the ancient bricks of St. Bride's Church, making even that building, which had seen a world that had changed over the centuries, look almost inviting. As their car drew up outside, Camille gave a sigh of regret and melancholy.

'I can hardly bear it,' she said, her voice wobbling. 'This shouldn't be happening, not to a young woman like Phoebe. Why, she'd hardly lived, particularly being married to a man like Edwin Carruthers.'

'Now then, old girl,' said Nathanial, patting her knee. 'Carruthers is a man stuck in his ways. And don't forget he was a good deal older than his wife.'

Camille glared at him as she got herself together to enter the church. 'And presumably, as a man, you think it makes it all alright, because he was an older man, stuck in his ways. Ottilie told me the things he said when he was visiting Harry at Kenilworth House. The man's a misogynist.'

Nathanial shrugged. 'That's as maybe, but he's a man who's about to bury his wife. He must be mortified.'

'Hmm, we'll see.'

They got out of the car and followed some of the other mourners into the church.

'You know Harry will be here, don't you. He and Carruthers are like that.' He lifted his hand with two fingers crossed.

'No, I didn't know,' Camille sighed. ' I suppose I should have realised. They are friends after all.'

'We'll sit at the back if you like. Harry will probably be at the front. You know how he likes to be the centre of attention, no matter what the occasion.'

'Unfortunately I do.'

'Are you giving everyone the evil eye?'

She turned to him frowning as they took their places in a pew at the back of the church, which was all that was available, as it was almost overflowing with mourners. 'The evil eye?'

'Don't they say that killers always go to the funerals of their victims?'

Camille sniffed and looked into the depths of the church, trying to place the identities of the other mourners. She shook her head and sat back in the pew. 'I don't know how I'm going to manage that. There are so many mourners and to be honest there are plenty I'm certain I've never met before. It could be any one of them.'

'A male?'

'Not necessarily. Women do kill you know.'

'I'm sure they do, but I haven't heard of many who would kill a horse.'

'Only their husbands?' Camille said, finding a small smile. 'To be honest there have been times...' She watched as Harry entered the church with Ottilie by his side. He marched purposefully up to the front and went immediately to Edwin Carruthers.

'Why on earth...? Why would he bring Ottilie? She's too young for such an event.'

'No younger than Phoebe's girl. Look.'

She observed as everything played out in the first few pews. It was as though she were watching a theatre production. Harry went to the front pew and shook Edwin Carruthers' hand as he rose to greet him, then sat next to him as if he were one of the family. Ottilie went to the children's pew and sat next to the little girl, the youngest of the children. Camille watched as she took the girl's hand, giving her a little smile as if to say, 'I'm here.' Camille's eyes filled with tears.

'She has such a soft heart,' she said, wiping the tears from her cheeks with an embroidered hanky.

'That was kind,' said Nathanial, sniffing back his own tears.

The funeral was over in just under an hour and Camille was glad to be in the fresh air, standing on the pavement outside the church.

'Where is she to be buried?' asked Nathanial.

'In the family vault at Kensal Green, but I won't be attending at the graveside. I need to get back to Birdcage Mews for Cecily and then on to Pratt Street. Just the thought of going there sends shivers down my spine.'

'Would you like me to come with you?'

Camille shook her head. 'I think it best if Cecily and I go alone. If Mr Bell is living I don't want him to feel he is being intimidated. We will tell him we are friends of Nellie. I'll let Cecily do the talking.'

'And you might want to change those clothes. Much too 'de rigueur' for a friend of a personal maid.'

'Perhaps you'd like me to wear sackcloth and ashes.'

'I wouldn't go that far,' said Nathanial as he lit up a cigarette. 'Have you spotted any likely suspects?'

'Only Chief Inspector Owen who is clearly here doing the same thing as I'm trying to do. No success for me, but maybe he can tell from someone's behaviour. He is an expert after all.'

'Oh, watch out. He's coming over.'

Chief Inspector Owen tipped his hat as he approached Camille and Nathanial.

'Lady Divine. Lord Fortesque-Wallsey. A very sad day.'

'Yes, indeed, Chief Inspector,' said Camille. 'There seems to be no rhyme or reason to it.'

His eyes met hers and Camille felt a slight frisson between them. Owen was a good-looking man, who must have been, in Camille's summation, early forties. His dark hair had been invaded by a few grey ones at the sides which gave him a distinguished look. Clean shaven, which was unusual for the fashion of the day, he was youthful with a lean body, and had a twinkle in his blue eyes.

'I suppose you've heard that old chestnut about the perpetrator always being present at the victim's funeral.' Camille nodded. 'Unfortunately, Lady Carruthers being so popular and well-known has brought everyone who is anyone out of the woodwork. I think it will be slim pickings here today.'

'What about at the graveside, Owen?' asked Nathanial. 'It's possible fewer people will go to the burial. Lady Divine will not be joining us.'

Chief Inspector Owen raised his eyebrows questioningly. 'You won't be attending, Lady Divine? I would have thought you of all people would have wanted to be present if someone stood out.'

'You could be right, Chief Inspector,' said Camille, smiling. 'I have an appointment later, but, yes, you're right. I should attend. I should pay my last respects to Phoebe even though I didn't know her very well. Yes, of course I'll attend.'

Nathanial's car took them to Kensal Green where Camille could see Nathanial had been correct about there being fewer mourners. This was the most difficult part of saying goodbye to a friend, regardless of how short that friendship had been. Camille and Nathanial hung back, allowing Phoebe's close family and friends to stand closer to the vault.

'How hideous,' said Camille, turning her face. 'Phoebe was so vital, so full of life. She would have been horrified if she'd known she would be walled up in that grotesque monument to death.'

'Darling, I don't think she'll know much about it. At least she's not being buried. How awful would that have been for her children.'

Camille watched the tableau, Edwin Carruthers standing stoically by the vault as his wife's coffin was slid into place, the children, their faces wet with crying but receiving no comfort from their father. Harry, placing a hand on Edwin's shoulder, then whispering something into his ear which facilitated a smile from him, and Camille wondered what on earth Harry could have said to him to warrant that reaction. Then her own little love, Ottilie, standing behind the children, a hand on Phoebe's daughter's arm, and one on the younger boys back. They both made watery smiles at her and Camille thanked all the stars in heaven that it wasn't Ottilie saying goodbye to one of her own parents.

She spotted Chief Inspector Owen standing a few feet away, straight-backed, his face unreadable. He was scanning the small gathering and Camille decided to do the same. Camille realised she knew, or at least had some acquaintance with most of the mourners, particularly the men who had come to the house to see Harry. She didn't know all of their wives, but as they stood in couples, one could see who was connected to whom.

Her eyes rested on a lone man, someone who would have very easily been called a dandy in days gone by. He wore a beautifully-cut suit with a tailcoat, not very often seen in the early twenties unless the occasion called for it, and wore an immaculate top hat that shone as though it had been polished. His shirt was pristine white, and at his neck a light blue cravat pinned in the centre with a large diamond. He stood with his feet slightly apart, leaning forward to rest both of his gloved hands onto a mahogany walking cane topped with a silver horse's head.

'Who's that?' asked Camille.

Nathanial followed her line of sight and lifted his chin. 'Ah, yes, one couldn't miss such a man. Have you never been introduced?'

'Never.' She frowned. 'Friend of yours? He looks as though he might be.'

'No,' said Nathanial, laughing. 'Not a friend exactly, although we have run into each other now and again, at the House, or socially, that's all.

He keeps himself to himself rather. A small circle of friends, The Honourable Richard Burrows. From an old family. Up North I understand. At least I think it's where his seat is.'

'How interesting. Does Harry know him? He knows most of the old families.'

'I doubt it.'

'Introduce me.'

'Why, Camille? I don't think Harry will appreciate it.'

'It may come as somewhat of a surprise to you, Nathanial, but I don't give a damn what Harry appreciates or doesn't. He and I are estranged and likely never to be together again.'

Nathanial raised his eyebrows. 'And what about Ottilie? Do you not care what she thinks?'

'For heaven's sake, Nathanial. I'm simply asking for an introduction. I'm not going to bed him.'

Grinning, Nathanial bowed his head. 'I'm very glad to hear it. Yes, I'll introduce you if you insist.'

'I do.'

They waited for the service at the vault to be brought to a close, and for the small gathering to disperse before Nathanial led Camille towards Richard Burrows, who nodded to Nathanial as he stepped into his eyeline.

'Lord Fortesque-Wallsey. I'm surprised to see you here.'

'Are you, sir?' Camille thought Nathanial sounded rather affronted. 'I am a close friend of Edwin Carruthers and therefore it is only right I should be here to support him. I hadn't realised that you were close to the family.'

'I am not a family friend, although Edwin and I have met in the House. I am here simply as a representative of someone who was close to Lady Phoebe, who unfortunately has been detained and cannot be here in person. It's a sad day is it not?'

'Certainly, sir, a very sad day. The lady was young and in her prime, a life cut short by a madman.'

'A man?' answered Richard Burrows. 'Was it a man? Has it been reported as so?'

Nathanial looked awkward. 'One is assuming so because of the severity of the attacks.'

Mr Burrows nodded. 'I see.'

Nathanial glanced at Camille and she widened her eyes at him as though to say, 'Get on with it.'

'The Honourable Richard Burrows, may I introduced my companion to you, Lady Camille Divine.'

Richard Burrows removed his top hat and bowed to Camille.

'Lady Divine. It is a pleasure to meet you.' He straightened and glanced over her shoulder to where Harry Divine was speaking with some of the other mourners. 'This must be rather difficult for you. I understand that you and Lord Divine are no longer together.'

Camille inclined her head and made a small smile. She made a point of looking straight into Richard Burrows eyes because she had always thought that the eyes were truly the windows to the soul, and gave even the tiniest thought away.

'Indeed you are correct, Mr Burrows, but because we have a daughter together whose happiness is paramount in both our hearts our estrangement is an amicable one. There will always be occasions when our paths will cross, although this was one occasion that I had never thought to attend. As Nathanial has so eloquently said, Lady Phoebe was such a young woman, and so talented. And the children...' Camille's voice broke off and she raised a lace handkerchief to her eyes. 'So very sad.'

'Lady Divine. Please allow me to escort you to Denham House,' Richard Burrows said, glancing at Nathanial as if daring him to object. 'One does not wish to see you in distress and I understand there will be some refreshment. We will go in my car. My driver waits outside the gates.'

Camille put a hand on Nathanial's arm. 'Would you mind, Nathanial?' She hardened her eyes over her handkerchief and he quickly got the intended message.

Chapter 13

In the short time it took for them to arrive at Denham House, Camille had summed up Richard Burrows. He had shown her every courtesy, helping her into the car because of her distress, which was real to a point, but she'd never been a crier, offered her refreshment from a small repository in the roomy passenger area which she refused, and asked the driver to drive at a gentle pace. Once the niceties had been delivered and either accepted or refused he spoke to Camille not at all.

At first she wondered if her distress embarrassed him. She was fully aware that some men felt they were put at a disadvantage when a woman shed tears or showed any kind of emotion. She took a deep breath and dabbed at her face, then replaced her handkerchief in her bag to show him she was now back in charge of her feelings, that conversation would be acceptable, but he did not take the hint.

She stole a few glances towards him. He was impeccably dressed, even more so than Nathanial. It was unusual to find a man who was even more exquisitely groomed than Lord Fortesque-Wallsey. His face was set, the jaw ridged, as he stared out of the side window. A few times she was sure he sighed with impatience. Although he had asked his driver to drive gently she was convinced he wanted to get to Denham House as quickly as possible. She couldn't help wondering why he had offered her his arm and insisted that she accompany him to the house. Could it have been for appearances? And if so why? Could he imagine that he was stealing a march over Harry because they would arrive at Denham House together? She smiled to herself. If it was the case he would be sorely disappointed. She was convinced Harry wouldn't have a care.

She turned her head and looked out of her window, feeling decidedly uncomfortable. She could not fathom why, but there was something about this man she did not like. On the surface he seemed kindly and concerned at her distress, but she began to wonder if he had feigned it simply so she would travel with him.

'You are not married, Mr Burrows?' She knew it was impertinent to ask a gentleman such a question, but also knew it would provoke some sort of reaction.

He turned to look at her with some surprise, as though he had just remembered she was sitting next to him. 'I...I am not, Lady Divine. And please, call me Richard. Mr Burrows seems so formal.'

'A little familiar perhaps, as we have just been introduced.'

He smiled which completely changed the landscape of his face. 'Oh, come now, Lady Divine. It is the new way is it not. Are women not requiring to be treated more like their male counterparts?'

'And would you approve if I subscribed to it?'

'I think we men know that women will never be equal to us. Surely females are far superior and always have been.'

She returned his smile. 'An excellent answer, although I can't help feeling you have very cleverly side-stepped how you really feel.'

The car pulled up outside Denham House and Camille was grateful for it. Again, Burrows showed her every politeness as he helped her out of the car, help she didn't need but allowed, but she couldn't help feeling that he was patronising her rather than being truly caring.

'Please, take my arm Lady Divine.' Camille reluctantly held his arm as they walked up the drive towards the house, but was determined to make her way to a familiar face as soon as they were given admittance.

Once inside, Camille inclined her head to Burrows to thank him, but assured him that she must attend to her daughter.

'Ottilie and I have yet to speak,' Mr Burrows, 'and we see so little of each other these days. I am sure she has found the events of today extremely distressing. Do forgive me.'

'Of course, my dear. No forgiveness required. A woman should never be parted from those she loves.'

Camille frowned as she made her way towards Ottilie who was sitting with the Carruthers' children. A strange remark, she thought, but then her eyes alighted on her daughter who spotted her going towards her and ran to her, a look of utter relief on her face.

'Mama.' Ottilie flung herself into Camille's arms. 'I have missed you, Mama. I wanted to speak with you in the church and when Lady Phoebe was put into that horrible vault, but Papa said I shouldn't make a fuss, that we were here for the children and not for me to see you.'

Anger flooded through Camille. How typical of Harry. He would use anything he could to keep her apart from Ottilie. How could he sink so low, she thought. I don't know the man at all. 'Darling, I'm sure Papa said it for all the right reasons, and you were such a support to the children. I was very proud of you.'

'Were you?'

'Of course, sweetheart. You always make me proud.'

They linked arms and found an empty chaise where they could sit together.

'I don't think Papa is ever proud of me,' Ottilie said sadly.

Camille looked at her in amazement. 'Ottilie, why would you say such a thing?'

'Because he wants to send me away to school. I thought when you and he...well, when he made you...I thought I would be the woman of the house, you know, do all the things you used to do. I know I would never do them as well as you, but, I thought it would be what he wanted. Instead, I'm to go to a girls' school, somewhere in Hampshire.' She stared at Camille, her eyes brimming with tears. 'Mama, I don't want to go. Why can't I go to a school in London? At least I could come home in the evenings, or even at the weekends if I'm a weekly boarder. I don't understand. And I'll never get to see you.'

Camille inhaled a deep breath. What she wanted to say to Ottilie was, 'Which is why your father wants to send you away to school. He knows it's the one thing that will hurt me more than anything else', but she didn't. It wasn't Ottilie's fight, it was hers, and it was one she would take on willingly.

'I'll talk to him, Ottilie. I can't promise anything because you live with him and he makes the decisions on your behalf, but I will speak with him, that I do promise. Have you told him you don't want to go.'

Ottilie nodded. 'He says I should think myself lucky that I've still got my parents and I'm not like the Carruthers children, having to go to one of my parents' funerals.'

Camille shook her head and turned away. She didn't want Ottilie to see the anger and disgust on her face. Harry was using Ottilie to get to her. It was unacceptable and something she would not allow. When she turned back Ottilie was still staring at her, waiting for her to put things right. Camille patted her hand.

'I don't want you to worry about this anymore. I want you to let me deal with it. I don't want you to be distressed by it any further.'

'Will you tell him that it will make me very unhappy? Will you beg him, Mama?'

'No, Ottilie, I won't beg him. Don't ever allow yourself to be put into a position where you have to beg another person for anything, but I will speak with him and tell him how distressed you are. Would you like to come back to Birdcage Mews with me?'

Tears coursed down Ottilie's face. 'More than anything, Mama. More than anything in the world.'

Camille flinched when she heard Harry's laughter ring out as he and his cohorts stood in the centre of the room, Edwin Carruthers included, drinking whiskey and smoking cigars, laughing at something one of them had just said, as though they were at a race meeting instead of Phoebe Carruthers' wake. What kind of men are these, she thought. Something must change.

Chapter 14

Camille was eager to leave Denham House. She had felt she was in a world alien to her, one she had left behind, even if in the beginning it had not been her choice. Was she ever like that? she wondered to herself. Had she ever been so cold, so dismissive of someone losing their life? She prayed not, hoped that the nurturing side of her had always come to the fore when someone needed help or consolation.

Her thoughts went to Harry. He was still her husband. She was still Lady Divine, but something told her that she might not be for very much longer. She had observed him in the middle of a room, one containing mourners, with Edwin Carruthers, a bereaved man one would have thought, and held court with his associates, actually made them laugh. They had swigged from well-filled whiskey glasses, and smoked copious amounts of cigars as if they were simply socialising instead of mourning the loss of someone who had been so brutally murdered, a young woman, a mother, whose children were sitting inches away from them and could witness the men's behaviour, watch them as they got increasingly drunk and laughed at some joke or other.

She shook her head as she made her way down the hall to the vestibule, her hand wrapped tightly around Ottilie's.

'Mama, you're hurting me.'

She turned to the voice. She had been so lost in her thoughts she had forgotten Ottilie was with her. 'Oh, Ottilie, darling. I'm so sorry. I just suddenly had a great need to get away from here.'

Ottilie nodded. 'I do think it's strange, Mama. Lord Carruthers isn't crying or anything. I thought he would have been. Don't people cry when they've lost someone? The children have cried all morning, particularly little Mathilda. She says she doesn't know what she will do now her Mama is no longer with them.'

'Yes. Usually we would expect it.' Camille couldn't keep the hardness out of her voice. 'One would think so.' She inhaled. 'But not in this case it would seem,' she said under her breath.

'But he's not.'

'Not what?' asked Camille frowning, her mind only half on what Ottilie was saying.

'Not crying, Mama. Are you listening?'

'Yes, yes, of course I'm listening. I think you should come home with me. Papa can collect you from Birdcage Mews.'

Ottilie frowned. 'Should I not tell him, Mama. How will he know?'

Camille waved her away and watched as she went back into the drawing room where a raucous laugh pierced the atmosphere, making Camille jump. Hot tears welled in her eyes and she wasn't sure if it was grief or pure anger. 'Bit of both I expect,' she said to herself as she waited in the vestibule for Ottilie to return, dabbing at her eyes with a fine-linen handkerchief edged with French lace. She looked at the handkerchief in the palm of her hand, thinking how inconsequential everything was.

'Madam? Madam?'

Camille startled at the sound of a girl's voice calling her. She turned in the direction of the voice and was surprised to see a maid, almost running towards her in her haste to speak to Camille. 'Madam, can I speak with you?'

It was one of the maids who had shown Camille into the drawing room when she had visited Edwin Carruthers after Phoebe's death. 'Yes, yes of course,' said Camille, her eyebrows knotted in a frown when she saw how distraught the girl was. 'Can I help?'

The maid bobbed a quick curtsey, then stood in front of Camille, wringing her hands. 'I'm not sure I should be speaking with you, Madam, but...well, me and the others, we know you was a friend of 'ers, Lady Phoebe that is, and, well, we've talked about it and we think you should know.'

'Know what exactly?'

'Before she died...was taken...she was gettin' letters, little notes, some not very nice, sayin' she should stop worrying about Nellie and get on with being a wife and mother 'cos it was all she was good for.'

Camille widened her eyes as the girl fidgeted from foot to foot, looking about her as if frightened she would be discovered. 'And these notes? How do you know about them?'

The girl pulled a face. 'She didn't hexacly 'ide 'em. I reckon she'd bin gettin' 'em for some time, but Nellie would 'ave put 'em away somewhere, but then, well she's not 'ere no more. We take...took it in turns to be Lady Phoebe's personal maid after Nellie left, and we all found one or more.'

'Do you still have them?'

The girl nodded. 'We hid them in her bedroom, Lady Phoebe's that was, in a chest at the bottom of the bed. Would you like to see them, Madam? Do you want them?'

'I would like to see them. This doesn't sound very good does it?'

'They're not very nice, and Lady Phoebe was such a lovely person. Treated us all lovely.'

'Can you get them now? I can take them with me when I leave.'

The girl hurried off, taking the main staircase stairs two at a time just as Ottilie joined her.

'Papa said I can stay with you tonight and tomorrow. He's going to a shooting party with Lord Carruthers and some of the others from the House. It means I can spend Christmas with you, Mama.'

Camille enveloped Ottilie in her arms. 'That's wonderful, darling. We'll need to go shopping this afternoon which will be lovely, and get you some new clothes for tomorrow with it being Christmas Day. Cecily and Knolly will be delighted that you'll be with us. I do have an appointment when we leave here. I'll take you to Birdcage Mews first because Cecily is coming with me, and perhaps you can do some cooking with Knolly. Would you like that?'

'Oh, Mama,' cried Ottilie excitedly. 'I would love it. And to go shopping with you too in all the sparkly shops. Oh, Mama, I'm so lucky.'

Camille's heart lurched at the happiness of her daughter. She knew she must do all she can to persuade Harry to allow Ottilie to live with her. She had to confess she was surprised that he didn't feel the need to spend Christmas Day with her, but then he was thinking only of himself as usual, and to put a shooting party before her on the most exciting day of the year, was, in her mind, unforgiveable.

'You say he's going with Lord Carruthers?' Ottilie nodded and Camille frowned. 'But what about the children?'

'They will stay here.'

'On their own?'

'With the servants.'

The maid who had spoken to Camille entered the vestibule from a side door, clutching a handful of notepaper in her hand.

'Here they are, Madam,' she said in a low voice. 'I hope they help you.' Camille glanced at her quizzically. 'We know you're trying to find out what happened. We'd all help if we could...but our jobs. Lord Carruthers would have our guts for garters if he thought we were getting involved wiv' things what don't concern us.'

'Thank you, my dear,' said Camille, smiling at her. 'It's very brave of you to do this. I promise I won't mention that you gave them to me, and yes, I will do my very best to discover what happened.' The girl nodded, her mouth a straight line, her eyes brimming with tears. Camille put a hand on her arm. 'I know how you feel, but the children. They need all of you.'

'They're staying here on their own tomorrow, poor little mites. It ain't right. They've already lost their Mama and they should have their father with them when they open their presents. It's not right.'

Camille inhaled a breath wondering if the thing she was about to propose was the right thing to do, but then decided to suggest it anyway.

'Will Lord Carruthers' driver be here tomorrow?'

'That he will, Madam. Lord Carruthers is going to Hampshire with Lord Divine.'

'Then may I suggest that he, the driver, brings the children to my house in Birdcage Mews in the morning. They can spend the day with me and he can collect them again after high tea. They can bring their presents, and we can have Christmas lunch together. What do you say, Ottilie?'

'Oh, Mama, it would be wonderful,' she breathed.

Camille turned to the maid who was smiling. 'Well?'

'Madam, that would be so lovely for them, to have some company and be with Miss Ottilie. I know they would enjoy it.'

'Right, well, let's consider it done. My house is number eight. The driver will not be able to take the car down the mews, so he must park in the road outside, but he can walk the children down. Will you tell him?'

The girl bobbed another curtsey. 'I will, Madam. And thank you.'

'Thank you, my dear,' Camille answered, 'and enjoy your Christmas Day. I'm sure it will be a lot easier for you all without having to take care of any charges.'

'Am I to tell Lord Carruthers?'

Camille couldn't help grinning. 'I don't think it will be necessary. By the time he returns the children will be back here in their beds, and if he discovers they spent Christmas with me, well, it'll be too late.'

The maid returned her grin. 'As you wish, Madam.' The maid turned to walk away then stopped. 'By the way, Madam.'

'Yes.'

'Lady Phoebe was due to have an exhibition at an art gallery in Bond Street in the New Year. I didn't know if you knew.'

'I didn't. Do you think it will go ahead?'

The maid shrugged and grimaced. 'I doubt it. I'm not sure Lady Phoebe and the owner of the art gallery agreed on the subject of her paintings. She had finished a load of pictures about suffragettes, painting them in their uniforms, and also some of the not so pleasant things that happened to them. I don't know if you know but some of them were made to eat.' She stepped a little closer to Camille. 'Shoved a pipe down their throats and poured stuff down so they didn't starve themselves,' she said in a whisper. She shivered. 'Sounds bloomin' awful don't it?'

'It certainly does.' Camille became thoughtful. 'So what did the owner of the gallery want her to exhibit?'

'Her animals and her landscapes, that sort of thing.'

'But not her suffragette paintings.'

'Oh, no. She'd already told Nellie about it and Nellie told us. Lady Phoebe was very disappointed. She told Nellie it was some of her best work.'

'Which gallery did Lady Phoebe exhibit her works?'

'Ooh, I dunno. If you don't mind waiting a moment, Madam, I'll ask the others.' She disappeared through the side door leading to the kitchen, and in moments was back again. 'It's the Yorke Gallery, Madam, in Bond Street. Even royalty buy their paintings there apparently. I can't imagine the likes of us would go in there.' Her face coloured to a bright pink. 'Well, me anyway. I didn't mean you, Madam.'

'Of course not, and thank you so much, my dear. What is your name?'

'Beatie, Madam.'

'You've been very helpful, Beattie. And please, thank your colleagues for their help, and don't forget about tomorrow. It'll be our little secret.' Beattie smiled conspiratorially and bobbed another curtsey, then went back to the kitchen.

'Where are you going, Mama?' asked Ottilie as they sat in the back of the car, a cab that had been hailed from them by the doorman at Denham House. Henrietta Street had never been so busy, with cars picking up mourners and dropping off great bouquets of flowers which Camille thought would go to waste as Edwin Carruthers did not seem to have time for the beauty in life, including his own wife.

'Cecily and I have an appointment, Ottilie,' she answered, hoping that the afternoon's visit would turn out well, while at the same time dreading having to go to Pratt Street which she knew had a reputation that wasn't to be envied. The street was not at the centre of one of the worst areas for vagrants, thieves, and vagabonds, but was near enough for her to be aware that she and Cecily must be cautious. In truth she wasn't looking forward to it but deemed it a necessity if she were to get a truthful picture about Nellie Bell's marriage. 'It shouldn't take more than a couple of hours, so if you can be ready by four o'clock, we'll take a cab to Knightsbridge for some serious shopping. How does that sound?'

'It sounds wonderful. So, do you have money, Mama?'

Camille glanced at her as they sat in the back of the cab and frowned. 'Yes, of course, Ottilie. Papa gives me an allowance, which allows me to put a little away for luxuries. I have very little to spend it on these days so shopping with you this afternoon will be a rare treat.'

'And he pays the rent for your house in Birdcage Mews?'

Camille stared at Ottilie, wondering why her questioning had taken such a turn. 'Yes, yes he does. Why, Ottilie?'

'So...he isn't an utterly horrible person then, is he?'

'Ottilie. Of course he isn't an utterly horrible person. He's your Papa. Why would you say such a thing?'

Ottilie stared up at her mother, her eyes sparkling. 'I heard you call him that once before you left Kenilworth House. I don't think he was being very kind to you.'

Camille breathed in and closed her eyes. This was what she had hoped Ottilie would never witness. Her arguments with Harry and the wranglings over his insistence that she leave Kenilworth House had been the moments that had brought her the most pain. 'Oh.'

'You told him you thought he was an utterly horrible person.'

'Did I?' She smiled at Ottilie with motherly affection. 'Darling, people say things in the heat of the moment. I'm so sorry you heard your father and I arguing, I'd hoped you never would, but we said things to each other we didn't mean.'

'Do you love him, Mama?'

An honest question deserves a truthful answer, Camille thought. 'I will always love him, Ottilie, because he is your father. When you were born it was the greatest gift anyone could have given me, and I will always love him for it. If you're asking me if I'm *in* love with him, then

I must answer honestly, no, I am not. And I'm sure he is not *in* love with me, but we will always respect one another and want the best for each other.'

Ottilie nodded. 'You won't live at Kenilworth House again, will you?'

Camille shook her head. 'No, darling. No, I can't think it would happen. But you have two homes now, and I can't wait for you to stay with me over the Christmas time, girls together.'

Ottilie leant against Camille and put her arm across her waist. 'I love you, Mama, so much.'

'And I love you, Ottilie. With all my heart.'

Chapter 15

'Are you sure about this, Lady Divine?' Cecily asked after Camille had left Ottilie with Knolly at Birdcage Mews.

'To be truthful, Cecily, I am not sure about it, but I can see no other way of discovering what happened to Nellie Bell. I'm just hoping her husband is still alive, but if he isn't, I understand neighbours in the community are best placed to know what happens within marriages of the people who live nearby.'

As they got closer to Pratt Street the atmosphere changed and another world presented itself from outside the car windows. The buildings were closer together, most were in terraces, and the brickwork on every house was dingy and black with soot. There were no gardens fronting the house, and every window looked as though it hadn't seen a cleaner for years. Some of the street-lamps were broken, and in the gutters was all manner of detritus that Camille did not even want to look at for fear of seeing something unsavoury.

'Oh my goodness,' said Camille. 'This is worse than I thought.'

'This isn't Pratt Street, Madam,' said Cecily. 'We're not there yet. Pratt Street is further in. A few streets more and we'll be there.' Camille nodded, wondering at the wisdom of her decision to venture into the area.

'Here it is,' said Cecily. 'Look, the sign. It says Pratt Street.'

Camille pushed herself forward on the car seat and looked out of the window and up to the street sign on one of the houses. 'Gosh, yes, but it's so filthy I'm surprised you spotted it. Well done, Cecily. Right, shall we get out of the car here. Here is as good as anywhere as I'm afraid I don't have a number, but we'll knock on some doors.'

Cecily glanced worriedly at her, but nodded and sighed and followed Camille out of the car and onto the street. It'll be me knocking on the doors, she thought, but kept her thought to herself.

They walked a little down the street. Camille felt uncomfortable and Cecily offered her arm which Camille took gratefully.

'Let's try here,' said Camille, stopping in front of one of the houses. 'This one doesn't look as run down as some of the others.'

Cecily looked at the paint peeling off the door and the grimy windows. 'It's number thirteen, Madam. Do you think another number might be better?'

Camille chuckled. 'I'm not superstitious, Cecily. Let's knock.'

Cecily shrugged and leant forward to knock on the door. She gave it a sharp rap and stood back, looking down at her feet. They waited for a few seconds but there was no reply. Cecily stepped forward and rapped on the door again. This time, the door was opened a fraction and the face of an elderly woman peered out.

'If you're collecting for anything, I've already given everything I can afford to the Salvation Army, so there's no need for you to be jangling your collection boxes at me.'

'We're not collecting,' said Cecily.

'Are you here to sing Carols then? I like Oh Come All Ye Faithful if you are. Traditional, that is.'

'No,' said Cecily. 'We're not here to sing Carols either,' said Cecily.

'Well, what you here for then?'

'We're looking for someone.'

The woman opened the door wider, looking interested now. 'Oh. Who? I don't know no one really. I'm a widow. I keep myself to myself.'

'We're looking for a Mr Bell. He was once married to a girl called Nellie. We wondered if you knew him. It's very important.'

The woman shook her head. 'No, ducky, sorry.' She wrinkled up her nose in thought. 'Bell. Bell, um, no don't remember anything about that name. Try number fourteen opposite. She knows everything and everyone. If anyone knows him she will.' They thanked the woman who slammed the door, shaking the crumbling paint from the wood, and crossed the road to number fourteen.

The paintwork on the outside of number fourteen was in a poor state, and the front door had been cobbled together with lumps of wood that were in a similar parlous condition. As they drew up in front of the house, Camille grimaced at the sound of children screaming and shouting from inside.

'Oh my goodness. What is that noise?'

'I think they're fighting, Madam, 'or perhaps it's their way of having fun.'

'Really? Well knock, Cecily. I want to get this over and done with. It sounds like a zoo and I don't want to stay here any longer than necessary.'

Cecily knocked on the door. The noise from the other side was deafening and didn't abate at their knock. There was no answer. Camille bashed the door with the side of her gloved fist.

'Well if that doesn't alert them nothing will.'

Moments later the door was dragged open and a teenage boy stood in the frame. 'What?'

'Could we speak to your mother,' asked Cecily.

'What d'you wan' her for?'

'We'll explain that when we speak to her,' said Camille losing patience. The boy didn't answer, but went back inside the house, where children were still screaming, and slammed the door.

'We're getting nowhere fast, Madam,' said Cecily when the door was opened again.

In the frame stood a woman of small stature. Her blonde hair was swept up on top of her head but looked in danger of collapsing around her face. Wrapped around her waist was an apron, filthy, the hems shredded and frayed. She pushed a stray lock from her eyes, then stood with her hands on her hips.

'Can I 'elp yer?'

'We're looking for a Mr Bell,' said Cecily. 'He was married to Nellie Bell.'

The woman crossed her arms in front of her chest and leant against the crumbling doorframe. 'Who wants to know?'

'We're friends of Nellie,' said Cecily. She glanced at Camille. 'At least, I am.'

The woman rubbed her hands together. 'How much do you want to know about them?'

Camille took a coin from her purse. 'This much.'

The woman grabbed it out of Camille's hand, bit on it, then put it in her apron pocket. 'They ain't married no more. Nellie left him.'

'Does he still live in Pratt Street?' asked Camille.

'Nah, he moved out. Don't know where he went.'

'Why did she leave him?' asked Cecily. 'I was very surprised to hear she was no longer with her 'usband.'

'I ain't surprised. Got a better offer d'int she?'

'A better offer?'

The woman crossed her arms in front of her chest again and raised her eyebrows. Camille gave her another coin which joined the other one in the woman's apron. 'Me and Nellie was friends, of a sort anyway. She told me that she'd met someone, another bloke, rich, got a nice 'ouse. He wanted her to leave Donald Bell. Wouldn't have no truck wiv her until she did, so she packed her bags and left 'im. Can't say I blame her. Old Bell weren't a looker. Older an' all. Quite a bit. I miss 'er though. She's a nice girl, a bit, what's the word, green I s'pose, yer know, ain't got much up top. Dunno why she married old man Bell. Maybe it was for a bit of security, but when this other bloke came along she saw the error of 'er ways.'

'Do you know where she was working?'

'Oh yeah, I know. One of them fancy 'ouses in Henrietta Street. I reckon that's what gave her ideas above 'er station. She'd saw 'ow the uvver 'alf live and decided Pratt Street weren't no good for 'er anymore, so she left. I ain't seen her since.'

Camille nodded and turned to walk away, and Cecily thanked the woman who closed the door with a slam. A piece of wood fell off the door but no one came out of the house to retrieve it and replace it on the door. It seemed to be the only thing holding it together.

'What a place,' said Camille. 'I shall never complain about anything again. How can she raise a family in such a house?'

'Don't think they have much choice, Madam. There's not much work about and the rents are quite high.'

Camille sighed. 'I suppose you're right, Cecily.' She smiled at her. 'Thank you for coming with me. It wasn't the most pleasant of things to do on Christmas Eve, but we've learnt so much. Now I must decide what to do with the information.'

'Will you tell Chief Inspector Owen, Madam?'

Camille nodded. 'Yes, but not until after Christmas. There are some things I must do until then. I know he won't be thrilled that I've been investigating, but I have a feeling we may have got much further than he has in his investigations. I may need you again, Cecily. I think it's so much better, and safer, when there are two of us looking into this.'

Cecily smiled. 'I don't mind, Madam. I'm quite enjoying it. It's different to my usual work. I like helping, really I do, and I'm keen to find out what happened to Nellie.'

They walked through the darkening streets, Camille holding Cecily's arm again, until they got to the lights of the high street where Cecily hailed a cab to take them back to Birdcage Mews. 'Christmas Day tomorrow, Madam. Sounds like we've got a lot of company coming.'

'Yes, we'll have a full house I think, mostly children, but I think that's rather wonderful don't you?'

'I do, Madam,' said Cecily with sparkling eyes. 'It's how Christmas ought to be.'

Chapter 16

The Christmas lights in Knightsbridge, Regent Street, and Oxford Street sparkled into the darkness leaving Ottilie breathless.

'Mama, this is so beautiful. I feel as though I've been in hibernation like a little hedgehog. Papa never wants to do anything like this. Thank you for bringing me here.'

Camille grinned and clutched her daughter closer to her, hugging her and enjoying her moment of happiness. 'It's my pleasure, Ottilie. I knew you would love it, and the dress you chose is perfect for tomorrow's celebrations. I can't wait to see you wear it, and of course, the Carruthers children. I sincerely hope they can find some enjoyment tomorrow, even though they have sadly lost their beloved Mama.'

'It was so kind of you, Mama, to invite them to Birdcage Mews. I know they'll still be sad. Losing ones Mama is a dreadful thing, but we'll try to make them happy, won't we?'

'Of course we will, and Knolly's Christmas lunch will cheer them up, I have no doubt. She's planning some wonderful things I hear.'

'Oh my goodness, yes she is. She showed me this afternoon. My mouth was watering all the time.'

'On that note, shall we go to Selfridges and have some afternoon tea. I'm sure you'll love it there.'

'Am I allowed? I thought it was only for ladies.'

Camille threw her head back and laughed. 'Yes, you're allowed, silly girl. And you are a lady, my darling. Lady Ottilie Divine.'

Ottilie grinned up at her. 'So I am.'

The restaurant at Selfridges wasn't as full as Camille had expected, and she and Ottilie got a table easily.

'I thought there would be more people having afternoon tea here,' she said, looking around at the empty tables. 'I imagined that Christmas Eve would be one of the restaurants busiest times. I'm surprised so many tables are free.'

A waitress came over to attend them and they ordered tea for two, including a selection of tiny sandwiches and cakes presented on a china cake stand.

'Oh, Mama, this is so pretty. And those cakes look scrumptious.'

'Scrumptious, eh. That's quite a word.' Ottilie laughed as she bit into a cake topped with cream which blew a blob onto her nose. Camille laughed and leant forward to clean it off with a napkin. 'Darling, I think you're meant to eat the sandwiches first.' She shook her head and smiled as the waitress returned to ensure everything was to their liking.

'It's all lovely, thank you,' answered Camille. 'I was just saying to my daughter that I thought the restaurant would be busier.'

The waitress nodded, then she glanced at Ottilie and lowered her voice so only Camille could hear. 'It's because of them murders, Madam, you know, of the ladies. We've had no end of cancellations because our regular diners want to stay at home where it's safe.'

'Oh, my goodness. I hadn't thought...'

'And there's been another,' the waitress whispered. She look pointedly at Ottilie. 'I won't say any more, Madam. I've no doubt it will be in the papers. What a way to welcome in the festive season.'

They made their way down Oxford Street. Camille was quiet and Ottilie kept looking up at her, concerned that her mother's mood had changed.

'Are you alright, Mama? Did the waitress upset you? You seemed to go very quiet after you'd spoken to her?'

Camille squeezed her arm. 'I'm fine, darling. Just thinking about tomorrow and hoping I've got everything ready. Oh, look, there's a newsstand. Wait here for a moment. I just want to get an evening paper.' She went across to the newsstand where an advertising board screamed the news that another body had been found. She went back to Ottilie and unfolded the paper, trying to prevent her daughter from seeing the front page.

'There's been another then?' said Ottilie.

Camille stared at her. 'Oh, Ottilie I didn't want you to see.'

Ottilie frowned. 'I can read, Mama, in French too, and a little Latin.'

Camille put her arm around Ottilie's shoulders. 'I know, of course you can. It's just...so awful. I'm trying to protect you I suppose.'

'Everyone knows about it. It's what happened to Lady Phoebe isn't it? The children know. The eldest boy, Marcus, spoke about it.'

Camille's hand flew to her mouth. 'Oh, the poor things. Not the little girl surely?' Ottilie nodded. 'Oh, dear.'

They found a cab which took them to Birdcage Mews. The sparkling lights had suddenly lost their allure for Camille, but as they got nearer home she shook herself and made up her mind to enjoy the next few days because she would be with Ottilie, and she wanted to enjoy their time together. She wasn't sure when Harry would allow them to be together again.

Once inside Cecily helped them off with their coats, then suggested that Ottilie went into the kitchen where Knolly had just made some shortbread biscuits in the shape of old-fashioned carriages, and couldn't wait for Ottilie to see them. Camille glanced at Cecily, and encouraged Ottilie to go to the kitchen, then drew Cecily into the drawing room.

'Do you need to speak with me, Cecily?'

'A telegram came for you, Madam.' She retrieved the telegram from her pocket. 'I thought it might be best if you read it alone. They're not often bearers of good news are they?'

Camille took the envelope from Cecily and nodded. 'Thank you, Cecily. That was very thoughtful of you.'

When Cecily had left her alone in the drawing room, Camille sat on the chaise and placed her thumb under the seal, tearing the envelope at the top. Inside was the telegram which she gingerly took out. She took a breath then unfolded it. Her heart began to thump in her chest and her breath came out in short gasps. She threw the telegram onto the chaise, then, taking a deep breath picked it up again, reading it slowly so that she fully understood the contents.

'Stay out of things that don't concern you,' she whispered aloud. 'Or you'll be next.' She put a hand across her mouth, then inhaled another deep breath. 'Nothing ambiguous about that,' she said to herself.

She folded the telegram and put it into her pocket as a knock at the drawing room door startled her.

'Sorry, Madam, but are you alright?'

'No, not really, Cecily?' She took the telegram from her pocket and handed it to her. Cecily's eyes widened with horror as she read what had been sent.

'You must tell the police, Madam. You really must. This is a threat.'

'But it's Christmas Eve, Cecily. Surely it can wait until after Boxing Day.'

Cecily shook her head. 'I'm sorry, Madam. I don't want to overstep the mark, but you should do it now. You've just had a telephone installed, Lady Divine, and you ain't...haven't used it yet, and Chief Inspector Owen gave you his card. Why don't you ring the station? Me and Knolly will keep Lady Ottilie occupied until you're done.'

Camille sighed with frustration then nodded. 'Alright. I'll do it now, but Ottilie is not to know about this. She knows too much already and she's only just turned eleven. I know young girls know more these days, but she's still a child.'

'We won't say anything, Madam.'

'When did you receive this, Lady Divine?' Chief Inspector Owen asked her, holding the telegram between finger and thumb. 'It's very clever to send a telegram and not a note. No chance of any useful fingerprints on it.'

'It came when I was out, Chief Inspector. I took Ottilie shopping in the West End and it must have been delivered then.'

Camille indicated for Chief Inspector Owen to sit down and he sat on the chaise which made her smile to herself. He was a tall man, and broad shouldered, and looked somewhat incongruous sitting on a pink chaise.

'Why is it asking you to stay out of things that don't concern you?'

This was precisely the subject Camille had been concerned about. She hadn't told Owen what had happened since the last time she saw him at Denham House, and when driving her home, he had specifically requested she leave any investigation to the police. She bit her lip and sat opposite him, her hands folded in her lap.

'Would you like some tea, Chief Inspector? It gets so cold when the night draws in.'

Chief Inspector Owen lifted an eyebrow. 'The last time we spoke, Lady Divine, I asked you implicitly not to involve yourself with any investigating. I'm assuming you ignored my advice, madam.'

'I may have done.'

'You may have done?'

She rose from the chair and walked around the room, feeling that she could think more easily and explain herself better if she moved about.

'The thing is, Chief Inspector, I made a promise to Phoebe Carruthers that I would find her maid, Nellie Bell. She specifically asked me to help her, as her husband, Edwin Carruthers, did not want her to go to the police about Nellie's disappearance. I felt strongly that it would have been wrong of me to give up the search when I promised Phoebe I would find her.'

Owen shifted on the chaise which he thought incredibly uncomfortable. 'And have you found her?'

'Not exactly.' Camille sat opposite him again, thinking how calm he was, so different from Harry.

'Not exactly? Can you explain what you mean by that?'

'We, that is, Cecily and I, discovered that Nellie had been married, well still is, to a Donald Bell, someone who is apparently much older than she. She lived with him in Pratt Street but then met someone else, another man, rich, from a different class I imagine, and she clearly fell for him because she left her husband for him.'

'Does Donald Bell still live in Pratt Street?'

'No, apparently not.'

Owen frowned. 'Then how did you come by this information?'

'We spoke to a neighbour.'

His eyes widened. 'You went to Pratt Street?'

'Yes.'

'On your own?'

'With Cecily, my maid.'

He shook his head, a wry smile on his face. 'Lady Divine, you do realise the kind of place Pratt Street is, don't you? It's a den of vagrants, drifters, and thieves...and worse. Why would you go there?'

'To find Nellie, Chief Inspector. A source told us she had been married and that she had lived in Pratt Street. There was nothing for it. We had to go.'

'Or you could have come to the station and seen me and I would have conducted an investigation, because I am the chief investigating officer on this case.'

'But you're not looking for Nellie, are you, Chief Inspector?'

He paused for a moment, staring at her. 'We have come to the conclusion that the events of Nellie Bell's disappearance and the recent murders may well be connected, although we don't as yet have any evidence to support that theory.'

She smiled, her eyes sparkling. 'So you will investigate?'

'Ah, well, the murders will take precedence.'

She lowered her chin, thinking how unfair life was sometimes. 'Because she is just a maid, and the murders have all been of high-society women.' It was a statement not a question.' But Nellie might be alive, Chief Inspector. The women are dead. If you think the two cases are connected surely finding her and her captor will mean you find the murderer. Isn't it possible that her captor might lose patience and do away with her like he has the other women...and the horse?'

'How on earth... It seems you have more than one source, Lady Divine.'

'I do, and I also have these.' She pulled the notes that Phoebe's maid had given her from her pocket. 'Apparently there were more, but it was thought that Nellie either hid them so Edwin Carruthers didn't see them, or had destroyed them.'

Chief Inspector Owen looked through each of the notes and read them in turn.

'There's one here asking her to meet with someone. Perhaps it was when she was murdered.'

'That is possible, but it looks older than the rest. To my mind it looks as though this may have been someone she had met before. It could be completely innocent of course. The handwriting is different.'

'The handwriting is different on all of them.' He shook his head. 'It could be that whoever wrote these was trying to make it look like there was more than one writer.' She nodded and he studied her for a moment. 'Do you have anything else to show me, Lady Divine? I hope you're not holding anything back.'

Camille rose from the chair again and went across to her bureau. 'Well, actually, Chief Inspector.'

She drew down the lid and reached inside, springing a secret drawer at the back.

'We found these.' She retrieved a letter and a small box from the drawer. 'It's a letter from Nellie's lover we think. And these earrings. They're really quite beautiful, and I don't think I would be wrong in saying that they are unaffordable on a maids' wages.' She handed the letter and the box to Chief Inspector Owen and returned to her chair.

'Who's we, and how long have you had these in your possession?' He opened the jewellery box and lifted out one of the earrings, then unfolded the letter.

'I'd rather not say who 'we' is, and I've had them almost since the murders began.'

'Where did you get them?'

'From Nellie's room at Denham House.'

'Before or after the police had searched there?'

'After.'

'I'm glad to hear it, Lady Divine, otherwise I could arrest you for perverting the course of justice. Removing evidence is a crime.'

Camille looked startled. 'Is it? I didn't know that.'

'Well, you do now, and may I suggest you don't do anything like it again. You, or whoever 'we', is.'

Camille pursed her lips, thinking that she would rather not commit to anything, but knowing she must placate Chief Inspector Owen, she nodded her agreement. 'Of course.'

'I mean it Lady Divine.'

'I'm aware of that, Chief Inspector. If I find anything else you have my word I will take it to the station.'

'I meant, Lady Divine, that I would prefer it if you were not to look for anything else. It seems from the telegram you received you may have put yourself in danger.'

'I admit, Chief Inspector that it has shaken me, but surely what the arrival of the telegram means is that I'm getting closer...to whoever took Nellie Bell, and I do believe someone did, or whoever is carrying out the murders. There has been another hasn't there. It's on the front page of the evening newspaper.' She rose and went across to an occasional table placed behind the chaise, and retrieved the newspaper. 'Lady Kitty Satchell was found late last evening, her body placed under a Christmas tree near Hyde Park.'

She lowered the newspaper and looked at Chief Inspector Owen, wondering if he had noticed the same similarities between the women as she, Carrie, Dorothy, Elsie, Ida and Cecily had.

'The women who have been murdered are all of a similar class. They have done something or been part of something that the murderer does not like or objects to. Why would he choose them otherwise. There is something about them, their lives, the way they conduct themselves that has put them in the path of the murderer.'

Owen nodded. 'Well, we do know that Lady Phoebe Carruthers was the only one who was married and had children. The others were all unmarried with no apparent suitors.'

'Do you think it's significant?'

'It might be.'

Camille sat in the chair again, then leant forward and pulled one of the notes she had given Chief Inspector Owen from the chaise longue.

'This note asking for the recipient to meet someone. It says, 'Meet me at the special place. Please.' Please, Chief Inspector? The wording sounds as though it is almost begging for the recipient to meet the person, but saying it nicely. I know Phoebe looked upon Nellie as almost a friend, but the truth is Phoebe was Nellie's employer. This note isn't a demand, it's a begging letter. And it looks older than the others but it doesn't mean it is, and the paper, it is not the same type? The other notes are written on a parchment with a slight watermark which unfortunately isn't clear. Perhaps the paper this note was written on was already old, a crumpled piece that had been discarded. A note written in haste and not planned.'

'That is possible.'

'Which means it could have been the last one that was sent, the one that made Phoebe leave the house that night.'

'But why would someone scribble a note so urgently?'

'Because they didn't have time to write a proper note, or perhaps the resources. Look, the words are practically scratched on, nothing like the others at all.'

'And how did the message get to Denham House?'

'A messenger costs nothing, Chief Inspector. A boy off the streets will take messages for a sixpence.'

'What are you suggesting Lady Divine?' Owen asked her, frowning.

Camille held up the crumpled note. 'That this note could have come from Nellie Bell, asking Lady Phoebe to meet with her, perhaps to help her in the situation she found herself in. It mentions a special place. Perhaps 'the special place' was a private joke they had between them, a place they went to get away from Edwin Carruthers, not an easy man to live with if I've read it correctly and from my own observations. The way he treats his children is testament to that. If we find the special place, we might find Nellie Bell...and the murderer. Perhaps Nellie was forced to write this note to entice Phoebe to their meeting place. I'm sure that if Phoebe had thought for one moment the message was from Nellie, she would not have hesitated in going to meet her. She was terribly worried about her, and if there *was* 'a special place' it seems only Phoebe and Nellie would have known about it.

'There is of course another possibility,' she said, staring off into the distance as she got her thoughts in order.

'And that is?'

'The note wasn't meant for Phoebe at all.'

Owen shrugged. 'You think it was meant for another member of the family?'

'Not the family, Chief Inspector. The note is not addressed to anyone. It could have been meant for Nellie. She may have been the recipient.'

Camille asked Cecily to show Chief Inspector Owen out. The aforementioned tea had not materialised as it seemed a trivial thing compared to the subject being discussed, and Camille wanted the Chief Inspector to understand that she wasn't trifling with him, that she was serious about the subject the was foremost in all their minds. Which was why she hadn't told him about the art gallery in Bond Street where Phoebe Carruthers was due to hold an exhibition of her work, the Yorke Gallery.

Camille was determined that she and Cecily would go there the day after Boxing Day to see the owner. She had wondered why he had not wanted Phoebe to show her new pictures at the gallery. It was part of history after all, women's history, yes, but that in no way lessened the reasons why it should be shown to a wider audience, and Camille knew it was the next step in her investigations.

It had pleased her when she had realised that she knew more than the police, and was relieved that he hadn't upbraided her too much for going to Nellie's room, or that she would not give him the names of the others who were helping her.

She smiled to herself. If he only knew, she thought, that he is so close to home, that just a little nudge and he would be very much the wiser. He knew Carrie Lawrence, and Dorothy Tremaine of course, and was aware of Elsie Dobbs and the way she earned her living, and of Ida Coyle, the cook at The Hotel. And Cecily had shown him into Birdcage Mews and out again. These were the women who had offered to help and done what they could to further her enquiries, and she was utterly grateful to them. Two heads are better than one, she thought as she locked her bureau, now divested of the secrets she had been hiding, and six is even better.

Chapter 17

Richard Owen made his way to where he had left the car on Birdcage Walk, from where Birdcage Mews with its pretty little houses and quaint cobbles led off, deep in thought. He had always known that the minds of women were different from the male of the species, but until he had met Camille Divine he hadn't realised just how much.

There was something about her, something vulnerable but at the same time incredibly strong, and he couldn't help but admire her for it. She had a spark about her, a lust for life that would not allow her to give up when things became difficult. Her stoicism in the treatment she had received from Lord Divine, her estranged husband, was testament to it, and he thought it was very likely unusual for a woman who had been raised in the upper echelons of society as she had to be so level-headed and logical.

She was so unlike his wife had been, a woman he had loved when she had allowed him to. He'd wanted to love her more but there had always been a barrier between them, a coldness which he had decided years ago had arisen when it was clear they would never have a family. It had grieved him that there was no longer affection between them, but before she had died from Spanish influenza she had alluded to their inability to create another life, and had said that it was the real reason for marriage, and that without children a marriage was not fit for purpose. It had hurt him dreadfully.

Now in his early forties and alone since 1918, he wondered about the years stretching out ahead of him. The work he did wasn't easy because most of the people he encountered during the line of his work were either villains or victims, which often made for unpleasant experiences, but he had always been proud that he had risen through the ranks from his beginnings as a humble police constable when he had first joined the force. He had thought that, Helen, his wife had been proud of him too, but he had always wondered why she had never complained about the late nights he sometimes had to keep, the long hours over the weekend when her friends were spending time with their families, and deep down he knew why. It was because she didn't care.

She had never told him she didn't love him, but she didn't tell him she did either. It was the indifference that hurt so much. She clearly wasn't concerned if he was at home or not, that she could manage perfectly well when she was on her own, and that when he was at home he was just someone to cook for or clean up after, not that he was an untidy sort.

He started the car and drove down Birdcage Walk onto Great George Street and travelled towards the station, thinking about what Camille had said and the notes she had shown him. He chuckled to himself. 'She'd make a damn good detective,' he said aloud to himself. 'Like a dog with a bone who won't give it up. We need more like her.'

He thought about the way she looked at him with her dark velvet brown eyes, and the fullness of her lips; her figure, and the way she wore her hair, bobbed in the fashion of the day, with a little curl on her cheek. She was a very attractive women, he couldn't deny it. 'Well, maybe not exactly like her,' he chuckled again. 'I'd never get any work done.'

Chapter 18

Camille and Cecily stepped out of a cab in Bond Street. Bargain hunters were already shopping, braving the cold weather, the grim, cold pavements underfoot where snow had turned to slush and lost its beauty. Bond Street was a bustling, attractive, compelling place that housed only the best of everything, home to shops in which only the rich could afford to purchase, and even with the sales their wares were out of reach of most of the inhabitants of the streets of London.

'Busy today, Madam. Busier than I thought it would be.' Cecily looked up at the long windows of the Metropol Hotel, sparkling with prisms of light from the chandeliers inside, then at Moffatts the Milliners, a huge shop with three beautifully dressed windows, places that Cecily knew she would never be given admittance. 'I thought the damp, miserable weather would have kept them away.' She looked into one of the shop windows. 'And the prices,' she said under her breath.

'Even the upper classes like a bargain, Cecily. They may have money, but you know what they say. A fool and his money are soon parted. And we're in Bond Street. What do you see?'

Cecily looked about at the people jostling for position outside the finest shops, the queues of eager shoppers waiting outside to enter. The clothes, well-cut and aimed at one-upmanship of their fellow shoppers. All were well-shod, a privilege of the rich. Shoes, or lack of them, told you who had a decent station in life and who didn't. Many a child had walked the streets of London with hand-me-down shoes that didn't fit, either many sizes too big, or with the toes cut out to accommodate too long toes...or sometimes no shoes at all.

'I see people who employ people like me, and the beautifully dressed windows of shops I wouldn't step foot in. This place isn't for me.' She glanced at Camille. 'Is it, Madam?'

Camille smiled. 'Because you are not a fool, Cecily. These shops and these so called sales are not what they seem, in fact, some of the prices are likely inflated.' Cecily's eyes widened and her mouth dropped open in surprise. 'Surely not, Madam. Why that's...that's criminal. It's not a sale is it, if they put the prices up?'

'It could be seen to be criminal, but it is not. Everyone has a choice. No one is being inveigled into paying the prices these purveyors are asking. Take the Yorke Gallery over there.' Camille lifted her chin and indicated the building on the opposite side of the street. 'They will do well today. I'm thinking that the prices they charge can only be afforded by the few. I've no doubt they raised their prices over the previous weeks, during November and December, before Christmas. They made a killing simply because of the festive season, perhaps selling to men whose wives could simply not live without a certain painting hanging on her wall, one she had seen on a previous foray to one of London's most elegant shopping streets. But look, the gallery has reduced the prices of the paintings it is exhibiting, no doubt back to the price originally being asked for it before the prices were raised to make the most of the Christmas rush. How wonderful. So now she sends said husband back to the gallery to purchase yet another to hang the other side of the mantelpiece, because it's a bargain. It's in the sales, and of course, he wants to save money, doesn't he? Should they not buy it before the price goes up?' Camille glanced at Cecily, grinning. 'So, now you know how it all works I think we should go to the Yorke Gallery and convince the proprietor that we are in the market for purchasing a painting at one of his inflated sale prices.'

'We are to purchase a painting, Madam?' asked Cecily looking concerned.

'Yes, I think so. We'll view the paintings at the gallery, take our time, become like any other purchasers who are interested in parting with their money for a canvas that could have been painted by a monkey.'

'Are you to be Lady Camille Divine, Madam. I think your name will carry a lot of weight.'

'Oh yes. I am who I am, Cecily, and if it paves the way to our successfully gleaning information about Lady Phoebe, so be it.'

They stood outside the gallery, perusing the paintings artistically displayed in the window, conversing as a lady would to her maid, pointing at the paintings on show, knowing that their presence was being watched from inside the gallery, presumably an interested owner who was thinking of his pocketbook, Camille surmised.

'Let's go inside,' she said to Cecily. 'I think our little performance has stoked some interest.'

Camille pushed the door open into the gallery. A bell above the door tinkled their arrival to the owner who had swiftly made his way into a small office towards the back of the gallery when he'd seen the impending arrival of potential customers, so as not to appear too eager.

'Ladies, ladies. A Happy New Year to you. How wonderful to see you, Lady Divine.'

Camille frowned. 'You know me, sir? I don't think we have been introduced.'

He forced a laugh. 'My lady. Anyone who is anyone of note knows of Lady Camille Divine.'

'And...you are someone, sir?'

'I...am the proprietor of the Yorke Gallery.' He pointed to a plaque on the wall above his head. 'Purveyor of art to the royal household. By appointment, as you see.'

Camille smiled and inclined her head. 'Indeed, sir. I'm pleased to make your acquaintance, Mr...?

'Riddell, Madam. Horace Riddell at your service.' He took Camille's proffered hand by the fingers and squeezed them. Camille stiffened. The feeling of his fingers holding hers wasn't pleasant, and was relieved she was wearing gloves.

She extricated her fingers from his with some effort and smiled politely again, but it did not reach her eyes. She couldn't help but to take in the manner of him, a pleasant-looking chap, but not broad and of slightly less than medium height. His brown hair was thin, and brushed back over his head, no doubt hiding a bald pate, making his face look rather moon-like. His skin was smooth and very pale, probably because he is forever in the gallery, she thought. Her eyes quickly took in the build of him. He doesn't need to be broad or tall, she thought, as her eyes flicked towards Cecily, not to overwhelm a woman. She wondered about Cecily's opinion of him.

'This is my personal maid, Mr Riddell. She accompanies me on my artistic pursuits, so her opinion is important to me.'

Riddell frowned. 'You must forgive me, Madam. I had no idea you were a subscriber to the arts.'

'Oh yes,' Camille said, airily. 'I'm terribly interested in all forms of art, particularly by women. Do you have anything to show us?'

She turned on her heel and began to walk about the gallery, peering at some of the paintings exhibited on the walls, and wooden easels in the centre of the room. 'I have a penchant for works by a female artist as I do believe they are gathering more interest in the artistic world.'

'Ah,' said Riddell, placing his hands together as though in prayer, and bowing slightly from the waist. 'We have a small number of female artists who exhibit here from time to time, although no one at present. We have some paintings that are of the moment from a talented young male artist who has, dare I say, exploded onto the artistic world. Up and coming and very of the moment you could say.'

'Mm,' said Camille as though deep in thought. She frowned, rather theatrically, Cecily thought, and she had to stifle a giggle. 'A little bird was mistaken then, when it told me that you were to hold an exhibition by the celebrated artist, Lady Phoebe Carruthers,' she turned to Riddell to gauge his reaction, 'now, sadly, deceased.'

Riddell stared at Camille for some moments, and she saw his throat move up and down as he swallowed away the dryness, obviously caused because it was a subject he did not want to explore. He turned away, walking into the small office to shuffle some papers on the desk.

'I was very shocked to hear of the terrible passing of Lady Carruthers.' He glanced up at Camille and she noticed that a pink flush was creeping up his neck. 'She...had exhibited here a few times, the paintings she created whilst on the continent, exotic, bright landscapes and seascapes, some of the desert. Beautiful paintings, exceptional, rather like the good lady herself. So many of us will never get to see such sights, only through the eyes of painters like her, and their artistic endeavours.'

Camille nodded, her expression a picture of condolence and understanding. 'And her paintings on suffrage?'

He inhaled, looking quizzical, tapping his fingers against his chin as though considering Camille's question. Cecily raised her eyebrows thinking that if she had ever seen a man display a false reaction, one was at that moment standing right in front of her. 'Her suffrage paintings, Lady Divine?'

'Oh yes,' said Camille, walking towards him. 'Oh yes, I have it on good authority that Lady Phoebe had painted a series of paintings depicting suffragettes in their fight for equality. I understand that some of the paintings were...well, let's just say rather too truthful for some tastes.'

Horace Riddell came out from behind his desk, his lips pressed firmly together, his fingers entwined into a tight ball in front of him.

'Ah, the truth, Lady Divine. The truth has many facets does it not?'

'I'm sure you're right, Mr Riddell, but I did not come here to discuss the vagaries of truth. I was assured that your gallery would be exhibiting Phoebe Carruthers' suffrage paintings, that in fact, an exhibition had been arranged, that is until her untimely death. May I ask if those paintings will ever be shown?'

Riddell shrugged and shook his head slowly. 'I know of no such paintings, Lady Camille. If they are to be shown at a gallery, I think perhaps your little bird was mistaken when he, or she, said it would be at the Yorke Gallery. The subject matter, is, as you say, a little forward thinking for some tastes, and as we are...' he pointed to the plaque on the wall above his head and Camille nodded, 'by appointment to the Royal household, I must take that household's feelings into consideration when I agree to show an artist.'

Camille took a pause. 'And are they so against suffrage? The Royal family?'

Horace Riddell walked to the gallery door and opened it so that the little bell above it tinkled.

'Of that I do not know, Lady Camille. You are probably in a better position to answer that question than I, but the Yorke Gallery caters to the tastes of aesthetes rather than those of a more confrontational nature. It is far safer.'

Camille and Cecily found themselves back on Bond Street. They paused outside the gallery for a few moments, Camille looking up and down the street, her thoughts in disarray.

'Are you game for a walk, Cecily?' she asked her maid. 'I feel in dire need to clear my head, and then have a cup of tea at the tearoom at Browns in Albemarle Street.' She began to walk towards Albemarle Street, threading her arm through Cecily's. 'You don't mind if I take your arm, do you? I just think we need to put our heads together and discuss what we've just heard from our Mr Riddell.'

'Of course, Lady Divine. Whatever you wish.' They were quiet for a moment as they walked down Bond Street. 'I didn't like him.'

Camille glanced at her. 'Didn't you? Why?'

Cecily frowned. 'Not sure, Madam, but he lied. He lied when he said he knew nothing about Lady Carruthers's suffrage paintings, in fact, I thought he looked as though he didn't want to talk about them. Something told me he knew very well about them. And...I don't think he should be assuming what the Royal family like or don't like.'

'I think he lied too, but is he our killer, Cecily? And has he taken Nellie Bell? Is he the attractive man of means who encouraged her to leave her husband for him?' She shook her head. 'For some reason, and please, don't ask me to explain, I don't think he is either of those men.'

'Well, he's not attractive if you don't mind me saying, Madam. He's not the type to swoon over, and leaving your husband is a serious thing. He'd need to be worth it wouldn't he?'

'And you don't think he is?'

Cecily glanced at her. 'No, Madam. He didn't make *me* swoon.'

Camille couldn't help but giggle. 'He didn't?'

'No, Madam,' replied Cecily, her voice going up a notch. 'He's no dishy film star, and that's a fact. Now, if he was like that policeman, Chief Inspector Owen, I would understand it, but he ain't...isn't...Madam.'

'Cecily!'

'I'm sorry, Madam. I was just trying to show the difference between them. The bloke at the gallery, oh, no, never. Nellie would never have left home for him.'

'What about Lord Fortesque-Wallsey?'

'No, Madam. He ties me up in knots sometimes with the things he says. I get flustered because I know he's only joking, but I'm not sure if I'm allowed to answer him. It seems easier and more suited to my station to say nothing.'

'Chief Inspector Owen and Horace Riddell are probably of a similar age.'

'Age is just a number, Madam. It don't mean anything. And it certainly don't in those two men. They're nothing alike.'

'No,' breathed Camille. 'I suppose not.'

They walked in silence until they got to Browns Hotel.

'I'll wait outside, Madam, whilst you're having your tea.'

'You will not, Cecily. You will join me. I think we could both do with a cup of good, hot tea, and some decent cake to go with it.'

Cecily looked horrified. 'But, Madam. I'm not dressed for...'

'Nonsense. You're always well turned-out, and neat and tidy. I won't have you waiting outside. It's much too cold.'

'Only if you're sure, Lady Divine.'

'I'm absolutely sure.'

'Can we choose a table on the edge of the room please, Madam? I would feel more comfortable not having to walk through all the other tables.'

The maitre d'hôtel approached Camille as they went into the busy tearoom which was full of chatter and clinking cups against saucers.

'Lady Divine. How wonderful to see you again. It has been some time.'

'So it has, Gerald. It's good to see you too. We'd like a table for two please, preferably on the perimeter if you have one. We may have to leave at short notice and we don't want to disturb your other guests.'

Gerald made a small bow. 'Of course, Lady Divine. I have the perfect table for you. Please follow me.'

He took them to a small table in an alcove. Cecily glanced at Camille gratefully and Camille nodded.

'This is perfect, Gerald. Thank you.'

'Tea for two, Lady Divine? And some petite sandwiches and pastries?'

'That sounds wonderful,' breathed Camille, looking forward to some refreshment, and putting Horace Riddell out of her mind. They were served almost immediately, but a few moments later Gerald returned holding an ice bucket in which sat a bottle of Browns' best champagne.

'Madam, I'm sorry to disturb you, but there has been a request to send champagne to your table. Do you accept?'

Camille was startled, but then scanned the room to see who it was who had sent an expensive bottle of champagne to her table. The Honourable Richard Burrows rose from his table and made a quick bow in her direction. She inclined her head towards him in thanks, then nodded to the maitre d'hôtel. 'Thank you, Gerald. You may leave the champagne.'

'Champagne, Madam? At tea? I've never heard of that,' gasped Cecily.

'It is sometimes taken at tea, Cecily, although not something I have subscribed to in the past. However, when one is gifted a bottle such as this,' she took the bottle from the ice bucket and peered at the label, 'one should always accept even if there is no possibility of drinking the whole bottle.'

Glasses were brought to the table and Camille poured champagne for Cecily. 'A little reward for assisting me, Cecily.'

Cecily took a breath. 'I've never had champagne before, my Lady.'

'Well, it's high time you did.'

Cecily took a sip and giggled when the bubbles tickled her nose. 'I hope you don't mind me asking, Lady Divine, but why would someone send a bottle of champagne to your table? Is it the sort of thing that's done all the time in your social circle?'

Camille smiled to herself, thinking Cecily terribly sweet. 'Actually, no, it isn't.'

'Oh, but...'

'That gentleman is the Honourable Richard Burrows. I met him at Lady Carruthers' funeral. I was curious about him so asked to be introduced. He was the only man there, apart from Phoebe's husband, who wasn't accompanied, and I thought it odd. He said he was attending as a representative of someone who was unable to attend, although he didn't say who it was. He insisted I travel with him to the wake at Denham House, although I can't think why.' She lowered her voice to a whisper. 'He's rather a strange man.'

'Why is he honourable? Has he done something honourable?' asked Cecily, also in a whisper.

'His father is a Viscount. I looked him up in Debrett's.'

'And that makes him honourable?'

'It makes him *an* Honourable. I suppose it's rather an old-fashioned thing, but it's how the aristocracy style themselves.'

Cecily shook her head. 'Couldn't be doin' with all that hoo-ha. Did you think he could be a suspect?'

'Indeed I did.'

'And is he still?'

'I'm afraid so.'

'Why?'

'Intuition. There's something about him. I'm just not sure. He's rather effete and dresses in the most meticulous way.'

'So does Lord Fortesque-Wallsey. I've never seen clothes like it. They must cost a fortune.'

'Yes, but this is different. When I sat in the car with Richard Burrows I got the feeling he's not particularly comfortable with women, and yet he tried to make an acquaintance of me. I felt rather uneasy in his company.'

'So that's two suspects we've got.'

'Yes, but I can't imagine either of them beating a woman to death and leaving her body under a Christmas tree, can you?'

'Not really, Madam, but then, p'raps we don't always know the real person, even when we think we do. People can hide behind a face, one that they like us to see when really what's going on behind it is very different.'

'Quite. And I think you've had enough champagne, Cecily,' said Camille, putting the bottle back in the ice bucket.

'Yes, Madam. So do I.'

Chapter 19

'I suppose I should tell Chief Inspector Owen about the visit Cecily and I made to the Yorke Gallery in Bond Street, and also about her suffragette paintings that seem to have gone missing.'

She and Carrie Lawrence were sitting at the big pine table in the kitchen at The Hotel, and with them were Dorothy Tremaine and Ida Coyle.'

'You've told him everything else I take it?' asked Carrie.

'Yes, I had to after receiving that horrible telegram. I must admit it made me wobble a bit. One doesn't want to be singled out for something like that.'

'Do you have any idea who sent it, Camille?' Dorothy asked. 'What did it say?'

'Stay out of things that don't concern you or you'll be next.'

'Oh, my goodness,' cried Ida. 'That's awful.'

'And Chief Inspector Owen knows about it?'

'Chief Inspector Owen knows about what?'

Elsie appeared in the kitchen, smoking a cigarette. Ida almost growled at her.

'Put that damned cigarette out, my girl. There's no smoking them 'orrible things in my kitchen.'

'Oh alright, alright, keep your wig on,' answered Elsie, dunking her cigarette in the sink.

'And now you can take that fag butt you've just left in my sink and put it in the kitchen bin outside. I don't want it in 'ere.'

'Well this is a nice welcome, I must say. I only came to find out 'ow you all were and this is 'ow I get spoken to.' Carrie, her sister, rolled her eyes, then glanced at Camille, shaking her head with exasperation. Elsie opened the garden door and threw the cigarette end onto the cobbles in the courtyard garden. 'Anyway,' she said, sitting at the table and pouring herself a cup of tea, 'you didn't answer my question. What does Chief Inspector Owen know about?'

'The telegram I received,' answered Camille. 'It was a threat, telling me to keep out of the investigation or I'd be next, presumably meaning I'd be the next woman beaten to death and left under a Christmas tree, although I imagine all the festive trees in the City and the shopping streets have been removed by now. I know Selfridges has already gone, but Harry Selfridge was so upset about Phoebe Carruthers's body being left underneath the Christmas tree at the entrance to Selfridges, he had them removed almost immediately.'

'This is a terrible business,' said Ida. 'Where's it all going to end? And still no word about that poor girl. At least she 'asn't been found under a Christmas tree.'

'So where is she,' asked Dorothy. 'She's been taken, surely, or would she not have been in contact with someone, a friend perhaps.'

'I'm sure she's been taken,' said Camille.

'And this art gallery?' asked Dorothy. 'Do you think it's significant?'

Camille sipped her tea thoughtfully. 'I do. I have two men in my sights, but of course I could be completely wrong. I wish I knew more about Horace Riddell, the owner of the gallery, but I'm not sure how I'm to manage it. There's something about him, not quite untrustworthy exactly, but his manner is not quite right, and when I mentioned Phoebe's suffragette pictures he denied any knowledge of them, in fact looked decidedly uncomfortable, yet the maid at Denham House assured me that an exhibition was due to take place, although she felt there had had to be some persuasion of the owner to show them. When I mentioned these pictures his behaviour changed, and he more or less showed Cecily and me the door. He said that his gallery was by appointment to the Royal family and that suffrage was a subject he thought the gallery should avoid, or words to that effect.'

'You should follow 'im,' said Elsie, biting into one of Ida's famous cream puffs. 'It's how you get to know people's comin's and goin's. It's the only way.'

'But how would you know when to be there and when not?' Carrie asked her.

'There is no not. You 'ave to be there all the time, from mornin' til evenin' every day, until he does something what gives you the information you're lookin' for.'

Camille's eyes widened. 'It sounds dreadful.'

'Where is the art gallery?'

'Bond Street.'

'Shame,' said Elsie with a full mouth, wiping puff pastry crumbs from her cheeks and rubbing her hands together.

'Why?'

'If it was a longer street you could 'ave sat in your motor and watched the gallery, but you'd be seen there. It's too short a street to hide in. You'd definitely be spotted. And if not by 'im by a copper, wondering why you're sitting in your motor all day. It's not usual behaviour is it, sitting in a motor all day, 'specially a woman. Don't look good.'

'So what's the answer?'

'Someone will 'ave to 'ang about, use the tearooms or coffee houses for cover until he decides to do something. Also, it's not good going in the front door. You've made a start, but you've only found out what he wants to tell you, and by all accounts that ain't much. What you need is to find out what he don't want to tell you. Someone needs to get in by the back door and 'ave a look round. If you're still suspicious, he needs to be watched.'

They all looked at one another. 'Perhaps you could hire someone,' suggested Dorothy to Camille, 'you know, to stand there all day and watch the premises. At least you'd know if he's up to anything.'

'And he'd need to be followed when he leaves the place,' Elsie joined in. 'He'd be a bit daft to dirty his own doorstep wouldn't he, specially a place like that? He might be doin' somethin' he shouldn't elsewhere. No one worth their salt, shits on their own patch.' Carrie grimaced and put her head in her hands.

Camille nodded. 'You're right,' she said, ignoring Elsie's language. 'Someone needs to be there. I'll hire someone. Detecting is all very well and good, but I think if I stood in Bond Street all day people would begin to wonder why. Many of the people who patronise that particular shopping area know me. I wouldn't know how to answer them if they asked me what I was doing. And if it got back to Harry there would be hell to pay.'

'You can hire me,' said Elsie. 'I'll do it.'

'Elsie,' cried Carrie. 'You can't do it.'

'Why not? I'm as good as anyone else. And I'm more of the street than you lot.' She chuckled. 'You're all so bloody soft. You 'aven't got a clue what it's like to get yer 'ands dirty.'

'I hate to say it,' said Dorothy, 'but she's right. She's the only one amongst us who would know how to carry on should she be challenged. Walking the streets is probably something she's more used to than we are.'

Elsie frowned. 'I've never walked the streets, Mrs Tremaine. I wouldn't lower meself. And may I remind you, I 'ave me own business what brings in a tidy sum.'

'When you say, hire you,' said Camille, 'you mean you'll want payment.' Everyone turned to look at Elsie. 'That is what you meant isn't it?'

Elsie took another cream puff from the plate and rolled her eyes. 'I s'pose if I said yes you'd all hate me and be on me back, like I was lettin' the side down. The sisters of witchery will turn on me no doubt.'

'That's right,' said Carrie. 'We will. You don't earn anything now do you, not yourself I mean. You earn off your girls while they're on their backs, so it's not like you'd be losing anything, Elsie. Just your time, that's all anyone's asking from you. And we all need to give something back sometimes. Even you.'

Elsie shoved the last of the cream puff in her mouth and sighed. 'Alright, alright, here you go again. 'Avin a go. There's no need to go on about it. Bloody 'ell, I try and do something good and I get 'auled over the coals again.'

'No one's hauling you over coals,' said Camille, 'and if you'd rather not do it...'

Elsie threw up her hands. 'I'll do it, and for free and gratis an' all, just to keep you bloody lot off me back. It'll be a relief if you lot would stop peckin' my 'ead. See. I can be nice.'

'Don't 'appen very often, though, do it?' said Ida.

Chapter 20

She had dressed to the nines, worn her most elegant clothes, and practised speaking properly, or 'proper' as she called it. Nathanial had thought it hilarious.

'What a charade,' he'd said, 'you, speaking like a lady. I'm not sure I like it, my sweet.'

'It don't matter if you don't like it,' she'd replied, chuckling. 'I'm a detectorist now, y'know. Not just a bunch of whores' madam. I've always told you there's more to me. I 'ave got a brain y'know.'

'You've never complained before. Those whores bring in your income.'

She'd turned her nose up. 'Yeah, bit boring though. A change is as good as a rest.'

'I suppose you'd rather be on your own back.'

She breathed steadily and smiled to herself. Keep yourself in check, she thought. 'No, Nat, I wouldn't. I'm true to you. Now I am, anyway.'

He gave her a sideways glance and pulled a face. 'Is she paying you, our illustrious Lady Divine?' She'd stared at him through narrowed eyes and he grinned. 'She isn't, is she?' He'd burst out laughing. 'So, you're doing it from the kindness of your heart. Now that is funny.'

'Y'see, Nathanial, that's the thing about you men, you don't know nothin' about the sisterhood.'

'And you're in the sisterhood, are you? Their sisterhood, those women who are nothing like you?'

'And why not? I'm as good as what they are.'

He realised he'd riled her and regretted it. 'Yes, my sweet, you are, in fact you're better.'

She sniffed. 'You don't need to go that far. I know what I am.'

Elsie walked slowly down Bond Street, peering in the shop windows, looking for all the world like an ordinary shopper, a woman of substance with enough money to buy anything she wanted. Of course, she *knew* she could buy anything she wanted, but she had no desire to change herself, to guild the lily so to speak. She was who she was, and it was enough for her.

The Yorke Gallery was the kind of place Elsie had never frequented before. She knew nothing about art and wasn't interested and didn't understand those who were. Why would anyone want to pay hundreds of pounds for a piece of canvas with a load of paint daubed on it? It was beyond her comprehension. Her mind was focussed on the task in front of her. She didn't make an issue of perusing the artworks in the gallery window, simply strolled by, peering into the window as she had with every other. If the owner had seen her passing by, he would have thought nothing of it, would simply have viewed her as one of the many looking for bargains.

She'd noticed a tearoom on the other side of Bond Street, almost exactly opposite the gallery. She smiled to herself. Perfect, she thought.

At least I can get meself a decent cup of tea. She entered and ordered a pot, hoping it would last her at least the morning. Choosing a table by the window, she sat herself in the chair with the best view of the gallery and prepared herself for a long wait.

Elsie left the tearoom intermittently, knowing she could not sit in the same chair all day because it would certainly arouse suspicion, and continued to stroll up and down Bond Street, crossing the road at various points, back and forth, back and forth, until she noticed the serving staff in the tearoom had changed and the next shift had taken over. At that moment she would go back inside, claiming the chair she had sat in previously and keep watch.

By six o'clock in the evening she had seen nothing to report. She knew before she had begun her watch that this indeed could have been a possibility, but was disappointed all the same. She took a deep breath. This detectorin' lark ain't much fun, she thought, leaning her cheek on her hand, knocking her hat askew and not caring if it didn't look elegant. And I'm gettin' bloody cold walking up and down all day, but I've said I'll do it now.

A movement from the opposite side of the street took her eye, and she watched carefully as Horace Riddell left the gallery, looked about him, then left and right, locking the door by pushing three keys into three different locks. When he'd done so he looked about again, up and down Bond Street, then pulled his overcoat more tightly around him, his warm breath floating around him in a mist. Elsie watched with narrowed eyes as he walked down the street, his chest puffed out, a look of entitlement expressed on his face.

'Think you're someone don'cha?' Elsie said aloud, sotto voce. 'Think you're someone special I'll bet. Think again, Mister.'

She paid for her tea and left the tearoom, keeping to her side of the road, her eyes permanently on Riddell's back as he walked purposefully down the street, nodding to an acquaintance here, shaking the hand of a customer there.

'Where are you goin' I wonder?' she said under her breath. ''Ome to the missus? Something tells me not.'

She followed him to Bruton Street, and then on to Conduit Street and Foubert's Place, keeping her distance but making sure he stayed in her sights. Then past Carnaby Street and beyond to Great Marlborough Street. From there he went onto Poland Street and Oxford Street, with Elsie not far behind, ducking in and out of doorways as the darkness engulfed her, the people of London pushing by her as they went about their business. She was cold now. The warmth from the pots of hot tea she'd consumed at the tearoom had only stayed with her for a short while, and now her fingers and toes felt like icicles, although perspiration rolled down her back with exertion.

'Bloody 'ell,' she said under her breath, puffing as she ducked into another doorway. 'Where the 'ell's he goin'?'

Elsie continued to follow him. He turned into Earnshaw Street where he walked to about halfway down, passing the slums and the lines of grey washing, stiff with ice and covered with soot from the tanning factories. He knocked lightly at one of the ramshackle buildings, three knocks, then two, then one, the door of which was dragged open, the bottom making a scuffing noise as it scraped the floor. He went inside without saying a word, and the door was slammed shut behind him.

Elsie stood on the corner, trying to get her bearings and hoping she could get a cab to take her back to the area where she felt safe, because this was not a street on which she wanted to linger. She looked about her, thinking of the house in Hanbury Street where she, Carrie and their two brothers were raised until they'd left home, she by choice when she'd married the brothel-keeper, Len West and had his baby, her daughter, Rose, and Carrie by force.

'This street is in a rookery, and 'e was expected by whoever was inside, no doubt about it.' she said frowning. 'What the 'ell is a man like Horace Liddell, who owns an art gallery on Bond Street, one of the poshest shopping streets there is, doin' in a stinking, rat-infested place like this?'

She turned on her heel and began walking towards Great Marlborough Street to hail a cab, her success emboldening her. 'You ain't who you say you are, Mister,' she said grinning to herself, 'and I reckon you're keeping somethin' interestin' in that 'ouse.'

Chapter 21

'So what do we have?' asked Camille as they sat in her drawing room at Birdcage Mews. She had invited everyone from The Hotel to join her for the evening, so they could discuss Nellie's disappearance, the murders, and specifically, what Elsie had discovered.

'More than the police, I reckon, ' said Ida. 'Why don't they know about Horace Liddell I wonder?'

'It's likely it's because people don't like speaking to the police,' said Cecily. 'They think that if they say too much they could put themselves in danger with them what are carrying out the crimes. The criminals of Whitechapel don't care about anyone. If you get in their way they do away with you.' Camille stared at Cecily, thinking she had never heard her say so much. Cecily put her head down and stared at her hands in her lap, her face flushed with embarrassment. Everyone was looking at her and she wasn't used to the attention.

'Cecily's right,' said Elsie. 'It's why the police are always on the back foot.'

Camille nodded. 'It was one of Phoebe's staff who told me about the Yorke Gallery and Horace Riddell. I'm only assuming they didn't tell the police the same thing. They would have been questioned, surely, but when she told me about the gallery, it all seemed a bit hush-hush.

I'm sure she didn't want Edwin Carruthers to know she was speaking with me, particularly about Phoebe's paintings. He is utterly against suffrage.'

'So what do we have?' asked Dorothy. 'It would be good to see it all written down. To be honest if feels rather confusing at the moment.'

Camille stood and reached behind her chair, pulling out a board that had been covered with paper.

'I thought we could use this. We can write the names of the victims on it, when Nellie went missing and when the murders took place, plus what Elsie found out yesterday.' She smiled at Elsie. 'You did an amazing job by the way, Elsie. I couldn't have done what you did, and to go into one of the rookeries on your own. That took some doing.'

Elsie sat up a bit straighter and looked pleased. She didn't often receive praise.

'I didn't think about it,' she said, 'just followed 'im. It was odd though, goin' from all those lovely shops and all those well-heeled people with money to splash, into a place like Earnshaw Street. I used to think Hanbury Street was run-down, but blimey, Earnshaw Street is much worse.'

'I wonder why he went there,' said Carrie. 'It can't be where he lives surely, a man like that. To have premises in Bond Street means money. He can't possibly live there.'

'It's not a brothel is it?' asked Dorothy.

Elsie shook her head. 'It ain't a brothel. I know where all the brothels are. I 'ave to, see. Got to keep your finger on the pulse to make sure no one's nickin' your punters. I'd know if it was a knockin' shop.'

'But we *do* need to know who lives there,' said Ida. 'Once we know that we can probably work out why old Riddell is goin' there. I know men, all men. After work they want feedin', I don't care what their station is in society. Now you can't tell me he was goin' there to get fed. Blimey, you'd need to be 'ard up to eat in a place like that. It don't bear thinking about. No, he was up to no good, you mark my words.'

'I'm inclined to agree with Ida,' said Camille.

They went quiet, all lost in their own thoughts.

'You don't think Nellie's there do you?' asked Carrie, quietly, breaking the silence.

'I was wondering that,' said Dorothy. 'It would make sense, wouldn't it, if she's being held somewhere. A street like that could hide all sorts of things.' She looked around at them apologetically. 'Not that I've ever been in a street like that.'

'It's not a place anyone would go if they've got any sense,' said Elsie, "specially after dark. They'd stick a knife between your ribs as good as look at yer, just to see if you've got coin on you. If you did they'd take it, and if you didn't they'd kick your 'ead in where you lay.'

'Oh, my goodness,' said Dorothy. 'Is it really like that?'

Ida nodded. 'You 'aven't lived, my girl.'

Camille began writing on the board with the beautiful fountain pen that had been a gift from Harry. She started at the top with Nellie's name.

'So here's Nellie. She's missing from her position at Denham House, and it would seem had a secret suitor. I'm wondering if her suitor is implicated in her disappearance. She had hidden a pair of expensive earrings behind a cabinet in her room, which we think were probably a gift from him, and a letter from someone who signed himself, B, in a copy of the book, Therese Raquin. I think she did that for the purpose, not necessarily because she thought something was going to happen to her, but because it was how she was feeling at the time. Perhaps she felt under a certain pressure to comply with her lover's wishes, and had left her husband because she thought if she didn't she would lose her lover. Therese Raquin had a lover who persuaded her that they should kill her husband so they could be together, but they were forever tortured, both the lover and Therese committing suicide to get away from the horror of what they'd done, the guilt and the nightmares. We have also learned that Nellie was married to a Donald Bell of Pratt Street, but left him when her suitor asked her to.'

'P'raps 'er bloke said, 'it's your 'usband or me,' said Elsie.

'Yes,' said Camille, nodding. 'I think that's likely. We also know that she was utterly loyal to Phoebe. Phoebe felt it was unlikely that she would have just upped and left her by choice, that even if she had wanted to leave she would have discussed it with her. Is everyone satisfied with that summation?' They all nodded.

'Next we have Phoebe Carruthers.' Camille wrote her name on the board. 'A woman of some standing, Lady Carruthers, married to Lord Edwin Carruthers, mother of three children, all who board at various boarding schools. She was a talented artist and had had exhibitions of her paintings around the world. Had travelled extensively. She was murdered, badly beaten and broken, and her body left under the Christmas tree at Selfridges. On her face was carved 'Emi', with a number one.' She looked away from the board towards the women sitting in her drawing room. Their faces were pictures of sadness. 'Is everyone alright to continue?' she asked them, her own eyes beginning to brim. Some of them sniffed away their tears and they all nodded again.

'We don't have to do this,' said Camille. 'If it's too much I can work this out alone.'

'No you can't,' said Elsie, her face etched with sorrow. 'You need us.'

Camille nodded. 'Yes. I do.'

She inhaled a breath and continued.

'Rowena Porter was the next victim. She was unmarried, yet it has been shown after autopsy that she had had relations the night of her murder.'

'But she didn't have a beau,' said Dorothy, looking wretched. 'She would have said I'm sure.'

'I think we must conclude that we don't know everything about these women. Most people have a little something they want to keep to themselves. Maybe Rowena also had a secret lover.'

'I think I've led a boring life, that's what I think,' said Ida.

'You're still with us, though, Ida,' said Carrie putting a hand on her arm. 'Thank goodness.' She smiled at Ida, who patted her hand.

Camille continued. 'Rowena's body was left under the Christmas tree at the Palace of Westminster.'

'I wonder why he leaves them under Christmas trees,' said Cecily. 'Seems a bit odd to me.'

'It must mean something to him...or her,' said Carrie.

'Rowena had 'Emi' and the number two carved on her face,' continued Camille. 'So we must assume the letters and the numbers are significant. She was an avid member of the suffragette movement and from a notable family. Her father is a wealthy businessman and primarily an importer. Next was Letitia Harvey-Milton who had 'Emi' and four carved into her face. I know nothing of her, only that like Rowena, she came from a notable family. I understand her father is a merchant. After her came Lady Kitty Satchell, 'Emi' number five. Her father is the Honourable Ernest Satchell and he is an important man in the East India Company.' She paused for a moment. 'So...there we have it.'

'You've forgotten the 'orse,' said Elsie.

'The horse?'

Elsie nodded. 'Yeah, the 'orse what was shot and had 'Emi' and three carved on its cheek. It's got to mean something.' Camille nodded and wrote, 'Horse Emi 3' on the board.

'Right,' she said, looking around at the others. 'There we have it. These women, and the horse, are the victims. Now I think we should look at the possible perpetrators. Unfortunately, this area is a bit...well, hazy. We have nothing concrete to go on, but I'm hoping that between us we may find something, a link perhaps, that will help us decide who this wicked person is.' She turned to Cecily. 'Cecily would you help Knolly in with the refreshments? This is the right time for a little break I think. It would be very welcome at this moment.' Moments later Knolly and Cecily returned with two large trays holding a large teapot, a tall, elegant coffeepot, and a selection of sweet biscuits. 'Tuck in everyone,' said Camille, encouraging Cecily and Knolly to stay. 'Hopefully this will be the fuel which will guide us to a solution.'

'It ain't just one person,' said Elsie as she munched on a biscuit after dipping it in her tea.

'You don't think so?' asked Cecily.

'Nah. And I dunno about it being connected neither.'

'Why do you say that?' Camille asked frowning.

'Instinct. This business with old Riddell. My gut is telling me he's up to no good, a shyster, slippery like. I reckon he's got 'is fingers in a few pies. I've known a life I don't deny it, but even I weren't 'appy about being in that rookery. Earnshaw Street is an 'orrible place, real seedy. Why would a bloke like 'im go to a place like that? It needs looking into. He's up to no good that one, all posh and toffee-nosed as he strolled down Bond Street with all his howdy-dos and whatnot, looking like a respectable businessman. Then takes 'imself to Earnshaw Street and an 'ouse that's almost boarded up. It don't add up.'

'She's right,' said Ida. 'It don't.'

'The problem we have is that I'm not sure we can do anything about it. Earnshaw Street sounds so dangerous, not the sort of place that any of us would want to go in to. I thought after the war, and everything that happened to this country, these places would disappear, but it seems they're thriving.'

'Course they are,' said Ida. 'No one's got anything, so they rob. Some people in this country are still scraping everything together and I doubt it'll get better any time soon. That sort of thing can bring out the worst in people if they're of that sort. There'll always be violence and robbing. That will never change.'

Camille pulled her lips into a straight line and sighed. 'I suppose I should talk to Chief Inspector Owen about it.' She rose from her chair and wrote Horace Riddell's name on the board, then the Yorke Gallery.

'Who else do we have?' asked Carrie. 'We're a bit light on suspects.'

'There's the man at Browns,' said Cecily. 'Madam thought he might be a suspect.'

'Who's that,' asked Dorothy frowning. 'Browns is one of my favourite hotels.'

'He was at Phoebe's funeral. I'd never met him before and I asked Nathanial to introduce me. He was unaccompanied and said he was there to represent someone who couldn't attend.'

Dorothy frowned. 'Now that is odd. It would be interesting to discover who the person was who couldn't attend. He didn't say I take it.'

Camille shook her head. 'He didn't, but you're absolutely right. I feel quite certain that whoever carried out these terrible murders was at Phoebe's funeral. As Elsie said, it's instinct. And Chief Inspector Owen was in attendance too, so he must have been of the same mind.'

'Who was this man?'

'The Honourable Richard Burrows. His seat is in Northern England, I understand.'

'So what was he doin' down 'ere then?' asked Elsie.

'He has contacts in the House of Lords. Knows Edwin Carruthers extremely well apparently.'

'"E said.'

'What do you mean?'

'Were they together at the funeral?'

Camille blinked at her, her mind racing, her thoughts hurtling back to the drawing room at Denham House. 'You know, I don't remember them conversing. When we got to Denham House I spent most of the time with Ottilie, but actually, I don't remember seeing him after that. Oh!' Her hand flew to her face

'What is it, Madam,' said Cecily looking concerned.

'His motor car.'

'What about it?' asked Dorothy.

'It wasn't there when we left Denham House. It was definitely not in Henrietta Street when Ottilie and I left. The doorman got us a cab and the street was very busy with mourners turning up to the wake and flowers being delivered, but I arrived in his motor car with him and I know where his driver left it, almost right outside the gates, and it wasn't there when Ottilie and I got into our cab.'

'So 'e'd left then,' said Elsie. 'Without speaking to Phoebe's 'usband about 'ow sorry he was, and without letting you know. You would 'ave thought he would 'ave told you at least, bearing in mind he arrived with you. He used yer didn't 'e?'

'I thought it was because of Harry. I would imagine every man would like to best Harry.'

'But it weren't.'

'No, no it wasn't. It was to get into Denham House without anyone thinking it was odd that someone had attended who wasn't well known to the family. Oh dear, that's awful. I helped him gain admittance. I feel quite sick.'

'But didn't you say that Nathanial Fortesque-Wallsey knew him?' asked Dorothy.

'Yes, but even Nathanial said he wasn't familiar with him. He only knew him because he'd seen him occasionally at events and sometimes at the House. The thing is he could have been visiting. Anyone can visit the House as long as they have clearance, and he doesn't look like the sort of man you would say no to. I wasn't comfortable in his company I must confess. I found him rather unfriendly and awkward. Oh dear. Now I have the shivers.'

'He sent you champagne, Madam. At Browns.'

Camille nodded. 'Yes, but he is feigning an association with me, one that I don't want and is unseemly. He asked me to call him Richard, too familiar don't you think after a first meeting? He sent a bottle of the best champagne to our table in front of a full tearoom at Browns. Clever, I think, and he wasn't alone. He was with someone at his table. I wish I'd paid more attention to whomever he was dining with.'

'Write his name on the board, Camille,' said Dorothy. 'I have a feeling our Mr Burrows is hiding something.'

'And what about Nellie?' asked Ida. 'The poor girl is still missing.'

'The thing is,' said Camille, 'we're rather depending that her 'friend' in Pratt Street was telling us the truth when she said Nellie's husband no longer lived there. He may not, but she certainly seemed to know a lot about them. It has given me pause I must say.'

'Perhaps her husband's name should go on the board too,' said Carrie. 'No one has actually spoken to him. We're only going on hearsay.' Donald Bell's name was written on the board.

'Now draw lines,' said Ida.

'Lines?'

'To connect them, and see where they cross.'

'Alright.' Camille drew lines between the names and stood back so that the others could see the result. 'The only person who doesn't seem directly connected is Richard Burrows. The gallery is connected to

Lady Phoebe, so that means Horace Riddell has a connection, although he seemed to have had little contact with her recently because of his refusal to show her paintings. Richard Burrows stands out. He has no connections with anyone.'

'Except this person he was representing at the funeral who he said could not attend. We need to find out who it was,' said Dorothy. 'And there's only one way to do that,' said Dorothy raising her eyebrows. 'Not a pleasant task.'

'I'm going to speak with Chief Inspector Owen first,' said Camille. 'There's something going on in Earnshaw Street and I'm hoping he'll want to know about it as much as we do.'

Chapter 22

'Lady Divine?'

Chief Inspector Owen came out of the side office he occupied at the police station in Agar Street, Charing Cross glancing at the young police officer manning the desk. 'You should have said it was Lady Divine who was waiting for me, Reynolds. Not just ' a lady wants to see you.'

Constable Reynolds lowered his head, his cheeks bright red. 'Sorry, sir.'

'Chief Inspector Owen?' cried Camille with a frown. 'I thought you were stationed at Brick Lane.'

He nodded. 'I was, but I've been seconded here because of the problems that have arisen over the last few weeks. I'm...I'm rather surprised to see you here, Lady Divine. Is there a problem that needs to involve the police?'

'I felt I should speak with you over some information that has been forwarded to me. I felt sure you would want to know about it. I'm hoping it will aid your investigation.'

He showed her into his office, a room with plain walls painted pale green, the plainness relieved by paintings of flora and fauna in bright colours. His desk sat underneath a window that had frosted glass at the top and wasn't dressed with curtains, and the rather utilitarian room smelt of Chief Inspector Owen's cologne which she was sure had sandalwood in it. Camille spotted a photograph on the desk, which she surmised to be Chief Inspector Owen's late wife.

'I've asked the constable to bring in some tea, Lady Divine,' he said as he closed the door behind them. 'I can't vouch for its quality I'm afraid. None of the constables in this station are good tea-makers, but it's hot, and sometimes it's all we need to cheer us.' He sat at his desk then looked at her, steepling his fingers together in front of him. 'Now, Lady Divine. What brings you into my part of the world?'

'I have discovered something. Regrettably, it's something I'm not sure I can follow up myself. I would very much have liked to, but I don't consider myself to be a stupid woman, Chief Inspector, and I know when there is danger.'

He sat back and stared at her. 'Please continue, Lady Divine. I'm utterly intrigued.'

'We...I have discovered that Lady Phoebe Carruthers was due to have an exhibition of her paintings before she died. It was to take place at the Yorke Gallery in Bond Street, but...well, she was killed and the exhibition didn't take place.'

Owen pulled a face. 'I'm surprised. She was a fine artist was she not? What was the reason for not showing them?'

'I'm afraid I don't know the real reason. I do know that Phoebe and the owner of the gallery, a Horace Riddell, had disagreed about the subject matter of the paintings.'

Owen sat forward, more interested. 'Which was?'

'Suffrage.'

'Suffrage? I thought she painted landscapes.'

'She does...did, but she had painted the pictures to support the suffrage movement. Apparently they were rather candid, truthful, rather too truthful for some tastes. Cecily and I visited the gallery.'

'You went there?'

'I was curious, Chief Inspector. The suffrage movement is in the news and making inroads into our lives whether people like it or not. Many have suffered because of it. Her paintings did not hold back on the subject.'

'You saw them?'

There was a rapping on the door which was then opened to reveal the constable with a tray of teas, and some biscuits arranged on a plate. The Chief Inspector's lips twitched into a smile when he saw them.

'Thank you, Reynolds. Very nice.'

'You're welcome, sir.'

Owen passed Camille a cup of tea. She looked into it and grimaced, but sipped it anyway. 'I did not see the paintings, Chief Inspector. My...source gave me the information. They apparently depicted imprisoned suffragettes being force-fed, and others being arrested in the streets.'

'Not pictures for the nursery then?'

'I should think not.'

Owen took a gulp of his tea then stared into the distance as his thoughts took over.

'Are you saying you think something has happened to these paintings?'

Camille shrugged. 'They must be somewhere, Chief Inspector.' She inhaled a breath, hoping what she was about to say would hit home. 'You do know what happens to the paintings of successful, deceased artists, don't you?'

'I would imagine their value increases.'

'Indeed.'

'And you think Horace Riddell, the owner of the Yorke Gallery has secreted them away until it's time to make a killing.'

'An unfortunate turn of phrase, Chief Inspector.'

'Yes. It was. I apologise.'

She grinned. 'No need. I'm not sure whether he has done so, or whether there is a reasonable explanation. I do know that Edwin Carruthers, Phoebe's husband, was incandescent about them.'

'He did not agree with her painting them?'

'He certainly did not. And I feel quite sure he would not have seen them, nor had them in his home. So, I'm wondering about the 'special place' that the writer mentioned in the note.'

'You think the paintings could be at this special place?'

'I think it's possible, yes.'

Chief Inspector Owen finished his tea. His eyes narrowed and he could not prevent a smile from playing on his lips.

'When you arrived you said you were not a stupid woman, which of course you are not, and you would not put yourself in danger, which I must say is something of which I'm extremely relieved.' Camille inclined her head and Owen rested his elbows on the desk. 'Is it because you have an idea of where the special place is, and it's somewhere you would rather not go.'

'Spot on, Chief Inspector.'

'And you found this out how, Lady Camille?'

'One of my so...'

'Yes, Lady Camille. I assumed it was one of your sources. May I ask where it is, this place you have found.'

'Earnshaw Street.'

Owen's brow crumpled as he pictured the street. 'Earnshaw Street? But that's in one of the old rookeries isn't it?'

'Exactly, Chief Inspector, and not so old by all accounts. And now you know why I did not think it would be safe for a woman like me to go there. I have it on good authority that anyone who goes there, and who isn't known to the inhabitants, is swiftly dealt with in the most brutal way, man, woman, or child. I am determined to discover what has happened to Nellie Bell and why Phoebe was murdered in such a horrendous way, but I would also like to be alive to tell the tale.'

'What makes you think Earnshaw Street is where this place is?'

'I had Horace Riddell followed.'

Chief Inspector Owen momentarily closed his eyes. 'By whom, may I ask?'

Camille smiled. 'You may not.'

Owen shook his head, knowing there was nothing to be gained from pushing the point. 'So, this Horace Riddell was followed by one of your,' he frowned at her briefly, 'sources, and they followed him to Earnshaw Street.'

'That's right.'

'You think that he doesn't live there?'

'Doubtful, wouldn't you think. He has a double-fronted shop on Bond Street where he sells paintings of high value. Why would a man of some means choose to live on a street such as Earnshaw Street when he could very likely live anywhere of his choosing. My source is sure that he went there for a reason. Please understand I would not dream of telling you how to do your job, Chief Inspector Owen, but I think it should be investigated.'

'You realise that I will not be allowed to gain entry to the address.'

'Why ever not?'

'I have no evidence, Lady Divine.'

'But have I not just given you some?'

'It's not evidence, however, I will send someone to check the address. If we feel there is something suspicious there I will obtain a warrant from the magistrate to search the premises.'

'But Chief Inspector, will that not just warn them that the police are interested in their activities? They would surely move anything that would incriminate them. Could you not obtain your warrant on information received?'

'We have to show good reason, Lady Divine. There must be physical evidence. Your statement is not enough I'm afraid. A magistrate will issue the warrant, but will not do so unless questions are answered with regard to the suspects. We don't have any suspects, there's no one we can name, only supposition. I doubt I'll get a warrant on that.'

'Horace Riddell?'

Chief Inspector Owen shook his head. 'Has he committed a crime, Lady Camille?'

'I...I'm sure he has.'

'It's not enough I'm afraid.'

'So will nothing be done?'

Owen smiled at her. 'Mr Riddell is not on our list of suspects, Lady Camille. I'm grateful to you for drawing my attention to him, but all we really have is a man who left his place of business and went to another address. Had it not occurred to you that his visit to Earnshaw Street might have more altruistic reasons?'

'Such as?'

'Perhaps he sponsors a poor family there.'

'I see.'

She shook her head and looked away, frustrated that the chief inspector had not taken her claims seriously. Then something occurred to her.

'So when he visits this poor family, he knocks on the door three times, then two, then one, like a code, and they will only answer the door on that knock, apparently without words of greeting, and he simply enters.'

The expression on Owen's face had changed. 'They used a code?'

'Yes, Chief Inspector Owen.' Camille rose from her chair.' However, I'm sure what you say is true, that he is simply visiting a poor family out of the kindness in his heart.' She looked at him sceptically, then smiled. 'Thank you for giving up your precious time to speak with me. Tell your constables to buy Twinings tea. It's so much more palatable.'

Chief Inspector Owen left his seat to open the door for her and followed her out to the front desk.

'We will investigate, Lady Divine.'

She looked up at him, one eyebrow raised. 'Will you? When? When 'the bird has flown', as they say?'

'When we can get a warrant to search the premises. That, I promise you'

She said her goodbyes and left, thinking that it was no surprise that so many criminals got away with their misdeeds when the police force's hands were so tied up in bureaucracy.

'Well, Chief Inspector Owen,' she murmured under her breath as she began the walk back to Birdcage Mews with a detour to Nightingale Lane. 'My hands are definitely not tied.'

Chapter 23

'I don't think we have any other choice,' said Camille. She was sitting with Ida, Dorothy and Carrie in the kitchen at The Hotel, sipping yet another cup of tea, although it was far superior to the one she'd had at the station in Agar Street. 'We know something is going on there, and by the time Chief Inspector Owen gets the warrant to search the place they will have moved on. We can't allow it to happen. It could mean life or death for Nellie.'

'So you really think she could be there?' asked Dorothy, as she stirred a complicated sauce on the range.

'I think there's every chance she could be there. My feelings are that her disappearance may have absolutely nothing to do with her lover, although of course it's still a possibility, and everything she knows about Lady Phoebe.'

'Do you mean her paintings?'

Camille nodded. 'It can only be the paintings can't it? Lady Phoebe was an exemplary wife and mother. There is nothing else so it must be the paintings. I'm curious as to where this special place is that the writer mentions in the note, and I'd also like to know where the paintings have gone. Edwin Carruthers is certainly not going to worry about where they are. He hated them after all.'

'Do you think they'll be worth a lot of money?' asked Ida.

'I do. When an artist dies their back catalogue of work usually increases in value. Lady Phoebe will no longer be painting so therefore her work will be sought after, by collectors, I shouldn't wonder.'

'So what will we do?'

'We must go to Earnshaw Street.'

Carrie, Dorothy and Ida gasped in unison. 'Surely not, Camille,' said Dorothy. 'Elsie said it's a dangerous place. Who of us would want to go there?'

'I can't imagine any of us will, but I have an idea.' She turned to Carrie. 'Carrie, could you ask Elsie to come and see me at Birdcage Mews. She visits here most days doesn't she?'

'She does, Camille. Are you going to ask her to go back to Earnshaw Street? You heard what she said about it.'

'I know, but whoever goes will not go alone. I have had some thoughts on the matter and I would like to discuss it with her. As she says, she is more of the street than any of us. She knows how the minds of these people work, and her knowledge will be very helpful.' She shook her head and rose to leave. 'I can't tell you how frustrated I feel. On one hand, Chief Inspector Owen had asked me not to get involved in looking for Nellie, but on the other the police seem hopelessly unable to do anything in the search for her. When I left the police station I had already made up my mind. We must do the thing that they seem unable to do.'

'This is a surprise, Lady Camille,' said Elsie, sitting in Camille's drawing room at Birdcage Mews. 'I never would 'ave expected you to summon me to your home, not on me own anyway. I've got this feeling that you want me to do somethin' for yer.'

'I do,' said Camille, pouring tea and offering a plate unwieldy with the pastries that she knew Elsie loved. Elsie, of course, took two. 'To be exact, I want to suggest something to you. You are not obliged to do it of course, you have the final choice, but I think it's the only way we're going to find out where Nellie is,' she paused, 'and what is going on at Earnshaw Street.'

Elsie paused, her hand staying in mid-air, delaying the moment when she would take a bite from the mille feuille in her hand. 'Earnshaw Street?' The pastry went back down on to the plate on her lap. 'Oh, my, Gawd. You want me to go there?'

Camille smoothed her dress over her thighs and sat opposite Elsie, leaning forward to make her point.

'You and Nathanial?' Elsie nodded, resuming her consuming of the pastry. As she bit into it, flakes of pastry fell onto her lap which she brushed off onto the carpet. Camille bit her tongue about the errant flakes. 'You have a certain friendship.'

'You know we do.'

'I'm doing my best to be delicate, Elsie. It is well-known, in some circles, that Nathanial, as fond as he is of you, prefers you to dress as a boy, when...when...' She sighed, not wanting to finish her sentence because she didn't know how to without giving offence.

'When we're in bed, yer mean.'

'Well, yes, actually, that is what I mean.'

'What's that got to do with someone going to Earnshaw Street? Or did you mean me?'

'The clothes you wear? Are they always the same?'

'No, course not. Depends what he wants. Sometimes I'm a ragamuffin, other times I'm an office boy, and we 'ave uniforms too. "E likes a bit of variety, does Nathanial.'

Camille felt herself getting hot and she stood so she could walk around the room and cool down a little. 'I'm sure he does, which is precisely what I wanted to talk to you about.'

Elsie frowned. 'You want me to dress up, as a boy?'

'As a policeman.'

'On me own?'

'No. With me.'

Elsie began to roar with laughter, blowing out even more flakes of pastry from her lips. She wiped her mouth with the back of her hand.

'Oh,' she said wiping her eyes. 'Oh, I'm sorry, Camille. I can't think you're being serious. Look at yer. You're all posh and toffee-nosed. And the way you speak, all proper like. 'Ow the 'ell are you goin' to pass yourself off as a policeman. And a man too. Not with them boosoms. What you gonna do with 'em. And even the police don't speak like what you do.'

'I could bind my...bosom, or pad myself to make myself look fat.'

Elsie put down her pastry and looked into Camille's eyes. 'Look, love, I don't want to offend yer, but, yer skin. You're a bit of a darky, ain'tcha? There's no darkies in the police.'

'A boy then. A ragamuffin, someone who was somewhere he shouldn't be, and you're knocking on doors to find out where he comes from.'

'And you think that'll fool 'em?'

'It might. We'll be taking them by surprise. They won't have time to think.'

'But 'ow's that goin' to 'elp us find out about Nellie?'

'It might not, but we'll be able to see who's there, won't we?'

Elsie sighed. 'You've got the bit between your teeth on this one 'aven't you?' She took another bite of her pastry. 'Alright,' she said with her mouth full, rubbing the pastry off her hands. 'I'll do it, but not with you. I'll take Cecily with me. She looks the part more than you do. She's skinny and she speaks right. You don't. And, Camille, you'd never pass for a boy. You're too, too, womany.'

'I think you mean ladylike, and I'm not happy about Cecily going. And I can't force her. She must agree to it. If she doesn't, well, we'll have to think of something else.'

Elsie shrugged. 'If that's what you want to do, but I won't go with anyone else. I'm tryin' to give us the best chance 'ere. I'll go as a policeman. I'm tall, and I know what to do with me 'air and face. I've been doin' it for Nathanial for months. If Cecily agrees I've got the clothes for 'er, a shirt and waistcoat, and raggedy trousers, all frayed at the edges. They'll do nicely.'

Camille frowned, a smile playing on her lips. 'Why, Elsie?'

'Why what?'

'Why can't Nathanial be happy with you the way you are? I won't pretend, I do think the relationship between you is rather odd, but clearly you have feelings for each other.'

'Don't ask me why, I 'aven't got a clue. It's what 'e likes.' She shrugged. "E comes across as all confident like, full of 'imself, but y'know, Camille, 'e's not really like that. He gets nervous around women, finds them a bit...much, if you get my meaning.'

'And that's why he likes you to dress as a male.'

'I think it is.'

'Do you love him?'

Elsie sighed. 'Love. Where does that get yer? Where did it get you? We give all the love we 'ave just to 'ave it thrown back in our faces. I'd like to love someone but...well, I 'old back if the truth be known. Len West really 'urt me. I 'ave to take some of the blame. I didn't check 'im out like I should 'ave. I don't know why he married me. I s'pose married men 'ave more respectability, but he never showed me any love, and Rose wouldn't 'ave know him if he'd 'ave walked right up to 'er, and 'e was her Pa. Dead now, of course. Just as well really.'

Camille looked into Elsie's face and realised they weren't so different. Both were women who had been let down by the person they should have been able to rely on the most. Both frightened to fall in love again.

'I've always had an affection for Nathanial,' she said. 'He's rather like a naughty little brother, always playing jokes and saying things others wouldn't say.'

'It's why I like him, Camille. There's no pretence. When 'e's at the 'Ouse it makes me right proud, it really does, to see 'im standing there trying to put things right. 'E's a different person when 'e's there. Strong, manly, and seems to know ever such a lot. And he 'as the respect of the other Lords an' all. Yeah, I am proud of 'im.'

Camille smiled. 'And he seems proud of you too.'

'Nah, he ain't proud of me. I ain't done nothin' for 'im to be proud.'

'I wouldn't speak too soon, Elsie. I think you might be just about to.'

'Yes, I'll go, Lady Divine. I've realised that talking about things don't get the job done. If the police won't do it then I s'pose we'll have to.'

'I'll look after yer,' said Elsie. 'I've been to some places in my time that would make yer 'air curl, so I know 'ow to talk to these people.' She glanced at Camille. 'When do yer think we should go?'

Camille shrugged. 'The sooner the better. We don't want them to suspect that anyone's on to them.'

"Ow about in the mornin'. I don't think we should go at night. For one thing, the bloke from the gallery might be there, and you said Cecily was with you when you visited it. If he claps eyes on 'er he might recognise 'er.'

'That's right, but I would imagine it's even more dangerous at night-time. The morning will be perfect.' She turned to Cecily. 'Now, Cecily. You're absolutely sure you will do this? Nothing will be held against you if you would rather not.'

'I want to do it, Lady Divine. Someone's got to. If Nellie *is* there we'll have saved her from goodness knows what. I know we don't know what's there and we might find nothing, and Nellie could be anywhere, but, yes, I want to go, even if it's to knock it off the list.

Chapter 24

'You can get a cab to the outskirts of the rookery,' said Camille. 'I don't think you should walk through the streets looking like that.'

Elsie and Cecily were in the drawing room of Birdcage Mews, Elsie in her policeman's uniform, Cecily looking for all the world like a lad who lived on the streets.

'Are you alright, Cecily?' Camille asked her.

'I am, Madam, although I'm not liking this stuff on my face. It feels very oily.'

'Greasepaint,' said Elsie. 'I use it when...well, yer know.'

'And you, Elsie. You look as authentic a policeman as I've ever seen. I can only imagine why Nathanial...'

'You don't know what I wear underneath, Camille,' Elsie replied, twiddling the bushy moustache stuck to her upper lip. 'He likes that an' all.' Camille grimaced as Cecily went bright red. 'Anyway, let's get this over and done with. Nathanial wants to take me out for lunch. He's right worried about what I'm doin' this mornin'. It surprised me to be honest.'

'It doesn't surprise me. I'm worried too, and I'm still not sure it's the right thing to do. I can't imagine what Chief Inspector Owen will say about it.'

'It'll be too late for 'im to say anything by the time this is over. "E 'ad 'is chance to do something about it an' 'e didn't. That was 'is choice.'

'We'll get out the cab at Dyott Street, then walk down to the corner where it meets Bucknall Street. From there we'll go on to Earnshaw Street. Dyott Street is far enough away for us not to be spotted by anyone from Earnshaw Street. You ready for this, Cecily?'

'I think so.' She looked up at Elsie with troubled eyes. 'I just don't want to let anyone down.'

'You won't. Don't say anythin', that's the best way, so they don't hear your voice, but I'm goin' to 'ave to grab you by the ear, and push you about a bit, to make it look real like. Understand?'

'I understand.'

They left the cab at Dyott Street and paid the fare, then walked towards the corner where it met Bucknall Street. Within a few minutes they were in Earnshaw Street.

'Looks different in the daylight,' said Elsie. 'Not 'alf so scary. It's 'orrible 'ere at night. It feels like the Ripper's 'iding round every corner.' She grabbed hold of Cecily's ear. 'Good job you're smaller than me,' she said. 'This wouldn't look 'alf so good.'

'Ow,' cried Cecily, clutching at her ear. 'Maybe not so real, Elsie. That ear is attached to my 'ead.'

Elsie walked Cecily down Earnshaw Street, peering in the filthy windows, some of them broken or boarded up, then knocked on a few doors so that it looked like she was checking every house in case they were being watched. She knew that people were wary in the rookeries, and if anyone they didn't know came onto the streets, they wanted to know about it. Of course, no one recognised Cecily.

'What would we have done if someone said they knew who I was, that I was their boy.'

Elsie stifled a laugh. 'Well they wouldn't have done, would they, yer daft ha'porth. No one knows you 'ere. That's the point of it. Tut.' She chuckled and shook her head.

'Do you know which house Riddell went into?' asked Cecily through gritted teeth.

'Yep, course I do. We're coming up to it now. Get ready to holler.'

They reached the door. It was the worst one in the street and looked as if it was only held up by the houses either side. Paint had flaked off revealing the rotting wood underneath, black with damp, and the piece of wood that had fallen off when Horace Riddell had gone into the house the night Elsie followed him was leaning up against the wall underneath the window, which was also rotting away. Obviously no one could be bothered to replace it.

Elsie rapped hard on the door with a truncheon that had been left at one of her brothels, and waited. No one answered. She tried again, harder this time, then peered in through the grimy window, dragging Cecily along with her. The windows were so filthy she couldn't see anything inside. As she was about to give up and suggest they leave, the door was yanked open, the bottom of it scraping along the step. Elsie dragged Cecily to the door.

Standing in the frame was a large man. His flabby arms and chest were covered in black hair, and he was wearing a dirty vest, and shabby trousers that were belted tightly under his huge stomach which protruded over the waistband. Unshaven, he stood on the doorstep, picking his teeth with his fingernail, a half-smoked cigarette in his other hand.

'Officer.'

'Do you know this boy,' said Elsie in a low, gravelly voice that Cecily didn't recognise. 'Throwing stones at doors he was, little wretch. I'm tryin' to find his parents if he's got any. He says he lives round 'ere but that's all he'll give me.'

The man looked at Cecily who was doing her best to hide her face while Elsie hung on to her ear. 'You new round 'ere? he asked Elsie.

'I am, sir, Constable West. And you are?'

He stared at her, his eyes narrowing into slits. 'What d'you wanna know that for?'

'This will be my patch from now on. Just getting' to know the community like. And tryin' to protect it from little gits like this.' She gave Cecily a shake who hollered at the pain in her ear. 'This is an up and coming area ain't it? Just want ter keep it that way.'

'Up and coming is it?' The man laughed. 'I ain't 'eard it called that afore. Me name's Donald Bell. Lived 'ere for the last two years. Used to live in Pratt Street. You won't find nuthin' on me. Got a clean slate I 'ave so no need for yer to go lookin'. We got some roughens around 'ere. They need takin' in 'and. Why don't you leave the lad wiv me. I'll see to 'im. He might talk to me whereas the police are thought of as shit on these streets to the people what live 'ere. The police 'ave never treated us very well. The people round 'ere get the blame for everythin'. Yeah, leave 'im wiv me. I'll see to the little tyke.' He leant forward to grab Cecily's arm just as Elsie pulled her back. Cecily hollered her displeasure at the treatment her ear was receiving, and she wasn't acting.

'I can't do that, sir. I wouldn't be doin' my duty as a police officer. He'll spend the night in the cells. That'll make 'im talk. He can't go around damaging other people's 'omes.'

'Donald?' A woman's voice came from inside the house. 'What's goin' on out there, lover. You've been gone ages.' A young woman joined Bell in the hall. 'Who is it?'

'The police.'

'What? Why?'

'Don't go gettin' yourself in a state. There's a boy 'ere been damaging front doors, little bastard. The officer wanted to know if I knew 'im.'

'It ain't one o' mine is it?'

'Nah, ain't one o' yourn. This is a pale, skinny lad, nothing like your three.' Cecily glanced up as the woman joined Bell at the door.

'Well, can't yer close the bloody door. You're letting all the cold in and the fire'll go out. In more ways than one,' she giggled.

'Yeah, yeah, comin' now.'

Cecily glanced away quickly and shut her eyes, hoping with everything she had that the woman hadn't recognised her.

'Carn't 'elp yer, officer,' said Donald Bell. 'Don't know the lad. Don't fink 'e's from round 'ere. You got your work cut out, you 'ave, if you're gonna be patrolling round 'ere. You look a bit young and nancy to me to be Earnshaw Street's police officer if you want my opinion. Reckon you need a bit more muscle. Nuthin' but thieves and petty criminals, that's what we got round 'ere. You wanna watch yerself, sonny, else you'll find yerself flat on your face wiv a boot on yer neck...or worse.'

The woman let out a shrill peel of laughter and slapped the man on the shoulder. 'You and your sense of 'umour, Donald Bell. You'll be the death of me that you will.'

The door was slammed in Elsie's face as she released the grip on Cecily's ear. She grabbed her arm instead and frog-marched her down Earnshaw Street to keep up the appearance of a police officer apprehending a villain.

'You alright?' Elsie asked Cecily as they got to the end of the street. As they turned the corner Elsie released Cecily's arm and she rubbed it wincing.

'You're stronger than you look. My ear,' she said, cupping her hand over her ear which was bright red. 'It's burnin', like it's on fire. Did you 'ave to grip it quite so hard?'

'Sorry, love,' said Elsie. 'Just wanted to make it look real. I think we got away with it, an' all.'

They turned into Bucknall Street, then Dyott Street and slowed down, looking behind them in case they were followed.

'No one there,' said Elsie. 'Think we did a good job there, Cecily.

'I know who the woman is. The one who was in Donald Bell's house.'

'What?'

'Can we get a cab? Lady Divine gave you enough money didn't she? Look, we're nearly in Shaftesbury Avenue. We'll get one there and then

I'll tell you. Oh, my goodness, I just want to go 'ome. I never want to come back 'ere again. It's awful.'

'I did say,' said Elsie, grinning to herself. 'Look, there's a cab now.' She lifted her arm to hail it and it stopped. When they'd climbed in the back Elsie stared at Cecily. 'Right, Cecily. Talk.'

'It was 'er, Madam,' said Cecily breathlessly, excited and anxious at the same time. 'It was definitely 'er.'

'I wonder what she was doing there.'

'It sounded like she was with 'im, y'know in that way. She called him lover, didn't she, Cecily?' said Elsie. 'She was forward with him, flirty, although God knows why. Ugh, he was 'orrible, and it makes me wonder what Nellie Bell saw in 'im. Why would she marry such a bloke?'

The discovery of the woman at the house in Earnshaw Street, who Camille and Cecily had previously spoken to when they had knocked on the door at 14 Pratt Street, had astonished Cecily. Her main concern at the time was that the woman did not recognise her, because if she had there would have been a price to pay, needless to say the grab he'd made for her at the front door would have no doubt been more successful. She shivered when she thought of it.

'Are you alright, Cecily?' Camille asked her. 'May I suggest you go up to the bathroom and wash off that brown greasepaint, then have the rest of the day off.'

'What about Knolly?'

'I don't think Knolly is very happy with me for sending you out on a 'dangerous mission' as she called it.'

'I'll go and see her first, tell her that I'm perfectly alright and that nothing untoward happened to me. To be honest I rather enjoyed the change, apart from nearly havin' my ear twisted off.'

'Yeah, sorry about that,' grinned Elsie. 'I got into me part a bit. I always go the extra mile when I'm dressing up for Nathanial. Forgot where I was.'

'And if Knolly isn't too cross, do you think you could ask her to bring us in a tray of tea and some sandwiches. I think we could all do with some refreshment.'

'I could,' said Elsie. 'I didn't eat before we left for Earnshaw Street. Nerves, see. Goes right to my stomach.'

'You were nervous?' cried Camille. 'I can hardly believe it. I would never have had you down as the nervous type.'

'I'm not usually, but going into one of the rookeries isn't my idea of a good time.'

'No, well, I don't suppose is.'

Once the tea and sandwiches had been delivered, and Knolly had given Camille a smile to show her that she forgave her for sending Cecily on a dangerous mission, Camille wanted to talk about the next step.

'We must do something now that we know they're in league with one another. It's clear that Nellie's husband and this woman have cooked up something between them, and something tells me it involves Nellie.'

'And what about Horace Riddell? It was only because I followed him there that we know about the 'ouse in Earnshaw Street, so 'e must be involved as well.' Camille nodded then gave Elsie a long stare. 'What yer lookin' at me like that for?'

'Your policeman friend, the one who visits you at Bucks Row.'

'What about him?'

'Is he an Inspector?'

'No.'

'A Chief Inspector?'

'No.'

Camille frowned. 'Not a constable, surely? Can they afford your...services?'

'No 'course they can't. 'E's 'igher up than all of 'em. 'E's the top dog. Pays well 'an all.'

'Top dog, eh? Is he a top dog who could organise a search warrant for Chief Inspector Owen?'

'He can do whatever 'e wants. 'E's in charge of all the stations in London, and all the police officers. If 'e wanted a warrant he'd be able to get one.'

'Elsie, we need that warrant. If we're to push this further that house must be searched. I'm sure there's no good going on there and we need to find out what it is. Are you in contact with him?' Elsie nodded. 'Could you be in contact with him today...now, as soon as possible?'

'When I've changed I'll go back to Bucks Row and send the messenger to 'im with a note. He'll want a bit of 'ow's your father no doubt, but it'll be worth it. I'll tell 'im to get the warrant sent to Chief Inspector Owen's station. Where is 'e?'

'At the Charing Cross station. Agar Street.'

'Consider it done, my lady. My friend knows all the magistrates around these parts, well, so do I. They're some of my best customers. Love my girls they do. They all know about each other, know they come to Elsie's for a bit of rumpy pumpy, but from what I 'ear it's something they don't discuss, like a secret club.'

'Will he ask why you want the warrant? It could be awkward if he does. I'd rather he didn't know about what we've been doing...what I've been doing. Chief Inspector Owen already disapproves of my involvement in the search for Nellie, and he told me in no uncertain terms to stay out of it. Of course I refused.'

'No, course he won't ask. He'll shake his 'ead and give me one of 'is looks, then call me a little minx. Then he'll chase me about the room for a bit with his truncheon in 'is 'and, and I'll pretend to be caught by 'im and he'll punish me. It's 'is little game. He loves it and 'e'll be like putty in me 'ands afterwards. Don't you worry, Camille. It's as good as done.'

Chapter 25

'Chief Inspector Owen. I wasn't expecting to see you today. I hope there's nothing wrong.'

'That depends, Lady Divine.'

'Oh, does it?' Camille nervously entwined her fingers in her lap. Chief Inspector Owen was looking at her askance. He's wondering why he received the warrant, she thought. And who from.

'It does. I received a warrant from a magistrate today for a house in Earnshaw Street.'

'Oh. Did you?'

'I think you're fully aware that I did.' He frowned. 'How did you manage it?' He held up his hand. 'No, don't say it. One of your sources I expect.'

She nodded looking contrite. 'We discovered something, Chief Inspector, something I'm sure you'll find of great interest.'

Owen sighed and sat wearily on the chaise without being invited. 'What exactly did you discover?'

'Nellie Bell's husband lives there.'

Owen sat up and narrowed his eyes. 'He does?'

'Yes, and so does the woman we spoke to in Pratt Street, number fourteen, who claimed to be a friend of Nellie's. I say she lives there, but I'm not certain of it. She was there this morning and was behaving in a rather familiar fashion with Donald Bell apparently, as though they knew each other very well. So there's the triangle, Chief Inspector. Nellie, Donald Bell, and the woman from Pratt Street. I'd say that was suspicious wouldn't you.'

'Was there anyone else there.'

'No one was seen, but that doesn't mean to say that no one else was in the house. Don't forget Chief Inspector, this is the house Horace Riddell went to after he closed his gallery. He knocked at the door and was given admittance. Strange don't you think?'

Chief Inspector Owen nodded and rose from the chaise. 'Very strange. I have men on the way there now and I'm off to join them. I hope this isn't a blind alley, Lady Divine. The force is very stretched at the moment what with the murders of those poor women, and we seem to have very little to go on. It's a conundrum, one that we need to solve and quickly before anyone else loses their life.'

Camille nodded. 'I have every confidence you'll find something, Chief Inspector Owen. Something is going on between those two, Donald Bell, and the woman from Pratt Street, who assured me she had not seen Bell for some time, that he had moved out of the street many months hence. Her behaviour towards him would suggest otherwise.'

'What are you doin' ere, Camille?' Elsie was standing on the pavement outside her address in Bucks Row, talking to Camille through a cab window. 'I can 'ardly believe you've deigned to be seen in Bucks Row.'

'Get in the cab, Elsie. The police are on their way to Earnshaw Street. I'm desperate to see what happens, aren't you?'

'Yeah, I am. I 'ad to do extras to get that warrant. I think I'm owed.'

'Get a coat and get in. I don't want to waste any more time.'

The cab took them from Bucks Row, through Whitechapel, and past the new Whitechapel Gallery and on to Holborn.

'How far is it?' Camille asked the driver.

'Just over three miles, Ma'am. You in a hurry?'

'We certainly are.'

'I'll do me best.'

'Can you stop on the corner of Earnshaw Street. We don't want to get too close.'

'What you two up to? You ain't spies are yer?'

Camille and Elsie glanced at one another and burst out laughing. 'Course we are,' said Elsie. 'Can't you tell?'

As they passed by the Old Bailey, Elsie nodded in its direction.

'That's where that lot'll end up no doubt about it.'

Camille sighed. 'I hope so, Elsie. Chief Inspector Owen will be less than pleased if we've sent him on a wild goose chase.'

'I hope so too. We could get done for perverting the course of justice, or at the very least wasting the time of the police. That's what my policeman friend says anyway. 'I 'ope you really need this' he said, 'cause if it's just to get your own back on someone you could be in trouble.' And he said not to mention 'is name, although God knows what 'e'd do about it if I did. There's nothin' he *can* do. He wouldn't want 'is wife to know what he gets up to at my place.'

Camille shook her head and looked out of the window. A frisson of nervousness went through her at the thought of Chief Inspector Owen's reaction if there really was nothing going on there. Please let Nellie be there, she thought, or something at least. Something.

The cab pulled up at the corner of Earnshaw Street. Camille paid the fare and asked the driver if he would mind waiting as they weren't planning to be long. He shrugged, then pulled his cap over his eyes and settled down for a nap.

'Come on, Elsie. This is the moment we've been waiting for. I must see what they find.'

'If they find anything.'

Camille grimaced. 'Please don't say that. I feel very nervous about it.'

Elsie squeezed her arm and they looked at one another, smiles on their faces.

'Do you think we could be friends, Elsie?' Camille asked her.

Elsie nodded. 'Yeah, but you'll have to drop your toffee-nosed ways, and get some decent tealeaves instead of that stuff you drink.' She grinned. 'I'd like us to be friends. I know we're different, but I think it's what makes friendships interestin'. Wouldn't be no good if we was all the same would it?'

Camille returned her grin. 'I suppose not. And I'll change my tealeaves.'

'What about the other thing?'

'One step at a time.'

As they reached the railway bridge that went across Earnshaw Street, Elsie grabbed Camille's arm.

'Quick. Let's hide in the arches. No one'll see us here. Look. The police. They're at the 'ouse.'

They watched as the police knocked on the front door of the house where Elsie had taken Cecily. There was no reply. They tried again, then Chief Inspector Owen commanded them to knock the door in. There was a loud crash as a small battering ram was used by two constables to force their way in. The door disintegrated into myriad jagged pieces and they heard a woman scream.

'That will very likely be the woman from Pratt Street,' said Camille. 'I'm sure she wasn't expecting this this afternoon.'

They heard shouting, a man's voice complaining at the treatment he was receiving at the hands of bent coppers, and Donald Bell, still in his vest and the same shabby trousers, was led out of the house by two police officers.

'What the bloody 'ell yer doin'?' he cried. 'I ain't done nuffin. All I done was look after 'em for 'im. I weren't receiving 'em. I weren't gonna sell 'em. I was just takin' care of 'em for 'im. He said they needed lookin' after.'

Chief Inspector Owen stood in front of him and clearly asked him something. 'I don't know who they belonged too. I 'fought they belonged to 'im, that's what 'e said anyway. I don't know why your arrestin' me officer, it ain't me what you should be arrestin', it's im, 'cause I ain't done nuffin.'

Camille turned to Elsie, frowning. 'What's he talking about, do you think?'

'I think we're about to find out.'

Donald Bell was handcuffed and a rough-looking blanket was wrapped around him. He was pushed into the back of a police car with a constable, as, moments later, the woman that Camille recognised from Pratt Street was also led out by two more constables. Her screams cut the air in two.

'God, she's got a mouth on 'er ain't she?' said Elsie. 'Bloody 'ell, I wish she'd stop all that. She's gettin' on my nerves.'

'She certainly knows how to scream that's for sure. And the language? I didn't know women knew words like that.' Elsie grinned. The woman was bundled into the back of a different police car, still screaming her head off, and could be heard as the cars drove past them on the way to Agar Street Police Station.

'They're heading for the cells I should think,' said Elsie as Camille grabbed her arm. 'Look.'

They watched as a dozen or more framed paintings were taken from the house. They had been wrapped haphazardly in torn sheets of newspaper; lengths of string tied around each one that did nothing to protect what was inside.

'Phoebe's paintings,' cried Camille. Tears filled her eyes as her hand flew to her mouth. 'They must be her suffragette paintings, the ones Horace Riddell said were so distasteful to him. He stored them in that house, somewhere no one would think of looking.'

'He probably paid Bell to store them in that dump. God knows what they're like now. They didn't exactly look well-cared for did they. Bloody 'ell, that Riddell's a right bastard ain't 'e. 'E's used your friend's death to make a pot for 'imself. Bet they're worth a fortune now.'

Camille wiped her eyes and Elsie looked at her with sorrow. 'Oh look don't go getting' all upset over it again. They're found now, Camille. They can be sold and the money can go to Phoebe's kids, or the suffragettes if that's what she wanted.'

'But what about Riddell?'

Elsie grabbed her arm. 'Come on, we'll get the cabbie to take us to Bond Street. We might as well see this thing through, Camille. You wanna see 'im arrested don't yer?'

'Nothing would make me happier right at this moment.'

They ran down Earnshaw Street to where the cab was waiting for them. Elsie banged on the window. The driver was fast asleep and almost jumped out of his skin, his cap falling over his eyes.

'Alright, alright, where's the fire?'

'There ain't no fire,' Elsie answered as she and Camille climbed into the back of the cab. 'We need to get to Bond Street and fast, mate, as fast as you can.'

He pushed his cap back on his head and started the cab. 'I knew you two was spies.'

Bond Street was as busy as ever, the January sales were still in full swing with shoppers desperate to get rid of their cash.

'I've got the perfect place for us,' said Elsie as they climbed out of the cab and paid the driver, 'and we'll get a cup a tea an' all. I'm parched.'

'So am I,' replied Camille. 'And I think I'm getting a cold. Damn. I don't need it at the moment.'

'You're alright,' said Elsie. 'Here we are. It's the tearoom where I sat when I was watchin' the gallery. It's right opposite so we won't miss a trick.'

They managed to get a table in the centre of the tearoom and ordered a pot of coffee.

'Fancy somethin' different today,' said Elsie. 'Would you rather 'ave tea?'

'Coffee's fine. I do hope it's Columbian.' Elsie pulled a face at her. 'Er, well, anything would be nice.' Elsie smirked then nodded towards the gallery.

"Ere we go. It's showtime.'

They sipped their coffee as they watched Chief Inspector Owen and two constables enter the shop by the front door. They heard the bell tinkle as they went in and Elsie giggled.

'Sounds so nice, don't it, the little bell over the door. Makes you think it's all nice and cosy like, friendly and all above board, instead of some nasty little shit making money out of a poor woman what's lost 'er life.'

'You're right. I think Horace Riddell is just about to lose the plaque in the gallery, which he is fond of pointing out so often that says, 'By appointment to the Royal Family'.'

'That won't save 'im. He stole those paintings and got Bell to fence 'em, no matter what 'e says about not receiving. They're stolen goods and they was in 'is 'ouse. He can squeal as much as he wants. Oh, look, the constables of taken 'old of 'im and 'e's tryin to wriggle away. Good luck with that, mate. You won't get away from them young buffs. They're a lot stronger than you are.' She glanced at Camille. 'Chief Inspector Owen ain't bad is 'e. I might give 'im my card.'

Camille stared at her. 'Don't you dare. He's a widower.'

'I don't care what he is. I wouldn't kick 'im out of bed that's for sure.'

They continued watching as the constables walked Horace Liddell out of the Yorke Gallery. Chief Inspector Owen locked the doors then followed them along Bond Street and got into the same motor car that the constables had pushed Liddell into.

'Bet that's a difficult conversation,' said Elsie. 'He'll be grilling 'im now, and serves 'im bloody well right.'

Camille nodded. 'We didn't find Nellie, though, did we, Elsie? I'm sure there's a connection to her. The fact that her husband was hiding Phoebe's paintings must say something. How could he be involved if not through Nellie?'

Elsie shrugged. 'So there must be a connection. Nellie worked for Phoebe. Nellie's husband is Donald Bell, the woman from Pratt Street knew them both. Horace Riddell knew Lady Phoebe.'

'And then there's the special place that the writer of the note mentioned.'

'Where's that?'

Camille looked glum. 'Who knows.' Taking a sip of her coffee she suddenly narrowed her eyes and said,' but if Horace Riddell knew Phoebe he very likely knew Nellie. Nellie went everywhere with her by all accounts, so when Phoebe went to the gallery, it's very likely Nellie was with her.'

'So you think Riddell knows more than he's letting on?'

'I do. And there's something else. Where is Phoebe's studio? I know she painted pictures of her travels, but it was from photographs that she took while she was in all of those exotic places. She brought them back to London and painted pictures from them, but where...where did she paint them? Would that not be her special place? She must have loved it there because it's where she did the thing she loved the most, her painting.'

'D'you think Chief Inspector Owen will think of that when he's questioning old Riddell? I mean, you've been working on it for weeks and you've only just thought of it. What if 'e's got 'er locked away somewhere to keep her quiet. She knew about Phoebe's paintings; knew they were of suffrage. She was a suffragette 'erself weren't she. D'you think Phoebe painted them for her?'

'I suppose it's possible. They were close, more than maid and lady. Phoebe told me they were friends, best friends I should imagine. When you're married to someone like Edwin Carruthers it's difficult to know who your real friends are, because people often only want you for your title and for the cachet you can bring to the relationship.'

Elsie frowned. 'Cachet. What's a cachet?'

'Cachet is status or prestige. People often cosy up to the aristocracy because it raises their own standing in life.'

'I couldn't care less.'

Camille grinned. 'I know, Elsie. It's one of the things I like about you. I can't imagine you cosying up to anyone just for the sake of your reputation.'

'Well there's the rub, Lady Camille. The one I've got ain't worth 'avin, and no cosying up's goin' to make any difference to it. Everyone knows what I am, and more important, I know what I am.'

'Do you think we should go to the station in Agar Street and speak to Chief Inspector Owen? What will happen to Nellie if Liddell has her locked up somewhere. He might be the only one who knows where she is.'

'What about 'er 'usband?'

'My instinct tells me he doesn't know, but the woman from Pratt Street might. I think we should go to the station, Elsie. If I'm wrong I'm wrong, but if I'm right it could save her life.'

Chapter 26

It took them more than half an hour to get to Agar Street. It was one of the busiest times of the day and Camille was getting impatient.

'Calm yourself,' said Elsie. 'We'll get there when we get there.'

'But what if we're right and one of them knows where she is?'

'P'raps Chief Inspector Owen's already thought of it.'

'And maybe he hasn't.'

'Look, we're nearly there. We're on William IV Street. We've only got a short way to go. When we get there you run in and I'll pay the cabbie.' Camille looked at her and raised her eyebrows. 'With money. I 'ave got money yer know. Probably more than you in your awkward circumstances.'

Camille climbed out of the cab and ran into the police station in Agar Street where Constable Reynolds was manning the desk. He frowned when he saw her.

'Lady Divine, isn't it?'

'That's right, constable. I must see Chief Inspector Owen.'

'He's in the interview room, interviewing a suspect. I'm not meant to disturb him.'

'Constable Reynolds, you must disturb him on this occasion. It could be a matter of life or death.'

His eyes widened and he nodded. 'Right you are, Madam. I'll tell him you're here.'

Chief Inspector Owen looked grim as he joined Camille by the desk.

'I take it you've heard, Lady Divine. We found Lady Carruthers' paintings being stored in the house in Earnshaw Street. You were right it seems. There *was* criminal activity going on there.'

'Am I right in assuming Horace Riddell was in league with Donald Bell to hide Phoebe's paintings, and then sell them when her catalogue increased in value because of her death?'

'Yes, spot on. Riddell's a slimy character.'

'How does he know Donald Bell?'

'I've questioned Donald Bell who told me he met Riddell through his wife, Nellie, a chance meeting on the street one day. Riddell knew Nellie through Lady Carruthers. When I questioned Riddell about why he'd chosen Bell to fence the goods, he said he knew as soon as he'd met him that he was the kind of man who wouldn't turn down payment for simply storing something, and with no questions asked.'

'The thing is Chief Inspector, my instinct is telling me that at least one of them, or maybe all of them know where Nellie is. If they are the only ones that do know, her life's in danger. They may have her locked away somewhere.' Owen nodded. 'I've been asking myself about Phoebe's studio.'

'You know where it is?'

Camille looked worried. 'No, I don't. It's not something we discussed because she was so worried about Nellie.'

'But Nellie disappeared before Lady Carruthers' was murdered, Lady Divine. If it was Riddell or Bell who took her, what would be their motive?'

'Yes, you're right,' nodded Camille. 'There's clearly a hole in my thinking.'

Owen frowned. 'Unless...'

'Unless...?'

'Nellie had a lover, did she not, a man out of her class.'

'It would seem so. The earrings and the note point to it. The note was written on good paper and beautifully written, the earrings not the sort of present many could afford.'

'Perhaps Bell decided to take back what he felt was rightfully his.'

Camille nodded, galvanised by his theory. 'And when Phoebe was murdered and Riddell asked him to store her paintings away from prying eyes, they agreed to keep her locked away because she may very well have disagreed with what they were doing. We know she thought the world of Phoebe. From what I know of Nellie I cannot imagine that she would approve of what they've been doing.'

'It's likely they all know where she is. If she has been taken and isn't with her lover, my money is on Bell taking her in the first instance, because she told him she wanted to leave him. Then Riddell got involved when he asked Bell to store the paintings.'

'And the woman from Pratt Street?'

'An Alice Price. We've got information on her, the only one out of the three that has a police record. Used to run a gang of thieves, robbing people as they came out of the big hotels near Hyde Park. She taught them what to do and how to do it. She's a real hard case. She knew the Bells didn't she, from when they lived in Pratt Street, knew that Nellie had met someone else, someone with money, perhaps pretended to be a friend to her. It could very likely have been her who told Donald Bell that Nellie was being unfaithful to him. It wouldn't surprise me if she's the mastermind behind all of this.'

Camille gasped. 'Really? A woman?'

'You shouldn't be so surprised, Lady Divine. Life in the rookeries is very different from the life you have known. The residents there will do anything for a coin, and more if they can get it. Life is hard there. There are no values, no morals, and life is cheap. They do what they can to survive. I'm not defending them. Some of them could find a decent days' work if they put themselves out a bit more and pulled themselves and their families out of the muck they live in, but they become inured to the way of life. I'd say most of them like the ducking and diving, the feeling they can get something for nothing, when all they have to do is stick their hand into the waistcoat of someone who has probably just paid a bar bill that would keep a family fed for a year.'

'So what will you do?'

'I'll change tack for now, question them about Nellie. I think she's more important than a few paintings, don't you?'

'Yes, Chief Inspector.' She smiled at him. 'My thoughts exactly.'

Elsie was waiting outside the police station, leaning against the wall and smoking a cigarette.

'Well, what did 'e say?'

'He agreed with me. If Nellie hasn't gone away with her lover, he is almost sure that they know where she is.'

'All of 'em?'

'Yes, and he said it wouldn't surprise him if the woman was the ringleader.'

Elsie frowned then dropped her cigarette end on the pavement and ground it out with her boot. 'Does he know 'er?'

'He knows *of* her. He said she has a criminal record, that she used to hire and train people to pick the pockets of people coming out of the hotels near Hyde Park.'

'So she would 'ave done some time then.'

'I would imagine so. I'm just praying that they do know where Nellie is, and that they tell Chief Inspector Owen before any harm comes to her.'

They walked down Agar Street and then St Martin's Place until they got to The Strand.

'I really can't walk any further, Elsie,' said Camille. 'I have a cold coming, my head's throbbing. It looks like another cab I think. Will you come to Birdcage Mews?'

'Will you be alright on your own?' asked Elsie. 'I need to get back to Bucks Row and see my Rose. I 'aven't seen 'er much today and I miss her. Her tutor will have gone by now and she'll be ready for a cuddle with her Ma.'

'Yes, yes of course,' said Camille, waving her away to another cab. 'If I hear anything from Chief Inspector Owen about Nellie, I'll send a message.'

'Got a telephone, ain't yer?' Camille nodded. 'I'm gonna get one. Don't know why I 'aven't before now. Yeah, get a messenger to me. If you need me tomorrer, I'll be around somewhere.'

Camille gave a watery smile. 'Thanks, Elsie. I couldn't have got through today without you.'

'Yeah, you could.' She smiled and Camille realised she was a woman who hadn't had much praise from anyone in her life before.

By the time she got to Birdcage Mews, Camille knew she needed one of Knolly's herbal potions.

'Oh, Lady Divine,' said Cecily as she opened the door for her. 'You're looking a bit peaky, Madam, if you don't mind me sayin' so.'

'I don't mind, Cecily, and to be honest I'm feeling rather peaky. Do you think Knolly could rustle up one of her toddies. My head is absolutely thumping.'

'Why don't you take yourself off to bed, Madam. Me and Knolly will sort things out here, and put off any callers. I'll get Knolly to bring you up one of her lemon and ginger potions with lots of honey. You really look as though you need something.'

'If a message comes from Chief Inspector Owen I want to see it straight away, Cecily. Please don't be frightened to wake me. It's very important. Have you heard about the arrests?'

'No, Madam. You can tell me about it when you're feeling better. And don't worry, Lady Divine. I'll let you know as soon as we hear anything.'

For the next two days Camille was firmly ensconced in her bed. She protested, was a terrible patient, but both Cecily and Knolly were insistent that she stay there to rest and sleep until she felt better.

'You have a terrible cold, Madam,' said Cecily who helped Camille with her day to day personal needs. 'You won't do yourself or anyone else any good by ignoring it. Please, stay in bed. Knolly says you must anyway, and what Knolly says goes.' Camille had sighed, but nodded and impatiently acquiesced. There was no point in taking on Knolly when she had the bit between her teeth, and Camille knew if she went against her, Knolly would never forgive her.

At then end of the second day, Camille sat up as Cecily brought her a dinner tray of soup and some toast.

'Are you sure we haven't heard anything, Cecily? No messages, nothing at all?'

'Mrs West and Lord Fortesque-Wallsey came to see you, but Knolly said no.'

'Nothing from Chief Inspector Owen?'

Cecily gave her a sideways glance. 'Well, yes, Madam.'

'What? What did he say?'

'They haven't found her, Madam. I'm so sorry. He rang this morning to find out if you'd recovered. He wanted to speak to you, but Knolly said no, that if there was anything positive to be passed on, she would pass it on.'

'And there wasn't.'

'No, Madam. I'm sorry. I know you're worried. Apparently the three people Chief Inspector Owen arrested aren't talking. He said to tell you he's sure Alice Price is in the middle of it all, that and other things, he said, and that she's probably told Donald Bell and Horace Liddell not to say anything about the whereabouts of Nellie Bell.'

Camille was distraught. 'But if she's locked away somewhere she'll die before anyone gets to her.'

'He said that was their main concern.'

'I must speak to him, Cecily. He must lean on Donald Bell. I think the man still has feelings for her. Will you help me? I know I'm wobbly but I'm not so ill I'm unable to speak on the phone.'

'Knolly's gone to the market.'

Camille smiled. 'Then time is of the essence. We do it now then we won't get into trouble.'

Camille sat in the big chair by the window. Cecily had wrapped a blanket around her and brought the telephone to her, dialling the number and handing the earpiece to Camille.

'May I speak with Chief Inspector Owen please.' Camille nodded at Cecily and smiled. The Chief Inspector was available. 'Chief Inspector. It's Camille Divine. Yes, yes, I'm much better thank you. I understand there has been no developments as to the whereabouts of Nellie Bell.' Cecily watched Camille as she listened to Owen's reply. 'I'm sure if you persist with Donald Bell, and explain to him that if he doesn't tell you where Nellie is she will die, he will relent. I think he still loves her, Chief Inspector, that he arranged to meet her, perhaps to talk, and she agreed. Once they had met, my guess is that he imprisoned her to keep her from running away. He is the key, Chief Inspector. I know a woman's heart. I know that she will have had some regrets and felt some guilt over what she had done. She had taken a lover outside of her marriage and it would not have come easily to her, whatever her reasons were. Alice Price has twittered into Donald Bell's ear and encouraged him not to do the right thing because it is what is best for her. She wanted Bell because he had the promise of easy pickings, the money Horace Liddell had promised him for storing the paintings, and perhaps a cut of the money earned on the sale of them. That damned woman knew all along what was happening to Nellie, even when Cecily and I went to the house.' There was a pause. 'The special place. We...that is, I think it could be Phoebe's studio. Edwin Carruthers must know where it is. Please Chief Inspector, question Bell about his love for Nellie, and speak to Edwin Carruthers. I think she could be locked in the studio. I believe the studio could be the special place.'

Chapter 27

'What's this about, Chief Inspector? I'm working and I don't appreciate being interrupted when I'm at the House. You've pulled me out of a meeting. We're debating the withdrawal of troops from Ireland and I need to be there. I have a speech to make.'

'Yes, sir, I realise that, but this could be a matter of life or death.'

Edwin Carruthers sat at his solid oak desk and indicated for Chief Inspector Owen to sit opposite. Owen looked around the study. It was the first time he had ever been permitted to enter the Palace of Westminster, and he was overwhelmed by the history that surrounded him, the gothic architecture, and the sense of quiet industry that went on every day, the making of laws and the heated debates.

Edwin Carruthers' study was the picture of elegance, wood-panelled, the windows dressed with ruby-red velvet curtains held back with gold tassels. The walls were lined with books of every size, and on a pedestal in the corner was a globe of the earth, an absolute beauty depicting every country of the world.

'We are investigating the disappearance of a woman, a Nellie Bell, someone we are aware you have knowledge of.'

'Yes, of course I have knowledge of her. She was my wife's personal maid until she absconded and disappeared to who knows where.'

'We are of the opinion she did not abscond, Lord Carruthers. We think she was taken by her estranged husband and imprisoned. We currently have him in custody, along with two others, Horace Riddell of the Yorke Gallery in Bond Street, and Alice Price, a woman with a police record, who has been working in league with the two men.'

Edwin Carruthers looked shocked. 'Horace Riddell? Surely not. His gallery exhibited my wife's paintings. She often had exhibitions there. Why on earth have you arrested him, man?'

'Because he stole your wife's most recent paintings on suffrage, stored them in a house in Earnshaw Street, and paid Nellie Bell's husband for the privilege.'

'He stored them in Bell's house?'

'Yes, sir.'

'Why?'

'Because on the death of your wife those paintings will have increased in value a thousand-fold. I have investigated the auction houses and some of your wife's paintings are being sold for thousands to collectors. Riddell had planned to store the paintings until they had reached optimum value, then would have released them, probably to galleries on the continent and America, so he could safely say he was the owner without being discovered as a thief.'

Edwin Carruthers rubbed his face across his eyes. 'I'm astonished, Chief Inspector. I had no idea.'

'Lady Carruthers' studio, Lord Carruthers. Where did she paint? Not at your home?'

'Oh, no, she never painted at home. She said she found it too distracting. We often have callers and she decided that she needed to paint elsewhere.'

'And where was that?'

'We have a small house in Duke Street, a few minutes' walk from Oxford Street. A small pokey place, but at the back of the house is a large orangery which was there when we bought it. The light coming through the windows was perfect for her. In some ways I think she preferred the Duke Street house to the one in Henrietta Street. She was never bothered by status or society. She was at her happiest when she had a paintbrush in her hand and a canvas in front of her.

'She wanted to be apart when she was painting, but not so apart she felt isolated. She could have built an artist's hut in our garden which, as you've seen for yourself, is substantial, but she said coming home in the evening was a pleasure to her, to walk amongst people in the busyness of life in the evening after a productive day. I think we were more alike than I'd realised.' He sat back in his seat and rubbed a hand across his face, his eyes bright with unshed tears.

'You know, Chief Inspector, one doesn't know what one has until it is no longer there. Phoebe and I led almost separate lives. Unlike some of the other Lords who take their seats in the House of Lords only occasionally, or some not at all, I am an active member. Sittings can be arranged for any time of the day or night depending on what is occurring in the country. I take my position very seriously. Phoebe was a woman with her own mind and her own talents. I admired her. Unfortunately I didn't tell her just how much and I should have, but of course it is too late now, and that I deeply regret.'

'What is the number of the house in Duke Street, Lord Carruthers?'

'Thirty-five. You'll want the key of course. Do you really think my wife's maid is there, locked in somewhere?'

'We don't know, sir, but we must investigate every avenue.'

Edwin Carruthers took a key from a drawer in his desk and passed it to Chief Inspector Owen. 'I'll make sure one of my constables brings this back to you, Lord Carruthers as soon as we've finished inspecting the house.'

'There's no hurry, Chief Inspector. The only time I entered that house was when we first purchased it. It was primarily for Phoebe's use. I may sell it now. I have no use for it.'

Chief Inspector Owen left Westminster Palace and returned to his motor car, left in Abingdon Street. He got in and slammed the door, reaching into the glove compartment for a packet of cigarettes he kept there for emergencies. He took one from the packet, lit it, then leant back in his seat, blowing out a plume of smoke, thinking of Edwin Carruthers and what he had said about Phoebe Carruthers. He missed her he said, although from what he had heard from Camille Divine and others, he was less than attentive when his wife was alive. His thoughts went to Mary, his deceased wife. Did he miss her? They were not close when she died from Spanish flu, and, in a similar fashion to the Carruthers' lived almost separate lives.

Owen had become used to his own company. There had been no children so there were no family ties of that nature, and his life was his own. In reality it always had been. Did he miss Mary? There were times when he did, but he realised that he had missed her when she was still alive. She had abandoned their marriage when the longed-for children hadn't arrived, saying marriage was for children. She hadn't seemed to realise that a good marriage was far more than that. He'd wanted affection, companionship, a shared love of interests outside of work, but they had never found that place of sharing. They had shared nothing apart from the same roof. He missed her, yes, but for the life they could have had together, the one that didn't materialise.

He started the engine and made for Birdcage Walk, hoping that Lady Divine would be well enough to accompany him. If Nellie Bell was being kept at the Carruthers' house in Duke Street, she would need the security the sight of another woman would give her, and he felt sure that Camille Divine was that person.

'How are you, Lady Divine? You certainly look better than you did a few days ago.'

'I'm well, Chief Inspector, although I feel as though I'm being held prisoner by Cecily and Knolly who are adamant I should rest. Well, I have rested and now I'm thoroughly bored.'

'I know it's a bit late in the day, Lady Divine, but I wondered if you would accompany me to Duke Street. I can assure you you'll be inside, either in the motor car or in the house, so there should be no danger of your cold getting any worse. You were perfectly accurate when you said that Phoebe Carruthers would have a studio somewhere. She and Lord Divine purchased a small house in Duke Street that she considered perfect for her studio, and it's a few minutes' walk from Selfridges on Oxford Street.'

Camille stared at him. 'Oh, my goodness, yes, it is. Of course I'll come with you. Let me get a coat. Do you think Nellie might be held there?'

Owen shrugged. 'It's possible. If she is I think the presence of another woman will help her.'

Despite Knolly's best efforts to intervene, Camille joined Chief Inspector Owen to investigate the house in Duke Street.

'It's a short drive, Knolly,' said Camille. 'Please don't fret so.'

'It's too early for an outing, Lady Divine,' said Knolly. 'You mark my words you'll be laid up again. Oh, well, I s'pose it's none of my business. Just don't be out too long.'

'Knolly will very likely not speak to me for a fortnight,' said Camille chuckling as they walked to the motor car. 'She calls it sending someone to Coventry.'

Owen glanced at her. 'It's nice to have someone to take care of you, Lady Divine. You seem to be very close to your staff.'

'I am. I'm very fortunate to have such loyal people working for me. They're more like friends really.'

'But they know who's boss.'

'Oh, yes, but I'm a gentle mistress.'

Chief Inspector Owen opened the passenger door for Camille, and she got in as he ran around the front of the car to the drivers' seat.

'How long will it take to get there,' she asked him. 'I'm very eager to see if Nellie's there.'

'About twenty minutes or so. I telephoned the Agar Street station from the Palace of Westminster. There will be two constables to meet us. We don't know what we'll find there.'

Camille's eyes widened. 'You went to the Palace of Westminster?'

'To speak with Lord Carruthers. I felt that waiting for him to return home would be counter-productive. I felt it was imperative to find out where Lady Carruthers studio was and go there today if possible. If Nellie Bell is there it's been three days since she last saw anyone, unless of course there are others working with Bell, Riddell and Price.'

Camille shivered. 'I hadn't thought of that.'

Chief Inspector Owen turned the motor car into Duke Street and pulled up outside number thirty-five.

'There it is, and there are the constables.'

'Oh it's a sweet little place. No wonder Phoebe fell in love with it.'

They got out of the motor car, and Chief Inspector Owen unlocked the front door with the keys Edwin Carruthers had given him.

'Let's take this quietly. We don't know if there is anyone else here and if there is, the element of surprise will be our strength. Lady Camille I'd like you to stay behind me if you will. Constables, you go in first. Search each of the downstairs rooms first in case there is someone else here. We'll follow you in, then I'd like you to search the upstairs rooms.

The constables went in the house, searching the sitting room, a dining room in the centre of the house, and a small kitchen. Chief Inspector Owen followed them in. When the downstairs had been searched he beckoned Camille in.

'Do you think there is anyone here, Chief Inspector?'

'No, I'm not expecting it, but we had to be sure.' The two constables returned from searching the first floor. 'Anything?' They shook their heads. 'Wait outside while we search for the missing woman.'

Camille followed Owen as he went into the kitchen. He felt the kettle on the range.

'Stone cold.'

Camille glanced at the table where she'd spotted some dirty cups and a plate with some mouldy crusts. 'This isn't right,' she said. 'Phoebe wouldn't have left those there, and when on earth were those sandwiches eaten. Those crusts are stale.'

'Lord Carruthers mentioned an orangery which Lady Phoebe used as her studio.'

Camille pointed to a half-glassed door. 'It'll be in the garden, Chief Inspector. Through there I should imagine.'

Owen gingerly opened the door and peered into the room. 'A lobby, probably leading to the orangery.' He went into the lobby and opened a door the other side which flooded the lobby and kitchen with light. 'This is it,' he said. 'This is the orangery, but why is the light on?'

They both stepped inside. The building was rather beautiful, square in shape with long floor to ceiling windows, and a glass roof, rising into a pinnacle, each with a blind over the glass sections for when the sun was too bright.

'This is stunning, and look at the paintings,' said Camille going across to a large canvas with a paint-spattered cloth draped over it. 'Should we look at this do you think? Would it be too intrusive?'

'I'm not sure it matters now, Lady Divine. There doesn't seem to be anyone here to object.'

Camille pulled the cloth from the huge canvas and gasped.

'A self-portrait. Oh, my goodness.' She stepped back to observe it, her eyes filling with tears. 'Oh, dear, oh, dear, I wasn't expecting this. But it's utterly beautiful, just as she was. How clever, how talented. Surely, Edwin Carruthers will want this. How could he not? It's almost as though she knew, Chief Inspector, knew that time was short for her.' She turned when Owen didn't answer. 'Chief Inspector?'

'Don't move, Lady Divine.'

'What? Why ever not?'

'Can you step back towards me. One step back, that's right.' He took her hand as she stepped towards him.

'What is it Chief Inspector? What have you seen?'

'There's something on the floor behind the large easel holding Lady Carruthers' portrait...can you see, and it runs towards the edge of the orangery floor.'

She glanced down then turned away, shielding her eyes. 'Oh, no. Oh, please. Is it blood, Chief Inspector?'

'Please, Lady Divine, stay by the door and don't step any further into the room. I want to examine the stain.' He stepped towards the easel, carefully negotiating the dark stain that had settled under the easel. He sank to his haunches, placing his forefinger on the stain, then rubbed his finger and thumb together.

'Is it blood?' Camille whispered.

He nodded. 'Yes.'

'Phoebe's?'

'I think we have found the place where Phoebe Carruthers was murdered. This was clearly her special place, the place where she felt most comfortable, and unfortunately the place where she lost her life. Edwin Carruthers said he thought she was happiest here. I can only imagine that she and Nellie Bell spent a good deal of time here, away from a man who showed his wife little attention, or offered her little affection.' He shook his head. 'She had that huge house in Henrietta Street, yet she would have rather spent her time in a street that is on the edge of one of London's old rookeries, a house that has seen better days, yet where she felt the most at home.'

'I didn't know her very well, Chief Inspector, but I got the impression that appearance and status meant nothing to her. She was a good person. A very good person.' Camille glanced at the portrait. 'I hope this portrait was a present to her children, and wouldn't have been wasted on a man who didn't care.'

Chief Inspector Owen stood and replaced the cloth over the portrait.

'A forensics scientist will need to come in here. We know that every contact leaves a trace. They will be able to check for fingerprints, and for anything else that has been left behind by the person or persons who killed Lady Carruthers. We'll nail them, Lady Divine, do not be in any doubt. If it was Bell, Riddell or Price, we'll break them down eventually.'

Camille looked out into the garden. 'But there's no sign of Nellie Bell. Should we not call out in case she's locked in a cupboard or closet?'

Owen indicated for Camille to leave the orangery, and they both stepped back into the kitchen. Owen went to the bottom of the staircase.

'Nellie Bell! If you are here please bang on the wall or a door if you are locked in and cannot escape. This is Chief Inspector Owen of the Agar Road police station. Please make yourself heard!'

He and Camille waited for a sound, any sound.

'She's not here, Lady Camille.'

Camille shook her head. 'Then where is she? I am convinced that they know, those miscreants you have held in your cells. What about the woman, Alice Price? Could she be the one you must press for information?'

They left the house in Duke Street and Chief Inspector Owen left the two constables posted outside.

'Wait for the forensic scientist. I'll contact them when I get back to the station. Someone needs to be here when he arrives.' The constables nodded and took their places outside the house. 'Alice Price is as hard as nails,' he continued as he and Camille got into the motor car. 'She has a confidence that is hard to comprehend.'

'I wonder why? Surely she knows she will be charged for storing stolen goods.'

'She wasn't storing stolen goods, Lady Divine. Donald Bell was. And she knows it. She is denying any knowledge of the paintings, which is quite ridiculous because they were being stored in the sitting room of the house in Earnshaw Street, that's if it could be called a sitting room. Some of these people don't care how they live but this was a sight to behold. It was utterly filthy.'

'How filthy?'

'Grim, black as soot. Dust everywhere.'

'The kitchen?'

'Unusable, at least anyone with their eye on preventing disease would not use it.'

'Her house in Pratt Street, Chief Inspector. It's number fourteen. I would say that is your next port of call. We all know that some families live in insalubrious circumstances, but she lives in Pratt Street, not Earnshaw Street. That is not her address. It is Donald Bell's address. She may live in reduced circumstances in Pratt Street, but no woman would want a kitchen like that. My guess is she wasn't living there with Bell, but stayed there during the day for appearances sake, to give the impression the house in Earnshaw Street was a family home rather than being used for hiding stolen goods.'

Owen nodded. 'Alice Price is to be released. We don't have enough on her to hold her. She's claiming she's not involved and knows nothing, and to be honest, there really is nothing to connect her to the paintings, but she is connected to Nellie Bell and her husband. When she's released we'll follow her. My guess is that she'll return to Pratt Street, her real home. There is nothing for her in Earnshaw Street, particularly now that Bell has been arrested.'

'Do you still think she's the mastermind behind all of this?' Something occurred to Camille. 'Oh, Chief Inspector Owen, you don't think she killed Phoebe, do you?'

He shook his head. 'No, I don't think she's the murderer. Lady Carruthers' death is linked to the others. To discover who murdered her we must find the connection. Unfortunately we've yet to do that.'

'When will Alice Price be released from Agar Street?'

'I'll keep her for as long as we're allowed. I'm not finished with her yet. There are still some questions I want to ask her, but it will probably be tomorrow morning. Then we'll see what that lady does.'

'I'm not sure she's a lady, Chief Inspector.'

He glanced at her as he drove out of Duke Street. 'I think you're right yet again, Lady Divine.'

- Chapter 28

When Alice Price left the police station she stepped out onto Agar Street and released a huge sigh of relief. Leaning against the wall, and resting her foot on the bricks she lit a cigarette and took a long pull on it, blowing out a lingering plume of smoke, one of complete and utter satisfaction.

She'd done it, beaten the coppers at their own game. They thought they could catch her out, but instead, she'd done the same to them, side-stepping every question, every insinuation, and leaving Donald and the other geezer to take the can.

This had always been the way she had dealt with things. Gone were the days when she robbed anyone herself. She had been caught a number of times when she was young, just a snip of a girl really, and had done time for stealing from those that could easily afford to lose a few coins, a pocket watch, or a solid silver hip flask. These items were her stock in trade, but when she'd realised that she could make even bigger pickings, well, a girl couldn't turn it down. Getting other people to do the dirty work had been the best idea she'd ever had. It had worked well until one of the little toerags she'd trained up had snitched on her to the police. She'd paid a heavy penalty for it, did time for it, but they never found her stash which had given her a great deal of satisfaction. All gone now of course.

She smiled to herself, then ran her hands through her dirty-blonde hair, thinking that a turn under the spigot wouldn't go amiss. She'd hated staying at Earnshaw Street. Her place was no palace but at least you could eat a meal there, no matter how scant, without finding a cockroach crawling about in it. Bell's place was beyond disgusting. She didn't know what had happened to him. He'd gone to seed and that was a fact. He might have been a bit older but he'd been a handsome sort until he let himself go.

It was all Nellie's fault. Donald had pined for her when she'd left Pratt Street and couldn't accept she was gone. If she'd hung around long enough to see the whole thing through the police wouldn't have got on to them, although who it was who knew what they were storing at Earnshaw Street she had no idea. She'd thought they'd been careful, pretending for all the world that she and Donald had set up home together, just an ordinary family, a couple who'd found love and were living together. Sometimes.

They'd been fairly certain that keeping the paintings at Earnshaw Street was fool-proof, but she'd discovered pretty quickly that Donald Bell was an idiot. She'd had to work hard to make him believe that she fancied him too. He still held a torch for Nellie, even though she'd got a lover tucked away somewhere. A rich one by all accounts, she'd told Alice, someone she wanted to set up home with. Alice laughed to herself. Well, she got that wrong didn't she?'

Why Nellie had been so against Alice and Donald taking the paintings she couldn't fathom. It was the perfect plan to make easy money, but of course Donald messed it up for them. It was his fault really. If he'd just accepted that Nellie didn't want him anymore they probably would have got away with it. The police had got suspicious, and those nosy bitches who'd knocked on her door that day probably had something to do with it. They'd been looking for Nellie, said they were friends of hers which she hadn't believed for a minute. The dark skinned one was never someone who would have been a friend of Nellie's, stuck up cow. Then that Lady What's 'er name, went and got herself murdered, which meant the paintings were worth ten times what they'd been worth before, and everything went up a gear. The geezer from the art gallery kept coming to Earnshaw Street to check on them, and she'd hated it. He didn't know about Nellie of course. It wouldn't have worked if he had because he would have started making demands. And no one demands anything of Alice Price.

She pushed herself away from the police station wall and dropped the cigarette end on the pavement, grinding it out with her foot, then absent-mindedly looked left and right trying to decide what to do for the best. She wanted to go home to Pratt Street. She hadn't seen her three boys and two little girls for days and she wondered how they'd fed themselves or what they'd got up to. It was no good expecting the fathers to turn up and keep them in check. They were four of the biggest wasters she'd ever met and she'd always regretted getting involved with them, but then again—she smiled to herself—there'd been some fun along the way. It hadn't been all bad. She just wished she'd kept herself clean and not got herself saddled with three unruly boys. Still, once she'd got them trained up they would earn her a pretty penny.

She pulled her jacket tightly around her middle, thinking she'd lost so much weight she could wrap it round twice. Donald said he didn't like skinny birds but he hadn't said no to her, had promised her a generous cut of the proceedings once the paintings had been sold. Old Riddell had promised them a pay-out but she'd always been disbelieving about that. She didn't trust him any more than she trusted herself, and that was saying something. She thought about Pratt Street and smiled to herself. She wanted to go home, she *would* go home, and face whatever was waiting for her there. Whatever it was she could handle it.

Chapter 29

Chief Inspector Owen drew on his cigarette, watching Alice Price from a window in the police station. She was a cocky woman who knew that they couldn't have kept her any longer for questioning, because the truth was she hadn't committed an offence, none that they could prove at least. He'd let her go reluctantly, because he felt she had her fingers in this rather unsavoury pie, that she was pulling the strings, particularly those of Donald Bell.

He winced as she dropped her cigarette end on the pavement outside, and watched as she ground it in with her boot, saw her look left and right, then begin a slow sashaying walk towards Charing Cross Road where she'd no doubt pick someone's pocket so she'd have the tram fare to Pratt Street, or even a cab if she got enough. If there was anything left she'd probably buy more cigarettes and a bottle of booze to celebrate her release. He shook his head and took a breath in, then went quickly out to the desk where two constables waited, dressed in civilian clothing.

'Right, she's gone. Follow her. Go now, and for Christ's sake don't let her see you. She's canny that one. Find out where she goes then come back here.' They both nodded and made their way out.

This is my chance, thought Owen. That bitch has got something to hide and I'm determined to find out what it is.

He sat at his desk and put his head in his hands. They were no further forward in the hunt for the murderer who had wreaked havoc over London during the festive season. They needed a lucky break, a fissure in the seemingly impenetrable barrier that was stopping them moving forward, first, to find out what had happened to Nellie Bell, and second, why four women were murdered in such a savage way, and why were they left under the city's Christmas trees.

It felt very much like the murderer was determined to spoil the party, as though he, or she, were saying, 'It might be Christmas but I'm dishing up death and destruction to remind the inhabitants of London that life isn't all Christmas trees and lights' and in the most ghoulish way. And the letters carved on the women's faces. Why would the killer go to the trouble of doing it? And what did it mean? The murderer could have simply killed the women and left them where they were murdered. Clearly they were moved from the place where their lives were cut short. Phoebe Carruthers had been killed in her studio and then her body moved, to be placed under the Christmas tree at Selfridges department store. Was the murderer trying to remind them of something...or someone? Emi. Could it mean Emily, a shortened version perhaps, someone who had also been murdered, or perhaps killed?

He went out to the desk, his hand rubbing his stubbled chin in consternation. He hadn't been home for hours and his darkened chin was testament to it.

'Reynolds?'

'Yes, sir.'

'I want you to go down to the records room. We're looking for information on a woman who was killed or murdered over say, the last ten years, with the first name of Emily. And make sure you do a good job of it. Don't skim, check every record. It's important.' Constable Reynolds frowned knowing it would be an onerous task. No one liked working in the dark basement that was the records room, and he wished he'd finished his shift before Chief Inspector Owen had thought of it. 'Just humour me, Reynolds, and frankly, I think working downstairs will be more beneficial to find out who murdered those poor women than you sitting at that desk drinking tea.'

'Yes, sir.'

Chapter 30

The plain clothed constables ran by the window. Chief Inspector Owen's door was open and as they entered the police station and passed the desk he called them in.

'In here, lads.' They joined him in his office, both panting from their run. 'Well?'

'She went to Pratt Street, sir. One of her boys let her in. We went down the back alley what runs down the side of the 'ouse. There's a blacked-out shed at the bottom of the garden if you can call it a garden. It's more like a junk yard there's so much rubbish in it.'

'What d'you mean, blacked out?'

'The windows,' said the other constable. 'They've been painted over like they don't want anyone to see inside. I wouldn't mind gettin' me nose in there.'

Owen nodded. 'And that's what we're going to do. I've already applied for a warrant. I'm waiting on it now.' Just as he finished speaking a courier arrived at the desk. 'In here, lad. You got that warrant I'm after?'

'Yes, sir.'

Owen rose from his desk, scraping his chair across the floor in his hurry.

'Right, we're in business. You two, get changed into your uniforms, and be quick about it. I want everyone on this. Get the other lads primed. Alice Price's lads aren't babies and if they run we need to catch 'em. She'll run too, if she's given half a chance.'

Chief Inspector Owen left his car on the corner of Pratt Street and walked to within a few houses away from number fourteen. The constables were positioned at different points in the street, and two were by the back gate near the shed.

Owen lifted his chin to one of the constables who walked up to the house and knocked on the door. Owen's mouth was a straight line as he waited, his teeth clenched tight in his jaw. His instinct was telling him that Alice Price had a lot to hide, and he wanted to know what it was.

The constable knocked again. No sound came from inside the house. It was quiet, as though there was no one there, but Chief Inspector Owen was sure Alice Price was inside. She'd been seen by his constables entering the house after being released from the station.

The constable looked at Chief Inspector Owen who raised his chin. The constable picked up a small battering ram then called out to the occupants in the house.

'Stand clear in number fourteen. This is the police. We are about to enter.' He paused for a moment then rammed the front door which took very little to break it down. Suddenly a child, a little girl, ran out of the house. She was filthy, her clothes in tatters, her hair in rats' tails.

'Grab her,' said Owen, running forward. One of the young constables made a lunge for her and caught her by her dress.

'Got you,' he said. The girl screamed in fear.

'Take her to the vehicle,' said Chief Inspector Owen. 'Sit with her. I expect there'll be others.'

A loud shriek came from the alley running down the side of the house, and then cursing. It was Alice Price.

'Did you get her?' called Owen.

'Got her, sir,' said one of the constables. He and another brought Alice out of the alley. She was shrieking at the top of her voice, turning this way and that, trying to get out of the constables' grip.

'What the 'ells goin' on?' she cried. 'You've frit my kids 'alf to deaf. I'll 'ave you for this, Owen, you see if I don't. You let me go. You've got nuffin on me, nuffin.' She kicked out at the ankles of the constables who simply held her even tighter. 'You bastards, you fink you can just smash me 'ouse up and get away wiv it. Well fink again.'

Another motor vehicle arrived driven by a police sergeant. He got out of the car and walked towards Owen.

'Want me to take 'er back to the station, sir?'

'One minute, Sergeant Turner. I want to check something.' He beckoned to one of the constables who was as broad as he was tall. 'Finch, come with me. I might need some muscle.' They walked down the alleyway at the side of the house and let themselves through a gate into the back garden.

'Oh my God,' cried the constable. 'What the 'ell is this, sir? It looks like a junk yard.'

'Stuff Price and her boys have stolen I expect. Have we got all the kids?'

Constable Finch nodded. 'Three lads and two little girls. We've got them in your car, sir. The lads are kicking up a stink.'

'Yeah, well they would.' He walked to the end of the garden. The shed the constables had talked about was as they'd described, ramshackle with painted out windows. 'I want you to get the door to that shed off its hinges, Finch. There's a padlock on the front but we need to get in there.'

'Alright, sir. No problem.'

Owen watched as Constable Finch lifted the door off its hinges and yanked it with brute strength away from the padlock, throwing it onto the pile of detritus already strewn across the garden. Chief Inspector Owen stepped forward to peer into the gloom inside. It was damp and cold, and smelt musty, a mildewy odour that hit the back of the throat. On a wooden trestle was a dusty plate with some crusts which had clearly been chewed by vermin, and a chipped mug containing the remnants of tea, stone cold, with a mouldy film across the top. Cobwebs hung like bunting in the corners, and he heard rats scuttling under the floorboards, making their getaway at the sound of two sets of footsteps.

At the back of the shed, in one of the corners, was what he thought was a bundle of rags. He stepped towards it and laid a hand on it, gently pressing down on it. A frantic cry of fear came from its centre, then a sob.

'Nellie. I'm Chief Inspector Owen. You're safe now, my dear. No harm will come to you I promise.'

'Go away.'

'We've arrested Alice Price and Donald Bell. You have nothing to fear now.'

Blackened fingers pulled a gap in between the rags, just large enough for a startled eye to appear. 'I have no clothes', Nellie whispered

Owen was astonished. 'They've taken your clothes?'

'To stop me from escaping. Alice...it was Alice.'

'We'll get you some clothes, my dear, and someone to help you.'

'Not you. Not you.'

'No, not me. A woman. I'll get a woman to help you.' He stepped outside to where Finch was waiting. 'Take the car and the children to the station. Get Constable Hannah Carter to feed them and make them comfortable, then go to Birdcage Mews. Tell Lady Divine what has happened and ask her to accompany you here, and to bring a set of clothes with her, plain, nothing fancy.'

Finch ran out of the garden, up the side-alley and down the street to the car. Owen went back inside the shed and sat on a small, broken table that had clearly been gnawed at. He shook his head at the monstrosity of some human beings and what they were capable of in the name of money.

'It's just me, Nellie. I'm going to sit here with you until we have some clothes for you. There's nothing to be frightened of now. Someone's coming to help you. It's all over.'

Chapter 31

'The poor girl,' said Camille as she sat in the chair he indicated for her. 'How could anyone treat another person in such an awful way?'

Chief Inspector Owen shook his head as he took a cigarette packet from out of his desk. 'It's beyond me, but in this job you see all kinds of things. I'm not sure I'm shocked anymore, just disappointed in the way people behave towards each other.' He offered her a cigarette and she took it.

'Thank you. I've been trying to stop but these last few weeks have been rather eventful. I've felt in need of some comfort.' She slid the cigarette into a long slim holder and held it out for him to light. 'What will happen now, Chief Inspector?'

'Nellie's been taken to hospital. She's actually in the Charing Cross Hospital at the corner of Agar Street, so quite close to hand. I want to keep an eye on her. I have a feeling Alice Price was violent towards her, took out her temper on her. You must have noticed the bruises and abrasions.'

'I'm afraid I did. The poor girl winced with pain even when she was pulling on the dress I took to the house for her. And that awful shed. She wouldn't leave it until she was fully clothed. She said she had been kept without her clothes for weeks, that they had brought her a blanket when it had got cold, and one of those ceramic bottles filled with hot water. It was all the heat they would allow her. They occasionally gave her a hot meal, mostly soup with some potato in it, but not much more. Apparently Alice took her clothes to stop her from running away. She knew that a woman would not want to be seen on the streets half-naked. All she had were her under-garments, and they were almost in tatters.'

'Alice Price will be charged with abduction. She may have got away with being in on the paintings theft, but she won't get away with locking someone in a shed against their will for weeks on end.'

'But what about her husband, Donald Bell? Surely he should be charged with abduction too?'

'Oh, yes, he will be? He took her first I'm guessing, sent a message to her asking to meet, then held her at Earnshaw Street.'

'So why was she being held Alice Price's house in Pratt Street?'

'I'm guessing it's because Alice didn't want Nellie to inform Lady Carruthers about where the paintings were being kept. As far as Phoebe Carruthers was concerned they were at the Yorke Gallery in Bond Street, but you say there had been some disagreement about showing them in an exhibition.'

'Yes, that's right. Phoebe was adamant that they be shown, but Horace Riddell had dissuaded her, saying they were in poor taste. It looks like he was going to use them for his own gain.'

'He's still saying he had nothing to do with the murders...swears blind he had no motive for killing Lady Phoebe or any of the others.'

'Unless he decided that if Phoebe was the only one killed the connection would be too obvious, so he killed other woman to put the police off the scent.'

'I wondered that, but unfortunately my instinct is that he's telling the truth, which means we're not much nearer finding out who the perpetrator is. The marks carved into the women's faces,' he shook his head again, 'they must mean something to someone, and he swears, under some pretty hefty questioning that would have given him some encouragement to tell us everything he knew, that they mean absolutely nothing to him.'

Camille stubbed out her cigarette in the ashtray and sighed.

'What about Nellie? I'm guessing you won't have had the chance to question her yet.'

'Actually, Lady Divine, that was something I wanted to discuss with you. She's in a pretty fragile state, not just her body but her mind too. We need to be very careful with her, gentle. I don't want to push her, and I don't think it would be a good idea for either me or one of my men to speak with her. I'd like you to do it if you have no objections.'

Camille was startled at first, then her face broke into a smile. 'I was under the impression my involvement wasn't required, Chief Inspector.'

He shrugged and returned her smile. 'Your presence has proved to be invaluable, Lady Divine. There are some cases I come across in my line of work that would certainly move further forward with a woman's touch, and this is one of those times. Nellie has already met you, was aware that it was you who brought her the clothes so that she could leave the shed and be seen again, even if she did look like a frightened rabbit when she came out of the side alley.'

'She did rather didn't she. Yes, yes of course I'll help, Chief Inspector, but I won't question her as such. I'll speak with her woman to woman. I think I'll get an awful lot further with her that way. If she feels she's being interrogated she'll likely clam up, and she may have some information we can use to find the murderer.'

'We, Lady Divine?'

'Absolutely we.'

Camille and Cecily went to the Charing Cross Hospital with a view to seeing Nellie. Camille knew they must gain her trust before she would be willing to speak with them, so they went armed with flowers and fruit, and a box of chocolates to cheer her up. Cecily was also there to make Nellie feel she was amongst friends. The last thing Camille wanted was for Nellie to feel she was being intimidated and Cecily had such a gentle way with her, particularly when someone need some care.

Before they had gone to the hospital, Camille had wanted to speak with Chief Inspector Owen. She had wondered if Nellie was aware that Phoebe Carruthers had been murdered. If not someone must tell her.

'As far as we know, she doesn't know about Phoebe Carruthers, Lady Divine,' answered Chief Inspector Owen. 'At least, *we* haven't told her. Of course, Alice Price might have decided to if she were being particularly unpleasant. Perhaps you could gently sound Nellie out.'

Camille's heart had sunk. It was one thing talking to Nellie about her experiences and trying to tease out any information she might have, it was quite another to tell her that her beloved mistress was dead, having been so brutally murdered.

Nellie had been placed in a side-ward and guarded by a constable which Camille was glad about. She hoped to be able to find something out about Nellie's lover, and it wasn't a conversation that could be had in front of a hospital ward full of patients who would be able to hear every word, even with the curtains closed around them.

The constable stepped aside when Camille explained who she and Cecily were. He had already been briefed by Chief Inspector Owen and had been expecting them.

'Constable Reynold's isn't it?' asked Camille.

'Yes, ma'am.'

'You seem to be everywhere, constable.'

'Yes, ma'am. It certainly feels like that sometimes.'

The small side-ward was a pleasant enough room, the walls painted primrose-yellow, the curtains patterned with flowers.

Nellie lay in her bed, her eyes closed, face parchment pale, the bruises even more pronounced now she had been bathed by the nurses and dressed in a white linen nightdress. Camille could see that she was pretty, would be again once the bruises had faded, but she wondered if the memories of her incarceration would fade as quickly. She was only too aware of how the mind and heart could remain in pain after the dust had settled. And now I must give her even more sorrowful news to add to her woes, thought Camille.

Camille and Cecily sat on the same side of the bed, on two rather uncomfortable chairs that had been placed against the wall. Cecily looked at Camille and pulled a face. Neither of them wanted to wake her.

'I'm awake,' came a weak voice from the bed. Nellie opened her eyes and turned her head towards them. 'Sometimes I think I'll never be able to sleep peacefully again.'

'Nellie, I'm Camille Divine, and this is Cecily, my maid. I believe you two know each other.'

Cecily smiled at Nellie, and Nellie shifted her gaze away from Camille and looked at Cecily. 'Yes, I know of Cecily. I think we met once at a party.'

Cecily nodded. 'It was Mary Robert's engagement party, held at The Lamb pub. It was a good night.'

'Yes,' said Nellie wearily. 'I remember it. It was.'

'Are you able to speak with us, Nellie,' asked Camille, aware that the girl was exhausted and probably not fit enough to answer any questions. 'There are a few things we'd like to talk to you about, but if you're not...'

'Might as well get it over and done with,' said Nellie. 'No point in letting all this drag on. I just want to get home to me own bed, wherever home is now.'

Cecily glanced at Camille and Camille took a deep breath. There's never going to be a good time, she thought. Just do it, Camille.

'Nellie, we need to talk to you about Lady Phoebe.'

Nellie swallowed hard and turned her head away from them to stare at the ceiling. 'I know about Lady Phoebe,' she said, her voice a whisper. 'Alice told me, and she took great pleasure in it, an' all.'

Camille momentarily closed her eyes and took Nellie's hand. Her skin was cold as though bloodless. 'I'm so sorry, Nellie. I know you and Phoebe were close.'

'She needed me, Lady Divine. She was so lonely. I know she had her painting and everything, but she didn't have a closeness with no one. Lord Carruthers...well, he's so stern, spoke to her like she was one of 'is children instead of 'is wife. And she didn't want them kids to go to boarding school. He sent them off as soon as he could and it broke her heart. The little girl, Mathilda, Lady Phoebe missed her so much. She would cry and cry. I didn't know what to do. I just wanted to 'elp 'er.' Nellie began to sob. 'What will I do now? I've lost the best mistress I've ever 'ad and I feel so guilty.'

Camille frowned. 'Guilty, Nellie? Why on earth should you feel guilty, my dear? You've done nothing wrong.'

Nellie turned away from the ceiling and looked at Camille. Her eyes were dark, as though haunted. 'But I encouraged 'er. I encouraged 'er because I said to 'er she didn't get no love from no one else, least of all from 'er 'usband, and she couldn't have it from the kids 'cause they weren't there no more. She didn't 'ave no one, and when 'e came along, so 'andsome like, and young too, younger than 'is Lordship, I 'fought they was perfect for each other. I shouldn't 'ave done it. I shouldn't 'ave. And now she's gone.' She burst into tears and Cecily stared at Camille with horror.

'My Lady...'

Camille put a finger to her lips to silence her. She knew exactly what Cecily was thinking. She allowed Nellie to cry, then went to the door to speak to Constable Reynolds,

'Constable, do you think Chief Inspector Owen would permit you to fetch some tea from the cafeteria. Please, get one for yourself. You must be parched standing here all day.'

'I'm sure he wouldn't 'ave no objection, Lady Divine.' Camille handed him some coins and returned to the side of Nellie's bed.

'Constable Reynolds has gone for some tea, Nellie. I'm sure we could all do with one.' Nellie nodded and Cecily stared down at her hands in her lap. They remained quiet until the constable returned with a tray of tea. 'Thank you, Constable. Tea,' she said, smiling at him. 'The perfect salve.'

'Certainly is, Ma'am.'

Camille gave Cecily a cup of tea and put one on Nellie's bedside cabinet.

'Would you like some help sitting up, Nellie? You can't drink tea lying down.' Nellie nodded and both Camille and Cecily stood either side, took an arm each, and helped her into the sitting position. 'Is that comfortable for you?' asked Camille.

'Yes, thank you, Madam,' Nellie said softly. They sipped their tea in silence until Camille felt it was a good time to broach the subject.

'Nellie, who was Lady Phoebe's friend?'

Nellie looked up at her as if just remembering she and Cecily were there. 'I...I don't know, Madam.'

'But I thought you said you'd met him. You said he was handsome, and younger than Lord Carruthers.'

She nodded a little. 'I didn't meet him exactly, Madam. He came to one of Lady Phoebe's exhibitions, at the Yorke Gallery in Bond Street. I always accompanied Lady Phoebe to one of her showings, then we'd have some supper afterwards, at a little restaurant just off of Bond Street.' She looked wistful. 'It was so much fun...a different world to the one I was used to.'

'And he introduced himself to her?'

'Yes. He bought one of her paintings, and then they began to talk to each other. They had a lengthy conversation too. I'd never seen Lady Phoebe look so happy, all sort of sparkly. I could see there was an attraction there, for both of them. He was very attentive to her.'

'You knew Horace Riddell?'

Nellie's face changed. 'Horrid little man. He was always tryin' to get Lady Phoebe to give him a bigger cut when she sold a painting.' She took a gulp of tea. 'I didn't like him. Not one bit. I told Lady Phoebe an' all an' she said she didn't like him either, but his gallery was in the shopping street most frequented by people who could afford her paintings, so she needed to stay there.'

'And what about her suffrage paintings?'

Nellie's face clouded over. 'Those bloody things,' she said in a whisper. 'They've caused so much trouble, an' I just don't know why. They're wonderful, Lady Divine. They look almost real, like a photograph. Horace Riddell didn't like what the paintings were about and refused to show them.'

'She left them at the gallery I take it?'

'I think she was 'oping to change his mind.'

Camille glanced at Cecily who raised her eyebrows. Both wanted to ask the same question.

'Why did you leave your husband, Nellie?'

Nellie's eyes filled with tears and she swallowed hard. 'I met someone, a nice bloke, and I 'ad a chance with 'im.' She shook her head. 'Donald had changed so much, Lady Divine. He was in thrall to 'er. Alice. Fought she was the bees knees cos 'e said she 'ad a brain on 'er. Alice Price told me she and 'im were carryin' on. He said he weren't but she wouldn't leave it. She said they'd got plans. I was away at Denham 'ouse so often I couldn't really do anything about it.' She sobbed and wiped her eyes with the back of her hand. 'I'd already decided that I wouldn't go with my new friend. I'd met him at one of the exhibitions. He was lovely to me, told me I was beautiful, but then I saw sense. He was out of my league. A different class, and I knew deep down it wouldn't work. Then one day when I 'ad a few hours off, I went back to the 'ouse in Pratt Street. She was there, wiv Donald, sitting at the table drinking whiskey, looking all the world like she lived there. So I packed me bag and decided to move into my room at Denham House permanently. And that's where I've been ever since, well, until it all went wrong.'

'And how did it go wrong.'

'Donald sent a note, for me to meet 'im, at the special place. I'd told 'im about it in confidence thinking 'e cared about me. Thinking 'e cared about Lady Phoebe. I was wrong about that.'

'The special place being Lady Phoebe's house in Duke Street?'

Nellie's eyes widened. 'You know about it?' Camille nodded. 'It's like 'e was beggin' me. 'Please' it said. 'E never said please. Not to me anyway.'

'So you went.' Nellie nodded sadly. 'Then what happened?'

"E said he'd got a different 'ouse. That he wanted a fresh start. 'E looked so bad, 'orrible, like 'e 'adn't washed for weeks. I'd never known 'im like that. It was like 'e'd given up. He asked me to go and see it. I couldn't believe it when he took me there.' She shook her head. 'Earnshaw Street of all places. When I asked 'im why he'd moved out of Pratt Street, 'e said, 'To get away from 'er.' I think 'e meant Alice.'

'But he didn't get away from her, did he?'

Nellie shook her head. 'She'd followed us to Earnshaw Street. I don't think she knew about 'im getting' an 'ouse there and she got right nasty. She locked me in the back scullery and I 'eard it all, 'eard everything, about 'ow Riddell was going to say the paintings 'ad been stolen from the gallery, but 'ad asked Donald to store them somewhere for 'im. She'd been with Donald when Riddell had asked 'im.'

'How did they know each other.'

'Through me.' She closed her eyes and then looked down at her hands still cradling the cup. 'Donald came to one of the exhibitions once. When I thought he was a proper man, a proper 'usband. Riddell must 'ave seen something in 'im, knew he was a wrong 'un.'

'So they kept you at the house in Earnshaw Street.'

'For a couple of weeks. I was so worried, Lady Camille. So worried about the mistress. I knew she'd think I'd upped and left 'er but I would never have done such a terrible thing. I thought the world of her. She took me into her world and made me see life differently. I thought she was wonderful.'

'Why did they move you to Alice's house in Pratt Street?'

'Alice said I was a complication they didn't need. That if Riddell found out I knew what was goin' on, it would be all off and they wouldn't get their money. She knew how close I was to Lady Phoebe. I'd told 'er enough times. I thought she was a friend. That was something else I got wrong. Clever she is. Very clever. She got a friend of 'ers to bring a cart to take us both to Pratt Street. She 'eld a knife to me throat, saying if I made a sound she'd do for me. And you know what…I think she would 'ave done. She would 'ave done anything to get 'er 'ands on the cash what Riddell had promised.'

Camille took a deep breath, knowing she had to ask.

'We found a letter in your room, Nellie. And a small box hidden behind the cabinet by the bedside. Were they yours?'

Nellie's eyes widened. 'No, Lady Camille. Of course not.' She rolled her eyes. 'You want to know who they belonged to?' Camille nodded. 'He'd given them to Lady Phoebe. The man from the gallery. The letter was for her, sent it to the 'ouse in Henrietta Street of all things. Fancy doin' that. If Lord Carruthers had found out about it,' she inhaled, 'only the good Lord knows what would 'ave 'appened.'

'And the earrings?'

'They were with the letter. She asked me to hide the letter and the earrings for her. She knew what would happen if Lord Carruthers ever got wind of something goin' on that shouldn't 'ave been.'

'And were they?'

Nellie looked sad. 'Not in that way. Not for Lady Phoebe. She was too much of a lady for that. They used to meet at the house in Duke Street. He'd watch her while she was painting, and they'd talk about things, things what she would've talked about with Lord Carruthers if he'd ever show an interest in 'er.

'One day, when she came back to Henrietta Street, she was so excited. Her friend 'ad commissioned her to paint a portrait of 'erself. Said he wanted it hanging in his study so he could look at it all day while he was working.' Tears filled her eyes again, and rolled unchecked, down her cheeks. 'It must've been the last thing what she ever painted.'

Camille strode down Agar Street towards the police station, and an interesting conversation with Chief Inspector Owen, with Cecily hurrying behind her in her wake, trying her best to keep up.

'What do you think, Madam?'

'I think we've found our killer, Cecily.'

'Who is he, Lady Divine?'

'I wish I knew, Chief Inspector.'

Camille and Cecily sat in Chief Inspector Owen's office, opposite him as he sat at his desk. A tray of tea and biscuits had been delivered by one of the constables, and the empty cups and untouched biscuits sat atop a filing cabinet.

'He's our killer isn't he,' said Camille, more of a statement than a question.

'I would say he is. The problem is that this relationship, if it can be called that, was a secret as far as anyone was concerned, apart from Nellie Bell, and she doesn't have a name for him.'

'We have an initial, B.'

Owen shrugged. 'That could mean anything. It could even be a pet name or a nickname.' He sighed and rubbed his chin. 'What we need is a sighting, or at least some idea of what the man looks like.'

'P'raps Nellie could draw 'im,' said Cecily. 'Or she could tell someone what 'e looks like and someone else could draw 'im.' Both Chief Inspector Owen and Camille stared at her and her shoulders slumped with embarrassment under their stares.

'What a wonderful idea,' said Camille. 'Well done, Cecily.'

Chief Inspector Owen smiled. 'Yes, it is. Well done.'

Cecily beamed.

Chapter 32

'No, that's not right,' said Nellie to the police artist. 'His nose is a bit longer, sort of pointed at the end.' She nodded and smiled. 'Yes, that's it.'

The police artist sat at the side of Nellie's bed, while Camille and Inspector Owen waited for the drawing to be finished.

'And his hair,' the female artist asked her. 'What colour is it?'

'It's very fair, almost blond but not quite.' Nellie looked closely at the drawing again. 'Something's not quite right. I think it's the eyes. They're too dark. If I remember rightly, his eyes were quite pale, blue, with pale blond lashes.'

'And his clothes? Was he well dressed.'

'Oh, yes,' nodded Nellie. 'I've never seen a man so well-dressed. His clothes were clearly from the best tailors. I learnt about these things when I was with Lady Phoebe.' Camille saw her swallow. 'She taught me lots of things.'

'Can you describe what he wore?'

'When I saw him at the gallery he was wearing a grey suit with a light-blue silk cravat, fastened with a diamond tie-pin. He was very smart, and handsome too.' She looked across to Camille and Chief Inspector

Owen frowning. 'I can't believe he killed Lady Phoebe. There must be some mistake mustn't there? He said he loved her. In his letter. He said he loved her. Why would he do something so awful to 'er? To want to hurt her like that? Surely it was someone else?'

'We don't know yet, Nellie,' said Owen. 'This is just to eliminate him so if he didn't do it we know we're looking for someone else and we can move on with our investigations.'

'And do you think 'e killed the others too, y'know, the other women?'

'It certainly appears so.'

'He seemed such a nice man. And so fond of Lady Phoebe.'

Chief Inspector Owen raised his eyebrows. 'If that is the case, Nellie, I think he has a strange way of showing it.'

When the artist had finished the drawing Chief Inspector Owen held out his hand for the sketch. He glanced at it then nodded.

'It's a good sketch. Would you say it's a good likeness, Nellie.'

She nodded. 'Yes, Chief Inspector. I think so. From what I can remember of him.'

Owen passed the sketch to Camille and she gasped. 'Oh! Oh my goodness.'

He stared at her. 'Do you know this man?'

'He...he looks like a recent acquaintance, someone who was at. Phoebe's funeral.' She looked into Chief Inspector Owen's eyes. 'I asked him if he had known Phoebe well and he said not, that he was at the funeral representing someone else. I never discovered who that someone else was.'

'It could be that this sketch simply resembles him.'

'Yes, yes of course, but that would be a coincidence, Chief Inspector, and I remember you once telling me that you didn't believe in coincidences. That when something appeared as a coincidence there was usually a reason for it.'

'I have always thought so. Who is the acquaintance?'

'The Honourable Richard Burrows.'

Owen raised his eyebrows again. 'Burrows? B? The initial signed on the letter to Lady Phoebe. Another so-called coincidence.'

Camille and the chief inspector left the hospital. They parted at the front entrance after making an agreement that Camille should send Richard Burrows a note, suggesting they meet at Birdcage Mews.

'Is it acceptable to you, Lady Divine? I don't want to rush into this with both feet. I think some gently worded 'interrogation' from you with regard to Lady Phoebe might lead us to what we're looking for.'

'It is acceptable to invite a gentleman to take tea as long as there's a chaperone. I could invite Nathanial Fortesque-Wallsey to join us.'

Owen nodded. 'I think that's a very good idea. We don't know what is in this man's mind. And it could be that he was the person who sent the threatening telegram to you. If it *was* him you would be in danger if you were to meet him alone.'

When Camille returned home Cecily ran up the kitchen steps to the hall to greet her.

'You have a visitor, Madam,' she said as she helped Camille remove her coat. She leant in closer and whispered. 'It's that nice man who sent us the champagne when we were at Browns. He hasn't been waiting long. Said he'd wait another ten minutes then leave 'is card.'

Camille felt the breath go out of her body. 'Mr Burrows?'

'Yes, that's it. Mr Burrows.'

Camille nodded and smoothed down the front of her dress. She could feel nervous perspiration trickle down her back and she wished Nathanial, and even Elsie, would arrive, even if they were without an appointment. 'Is he in the drawing room?'

'Yes, Madam. And he's had a sherry. I hope it's alright.'

Camille smiled. 'Yes, of course it is, Cecily.'

Cecily returned her smile. 'I'll take your coat upstairs to hang up.'

Camille wanted to ask her to stay but decided she was being ridiculous. Cecily was in the house, and so was Knolly who wouldn't brook any nonsense. She was safe. She had to believe it.

'Mr Burrows. How lovely to see you.' She held out her hand for him to take in his. 'I'm so sorry to have kept you waiting. I had an appointment.'

Richard Burrows nodded and bowed before sitting in the tub chair.

'I should have made an appointment, Lady Divine, but I'm leaving London tomorrow morning and I didn't want to leave without saying goodbye.'

Camille sat on the chaise and smiled, hoping her smile didn't look wooden. 'Oh that's a shame. Have you had enough of us here in London, Mr Burrows? It can get quite frantic at times I must admit, and of course, the past few weeks have been...well, let's say difficult.'

'Yes, indeed.' He paused crossing one leg over the other. 'I'm going back to Northumberland. Father has taken a turn for the worst and I feel we...I...should be with him.'

Camille showed her concern. 'Yes of course. I hope it's not serious.'

'He's very elderly and has many ailments. I don't think it will be long.'

'I am so sorry, Mr Burrows.' He nodded his thanks.

'I understand you have been helping the police with their investigations, Lady Divine.'

Camille's stomach began to roll. 'Only in a very amateur way, Mr Burrows. Before Lady Carruthers was mur...was taken from us, she had asked me to enquire into the whereabouts of her maid, Nellie Bell.'

'Ah, yes.' He feigned a frown. 'Did I not read something in this morning's rag about a Mrs Bell who had been incarcerated at a house in Pratt Street.'

'Yes, Mr Burrows. It is the very same. She was extremely close to her mistress and was distraught when she discovered what had happened to Phoebe. I understand she often accompanied her mistress to her art exhibitions at the Yorke Gallery in Bond Street.'

'And you helped to find her?'

'In a manner of speaking.'

'And where is Miss Bell now?'

'I believe she is in hospital, Mr Burrows. She had been badly beaten.'

He nodded again, frowning to himself. 'And...which...hospital is taking care of her?' he asked airily, as if it was a question anyone would ask.

'I...the name escapes me, Mr Burrows. Somewhere in London I shouldn't wonder.' Camille rose from her chair and went across to the decanter. 'Would you like a sherry?'

'A sherry, er, no, no thank you.' He rose from the chair and pulled on his gloves. 'If you should discover the name of the hospital perhaps you could let me know. I would very much like to send the girl some flowers, in honour of Lady Carruthers. I understand she was fond of Poinsettia. The brightness of the flowers I should think.'

Camille thought quickly. 'And should I discover the name of the hospital, how should I contact you?'

He fumbled in his top pocket for his card case, then requested a pen which Camille found for him in her bureau.

'I'm staying at Claridges. You can reach me there until tomorrow morning. This is the number.' He passed his calling card to Camille and she accepted it.

'How did you discover Phoebe liked Poinsettia, Mr Burrows? Is that not something only a close friend would know?'

'Er, er, I believe Edwin Carruthers may have mentioned it. He...he adored his wife you know. Loved sending her flowers.'

He looked around the room, then nodded to Camille. 'I should go. I've taken up too much of your time. Thank you for receiving me, Lady Divine.'

'You're welcome, Mr Burrows. Will you return to us one day do you think?'

'Yes, yes. I'm sure when things have settled, we...I will return to London, Lady Divine.'

'Mr Burrows. It's Lady Divine. I'm sorry to disturb you at dinner. You asked me to inform you if I discovered the name of the hospital where Nellie Bell is being cared for.'

'Yes, Lady Divine. Yes I did. Do you know it?'

'I thought it was so thoughtful of you to want to send the poor girl some flowers. She has been under such dreadful duress and spends much of the time asleep. One only wonders what will happen when she is discharged. She is at the Charing Cross Hospital in Agar Street. If you telephone and enquire at the desk they will let you know which ward she is on.'

'You have been very helpful, Lady Divine. Thank you.'

'It's my pleasure, Mr Burrows.'

Chapter 33

Night had drawn in, and a light rain fell on the streets of London. Mist surrounded the tops of the streetlamps in tendrils, swathing each one in a ribbon of haze. Underfoot, the pavements were covered in a thin layer of wet mud, detritus from the carts that still traversed the city with their contents of coal, or vegetables from the farms, still covered with the soil in which they had grown. Overlaying this was the dung from the horses that pulled them and the aroma that accompanied it.

Agar Street Police Station was ablaze with lights from the offices and front desk, reflecting yellow beams onto the wet pavements outside. The familiar blue lamp above the entrance shone like a beacon of security and strength. Charing Cross Hospital, on the corner of Agar Street, was also a hive of activity. It was the night for late night visiting, so at eight o'clock concerned relatives and friends were still being given admittance.

Nellie Bell lay in her bed, her eyes closed, her arms on top of the coverlet. She had eaten well that evening, the first meal she had consumed without it causing her pain where Alice Price had kicked her in the stomach. She had done so more than once, and had clearly received pleasure from it, her cruelty etched on her face as she delivered each blow. Her cruel actions had shocked Nellie, dismayed her, and caused her untold pain.

She knew she had done wrong, that she should not have found an affection with someone else, a man who was already married, had a family, but he had given her the thing that Donald had not. He had given her respect.

Donald had not appreciated that Nellie worked for a wealthy family, in Henrietta Street no less, one of the wealthiest streets in the capital. He did not like it that her income was keeping them afloat, that the work he found, as intermittent as it was, did not. He had said he was the man of the house, that what he said was how things would be, and that just because she worked at some high falutin' house and ran around after Lord and Lady What'sIt, she was still just a maid and that was all. It didn't mean she was better than he was.

Nellie knew he had treated her badly. Anyone would have said the same. When he had proposed marriage to her, he had been a different man, a kind man, a man who took care of his appearance and told her he wanted only the best for her. He was older it was true, but this had not perturbed Nellie at all. Age meant nothing to her. It wasn't important, and because she had craved having someone she could call family more than anything in the world, she had accepted readily. He had treated her well at first, at least, he had, until Alice Price came on the scene. Her arrival into their lives had changed everything. Donald changed, became harder, brittle and more demanding. He wanted her to take things from Henrietta Street, things that wouldn't be missed, he'd said, like the odd ornament that might be valuable, or a piece of silver that they no doubt had many of. They can afford it he'd kept saying. It means nothing to them. You must come across things, he said, in drawers, on shelves that no one would miss if they weren't there.

He wanted her to steal from her employers, thought it was their right to take things because the Carruthers's had so much and they had so little. What she hadn't known until later, was that it was Alice who had persuaded Donald to press Nellie into stealing from Lady Phoebe, that she had said what was the point of her working in such a place if she didn't make the most of it, and that if she worked there she would have something down her bloomers every day. Donald had liked it, had enjoyed Alice's rough ways, but it had sounded the death knell for their marriage.

At first Alice had led Nellie to believe she was a friend, had encouraged Nellie to confide in her about her life with Donald, had pressed her on the man she had met, who had come into her life and had meant so much to her. But of course, with Nellie staying at Henrietta Street so regularly for work, Alice had inveigled her way into Donald's affections. When she had discovered that Horace Riddell was paying Donald to store Lady Phoebe's paintings, she had massaged his ego, told him he was too good for Nellie, that they should become a team, set up house together at his new place in Earnshaw Street, and share the money that Riddell would pay them, for storing them, and for the cut of the profits he had promised once the paintings were sold.

Nellie turned onto her side and stared at the door. Her life had changed and would continue to change because when she left the hospital she would need to find another position. Lady Divine had promised she would help. She knew the right people, and had said there were always positions for capable and loyal maids.

Nellie wondered if she would get any visitors that night. It was filthy outside and she couldn't imagine anyone wanting to venture out from their nice warm nest, but sometimes people did things that were unexpected. She hoped so. She truly did.

Chapter 34

Richard Burrows replaced the receiver on the candlestick telephone and thanked the concierge. He paused at the desk for a moment, deep in thought. He had come this far and was due to return to Northumberland the next morning. Should he take the next step?

He walked through the foyer of Claridges Hotel and got into the lift. Inside was as decadent and luxurious as the rooms, with a velveted banquette at the back for those who would rather sit than stand, and mirrors on the upper half. He stared at his reflection in the mirror and inhaled a breath deep into his lungs, arguing with himself about what should be done. A decision needed to be made, and fast.

The lift-operator greeted him like an old friend.

'Mr Burrows, sir. Did you enjoy dinner, sir?'

Burrows nodded. 'I certainly did. I wouldn't expect anything less.'

'And your guest?'

'My guest?'

The lift operator looked at him askance then made an apology. 'Oh, I'm sorry, Mr Burrows. I thought you had a guest with you.'

Burrows faltered. 'Oh, well, yes, a member of my family. They took dinner in my room. Not feeling their best you understand.'

'Oh, yes, sir. Can happen to the best of us.'

Burrows made a smile but it didn't reach his eyes. 'Indeed.'

In his room, Richard Burrows began to pack. He thought about the arrangements he had made for the morning, a cab to take them to the station, then a train to Northumberland. If he changed his decision he would also need to change the travel arrangements, to check-out of Claridges that evening, and organise a cab to take them to the station. He wondered about the trains to Northumberland, and made a call to the concierge on the hotel's internal telephone.

'Would you mind checking it for me?' he asked the concierge. 'I'd like to know within the next few minutes if it's possible. Many thanks.' A few moments later the concierge returned Burrow's call. 'Kings Cross you say. For half-past nine? Yes, yes, please book two one-way sleeper tickets to the Morpeth Station in Northumberland. Yes, yes, thank you. And a cab from outside Claridges within fifteen minutes. Let me know when it arrives.'

Fifteen minutes later Richard Burrows stood on the forecourt outside Claridges looking up into the fine rain and damning the weather, as the cab driver loaded the luggage into the cab.

'Agar Street, please, cabbie. The Charing Cross Hospital.' The driver bobbed his head and started the engine as Burrows climbed into the back seat. 'How long will it take to get there d'you think?' asked Burrows.

'About twenty minutes, sir. Nasty night.'

'Yes. Yes it is.'

Half an hour later the cabbie pulled the motor car up beside the Charing Cross Hospital in Agar Street.

'Here you are, sir,' said the cabbie.

'Do you think you could wait for about ten minutes, then take us onto Kings Cross Station. I'll pay you both fares then.'

'It's alright with me, sir. Ten minutes you say? I'll have to charge you waiting time if it's too much longer.'

'Oh no, it won't be longer than that. It's just a short visit.'

He got out of the cab and made his way into the foyer of the hospital. The inclement weather had kept people away so it was relatively quiet. At the desk he was directed to the second floor, Ward 5. He declined the lift and took the stairs. Within moments they were on the second floor. Down the corridor was the sign for Ward 5. They walked down the corridor, looking into the half-glazed doors of the side rooms.

He put his hand on the door handle and pushed it down. He opened the door with as much quiet as he could., The room was in darkness. On the hospital bed, covered by newly starched sheets and a fresh coverlet, lay Nellie, her eyes closed, her breathing steady. He pursed his lips and released a sigh of relief. She was asleep. He looked across at his brother.

'Is this her?' Anthony Burrows nodded and took a knife from the inside pocket of his jacket. 'Is there no other way, Anthony?' Richard Burrows asked him. 'Could we not take her with us?'

'She knows too much. She can identify me. I've done so much, achieved so much. Why should I allow this girl to put a stop to my achievements? There are so many more of them who need to learn a lesson. They're wicked these women. They must be stopped. I did all this for Emily, in her memory. It was the suffragettes who killed her, and that damned horse that trampled her, and this girl is a suffragette.

Phoebe told me how involved this girl was. It was why Phoebe painted those damned pictures...obscene, dreadful, lying images of women trying to get their own way as usual. No, Richard. This is the best way. It'll finish it once and for all. And I'll have justice for Emily.'

'Emily made her decision, Anthony. No one forced her to do what she did.'

Anthony Burrows turned to Richard and glared at him.

'She did it for *them*,' he spat. 'For those damned women who think their station in life is so far below them. She did it to further their cause and it killed her. Wonderful, loyal Emily, who was clearly easily swayed by this wicked movement of witches and sirens. She was my confidant, my friend. Every Christmas she and her family would return to us in Morpeth. It was the highlight of my year. And now she's gone.

'I can only pray my actions have stopped the upsurge in their activities. It has gone far enough.' He turned his attention to Nellie, his lip curling in disgust. 'I cannot allow this woman to live, to spout her evil rhetoric and expect men to change the way we live just to suit their ideals. This is the only way.'

He stepped nearer the bed and raised his arm. The blade glinted in a beam of light from the corridor as it swept down towards Nellie's chest.

Chapter 35

Camille sat in the waiting room at Charing Cross Hospital. She kept perfectly still, her legs crossed, her hands folded together in her lap. At her elbow was a cup of coffee, undrunk and stone cold. She turned her head to look out of the window. Outside was pitch black. There were no stars, just a sweep of rain that had increased in its intensity, pattering solidly against the glass. She sighed and closed her eyes momentarily, wishing she were at home in the sitting room at Birdcage Mews, a place of safety and peace. By her side sat Cecily, her loyal maid, who was equally as quiet. Her face was pale, her eyes rimmed with red where she had shed many tears. It had been a long night, a fateful night, one she would never forget.

The door to the waiting-room opened and Chief Inspector Owen stood in the frame, a steaming cup of coffee in his hand. He sat three chairs away from Camille and leant forward.

'How are you, Lady Divine? This has been quite a night.'

Camille dabbed at her eyes and nodded. 'It certainly has Chief Inspector. It's difficult to countenance how much hatred someone would hold in their heart.'

'You have realised then what this was all about.'

'I have...Emily Davison, the suffragette who was killed by the King's Horse, Anmer, when rushing out onto the racecourse at the Derby. What I don't understand is why Anthony Burrows felt it was necessary to kill other women.' She stared at him, her eyes still wet with tears.

'Because he held a torch for Emily. He'd met her on one of the family's visits to Morpeth in Northumberland during the Christmas festivities. It's where the family originally came from, although Emily wasn't born there. Apparently she and Anthony had struck up a close friendship, and when she was killed he blamed her death on her association with the suffragettes.'

'Is that why he struck up the friendship with Phoebe? He deliberately went to one of her exhibitions to meet her because he knew she supported the cause, and also because of Nellie's involvement.'

'Indeed, although I'm not sure he had planned to kill her. I think it was Lady Phoebe's suffragette paintings that did pushed him towards his dreadful crime.'

So, Emi, the word carved into their faces, was for Emily Davison. A reminder to everyone of what happened to her.'

'We believe so.'

'But she made her own choice.'

'She did.'

'She was a staunch feminist and suffragette. I remember my parents telling me about her, and Harry saying she got everything she deserved, which was a dreadful thing to say.'

'He doesn't approve of the suffragette movement then, Lady Divine?'

'Indeed he does not. I understand there are many men who believe the same way.' She eyed him waiting for a response regarding his own thoughts on the matter, but he made none. 'So, what happens now?'

'Richard and Anthony Burrows have been taken into custody. Anthony Burrows has been charged with murder. Richard Burrows will be charged with aiding and abetting a murderer. He will also face a sentence.'

'Will Anthony Burrows face the hangman's noose?'

Chief Inspector Owen shrugged. 'That very much depends on what the doctors say when he had been examined by them. He was raving when we caught him. If it is proved he is of sound mind then yes, he will.'

'It's what he deserves,' said Cecily quietly. 'After what he's done. He's a wicked man. All those girls lives lost and for what. Somethin' that 'appened ten years ago. No one forced her to run out in front of the 'orse, did they?'

'You're right, Cecily,' replied Camille. 'They didn't. In fact the suffragette movement were not aware she intended to do so.'

'And poor Nellie.'

'She was very frightened, but very brave. She did exactly as we had instructed her, pretended to be asleep so that Anthony Burrows thought he would have a clear way to killing her, so she could not identify him. She was the only one who could. I and three of my constables were waiting in the bathroom next door. As he was about to deliver the blow we arrested him and his brother, but not before we had heard everything he said while standing over Nellie. It was a confession, and we all heard it.'

'Is she alright?'

'A little shaken, but relieved it's over. You can go and see her now if you like. I think she could probably do with some female company.'

Camille rose from her chair. 'Well, we girls like to stick together.'

Chief Inspector Owen nodded and smiled. 'So it would seem, Lady Divine.'

Chapter 36

Camille got out of the cab, paid the driver and walked up the long driveway to Kenilworth House. At last spring had begun to show itself in the arrival of a swathe of daffodils across the lawn, and the tiny crocuses that had popped up between the flagstones. She couldn't help but smile. She had loved this time of the year in this wonderful house, and the prospect of seeing Ottilie again filled her with delight.

When Phillips had returned to Birdcage Mews, he had done so with renewed vigour, and had happily taken to planting up window boxes, planters, and baskets of hanging flowers for Camille, that were now blooming with the delightful colours of yellow, purple and pink to welcome spring to their door. She had been very glad to welcome him back, and he was equally as pleased to have returned, as was Knolly and Cecily to see him. He had been missed. The tired look had left his eyes and he explained to Camille that his stay in Ampthill had been a wonderful rest. Camille suggested that perhaps he was ready to retire, but he had simply chuckled and said, 'One day, my Lady. One day.'

The new butler at Kenilworth House gave her immediate admittance, unlike the last time she had visited. She was directed into the study where Harry was sitting at his desk, smoking a huge cigar. He got up when she entered the room.

'Camille, my dear. How delightful to see you.'

Camille frowned a little to herself. If this was Harry being patronising towards her it was working. 'Is it? I'm surprised to hear you say that, Harry.'

'No, no, we can be amiable towards one another can we not?'

She sat in the leather chair opposite his desk and he resumed his seat. 'I suppose so.'

'You've come to see Ottilie I expect.'

'Of course, but when you spoke to Cecily you left a message with her. You want to speak with me about something. Is it important?'

'I rather think it is.' She stared at him as if to say, 'well get on with it.' 'This is not an easy conversation, Camille, but one I feel we should have. Are you satisfied with the arrangements we have made since our estrangement?'

Camille nodded. 'Until now, but you know that the house in Birdcage Mews is only mine for another two months. David Lawrence wishes to take back possession to move his wife and children from The Hotel to Birdcage Mews. I was aware of it, but of course time goes so quickly.'

'When you're having fun?'

'I wouldn't put it quite like that.'

'I understand the police have a lot to thank you for with respect to discovering Phoebe's killer, and the killer of the other women.'

'I did what Phoebe asked of me. It led to a more...complicated investigation.'

'You seem to have a propensity for finding yourself in hot water, Camille. It rather follows you about.'

She didn't reply to this as Harry had said it as a statement, and not a question, so she didn't feel it needed an answer.

'This cannot be what you wanted to see me about, Harry.'

'I want us to discuss a divorce.'

Camille stared at him, her heart racing. She knew it had to happen at some point, they couldn't go on the way they were, they were estranged with no likelihood of returning to their marriage, but the thought of divorce shook her.

'Do we not need a reason for it? The courts will demand it surely?'

'They will, which is why I have decided to admit my part in it.'

She frowned. 'Your adultery?'

He nodded. 'Indeed.'

'But your reputation.'

'Will survive.'

'You seem very sure of it.'

'I am. I have many, well let us say, sympathisers.'

'Sympathisers?' Anger sent heat through her. 'Was our life together so terrible that you need sympathy from others.'

'No of course not.'

'Then why...?'

'I just meant that my colleagues in the house will not hold it against me.'

She smirked at him. 'Of course they won't. They are no doubt doing the same thing.'

Harry shrugged. 'That is not for debate here. I will begin divorce proceedings within the month. You need do nothing.'

'And Birdcage Mews? Where am I to live when David Lawrence takes back his house?'

'Ah, well, that is the other matter I wished to speak with you about. I have purchased a house for you.'

Camille swallowed hard. She could hardly believe it. He had always said he would not buy her a house.

'Where is this house? I hope it's not too far away from here, Harry. I hope you're not trying to get rid of me. I will not take it up if I cannot be near to Ottilie.'

'It's in Duke Street.'

Her eyes widened and she trembled. 'What?'

'The house that belonged to Edwin and Phoebe Carruthers. He has no use for it now, said it's a millstone around his neck, so I bought it. Got it for a good price too.'

She stood and faced him. 'You expect me to live in the house where Phoebe Carruthers was murdered? Is this some kind of joke?'

His face hardened. 'It is not a joke. The house is being renovated as we speak. You can choose your own décor and furniture, your own wall coverings. I do not wish to pay for another lease on a house I don't own. It's perfect for you, and has enough room for a small staff.'

'You've been there?'

'Of course. I wouldn't purchase a house I hadn't seen.'

'Did it not occur to you that it might not suit me, Harry, because of what happened there?'

'I have never had you down as the squeamish sort, Camille. The opposite I would have said.'

She shook her head in dismay. 'I think you have been rather insensitive, but it seems I don't have a choice.'

'Exactly.'

'And Ottilie. My request to you. Have you considered it?'

'I have.'

'And?'

He took a long pull on his cigar. 'She is permitted to stay with you for half the week, the rest of the week she will stay here at Kenilworth House until she becomes a boarder at a school in Hampshire.'

Camille held her tongue. She would never allow Ottilie to go to Hampshire, but she also knew she had won a small victory that Harry had agreed to allow Ottilie to live with her. 'I'm grateful.'

'Ottilie is in the garden. You may tell her what we have agreed. The renovation to the property in Duke Street will be finished in one month. May I suggest that you visit occasionally to see that all is being carried out to your instructions.'

Camille realised she had been dismissed. She walked towards the study door and put her hand on the doorknob.

'And Camille.' She turned to him. 'A quieter life for you might be best, don't you think? Let the police do their job, and you do yours of raising our daughter to be prepared for the life ahead of her.'

'Yes, Harry. Of course.'

Camille went into the hall and made her way to the garden door. Through the glass she could see Ottilie, sitting at a wrought iron table, a small easel in front of her, her paintbox and brushes at her elbow. Camille grinned to herself.

'That is exactly what I have in mind.'

The next investigation for Camille Divine in The Camille Divine Murder Mysteries

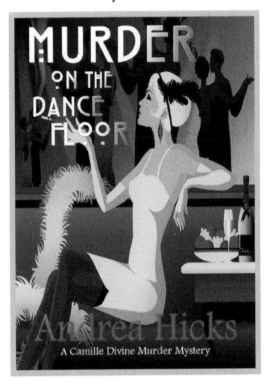

Note from the author...

Thank you so much for reading the first investigation for Camille Divine. Her character began life in the last book of the **99 Nightingale Lane Series – The Hotel,** which drew to a close Carrie Dobbs' journey through the Great War and into the 1920s. Like all periods in history, seemingly, it was the worst of times, it was the best of times. Of course The Great War was one that remains forever in our hearts and minds. So many young lives were lost, so many were hurt and so many families broken, but from within that background there were many heartening stories too, like how people pulled together during a time of great hardship, and how women were relied upon to do the jobs that our fallen men, and those that happily returned, were responsible for before they left for war. Carrie's story is uplifting as well as heart-wrenching at times, and I hope, if you have read it, that it claimed your heart. If you have yet to read it, I hope you will give it a try.

Camille Divine's stories are set in 1922 onwards. She is a woman of great character, strong, dependable...and very curious, which is why she finds herself in so much hot water. She is also kind and caring, and her personal backstory shapes her personality and the decisions she makes. Her next adventure, **MURDER ON THE DANCE FLOOR**, gets her into trouble yet again, simply because she tries to help a friend and finds herself in the middle of another murder investigation. And beyond that, **THE BRIGHTON MURDERS,** a tale of intrigue and memories that leads Camille and her loyal maid, Cecily, into even more turmoil.

Another investigation for her, another mystery for us to enjoy. I hope you grow to love her as I have.

Best wishes,

Andrea

Printed in Great Britain
by Amazon

10591500R00189